Freeborn Girls

Two women. Two ferocious times. One dream

Sally Keeble

ELEANOR PRESS

To freeborn girls the world over

Contents

CHAPTER 1
London: 5 June 2019

I t was the summer of my undoing.

The summer Stephanie came.

Not that it was her fault, of course. Nothing that happened that summer was down to her.

But the image of her in the doorway of my parliamentary office that June morning was the last fixed point before life unravelled: neat grey suit, string of pearls, sensible shoes: "Hi, I'm Stephanie Gardiner, your American intern."

She'd managed to get past security and arrived unannounced at my office three floors up in Portcullis House in Parliament, epicentre of the political universe. I shrugged off a moment's discomfort and held out my hand, already hot from the aggravations of the day. "Frances Quilter. You're very welcome."

Her hand was cool.

I hadn't wanted an intern, least of all an American. But her Rust Belt university had phoned so often asking for a placement, and given her such glowing references that in the end I said, "OK, three months this summer." Then shoved her to the back of my mind, behind the daily grind of committee meetings and casework lightened by flashes of shame or glory that make up the life of a backbench MP.

One of those highlights was about to happen. It was a Wednesday morning, and I was number eight on the list of MPs drawn in the ballot to ask the Prime Minister a question at her weekly question time in the Chamber of the House of Commons.

I planned to raise the plight of the Cooper Estate, a patch of '60s council housing in my constituency down the Old Kent Road. It was due to be demolished as part of a multi-million-pound regeneration scheme, with the loss of 800 housing units. No, not units, homes where people had lived, fucked, raised families, fought, died, survived, despaired, laughed, dreamed and clung on. And from which they were about to be kicked out into... That was the problem. There was nowhere for them to go.

So I left Stephanie with Joey Malone, a recent graduate who combined running my office by day with doing stand-up in a local club at night. He was well dressed if his jeans were clean, and his eyes were agog at Stephanie's suit and pearls. He said, "Yo," spun his chair round and cleared a space for her on the work surface. She smiled.

I parked the issue of what she might do for the summer, grabbed a red jacket from the hanger behind the door, touched up my face and scurried along the corridor to the glass-fronted lift that took me down to the café-studded atrium on the ground floor of our office block.

Here on the white marble paving, plots were hatched, confidences betrayed, reputations shredded.

On normal days, it was a gossip-fest.

Today it was peak toxic.

Three years on from the referendum, Brexit had claimed another Prime Ministerial scalp. The teetering government had taken a bollocking in elections to the European Parliament the previous week—terminal for the Prime Minister, who'd announced her resignation; opportune for her enemies in her own party, who'd been circling for months; bliss for those of us in opposition; adrenaline for all the political junkies flooding towards the Chamber of the House of Commons.

Adrenaline was all we had. Three years of fighting over Brexit had been made worse by tribal warfare. Not between our two main political parties, but within them. We fought over the fundamentals of how to run our fractured country. We took no prisoners. We knifed our leaders as surely as we turned on our friends. The atrium in Portcullis House was littered with political corpses. As we streamed past—and sometimes over—them to reach the underground passage to the Palace of Westminster, we were all running on personal and political empty. It was only adrenaline that kept us going.

Gerald Bryan, an MP from up the M1, bowled past talking volubly to his researcher, an earnest young woman in a pink top and heavy black glasses with a computer bag over one shoulder. Built for comfort, with a personality to match, Gerald greeted me mid-sentence—no let-up to his torrent of words—with a phone gesture, hand stretched ear to mouth, and when I nodded, he did a thumbs up.

Behind him was an MP from a constituency near mine, locked in conversation with a young man on the make, a fresh-faced MP who was already a ministerial bag-carrier. A one-sided conversation, it looked like. His jaws were clamped shut. Hers moved overtime. Nice woman, terrible politics.

Next came one of my party's grandees, a man who'd never given up his leadership ambitions, with an ego as brittle as his temper. He blanked me, the bastard.

"Frances." Toby Davis was loitering by the down escalator. He'd been the catch of the politics course at our Midlands university. I'd arrived, a teenager off a council estate, my life bounded by the river Thames, the south circular road and my mother's benefits. Feeling like I'd landed on the moon. He'd been way out of my league with his skiing and yachting and parental slush funds. Just before we'd all graduated, a mutual friend said Toby had confessed he couldn't help but fancy me. Soon after, he'd married a nice woman from the suburbs and then I heard he'd become a political consultant. He'd kept his svelte figure, but his once curly blonde hair was now cut close to his head, and faded to a dull grey.

"How nice to see you." Toby smiled, but his eyes were searching behind me for someone more influential among the figures passing by.

"What are you working on these days?" I asked.

"Regenerating south London. You know, restoring life to the inner city. Talking of which, the Cooper Estate's in your patch, isn't it?" Fleeting attention. Spark of interest.

"Yes. What's that to you?"

"We must catch up sometime. I'll ring." In other circumstances, we might even have brushed cheeks. But the tide carried me on and down the escalator.

Lurking at the bottom was Hugh, one of the whips, the senior MPs charged with keeping us backbenchers in order. A chunky northern MP, he had a soft burr to his voice that always tricked me into thinking he was kindly. He'd been trying all week to get me to ask the Prime Minister a question about what social cohesion meant to a government full of toffs. I'd told him I wanted to ask a clever question about the American presidential visit that might get me noticed. But he'd said people higher up the pecking order were doing that. "There's all the D-Day stuff going on," he said. "You could talk about the government's shocking defence cuts and your father's heroic war record."

I'd grimaced. What war record? Come to that, what father?

"I'll ask a question about my constituency," I'd said.

"Don't be too worthy," he'd answered.

Today he greeted me with a look that was part favourite uncle, part grand inquisitor.

"Whatever you ask, Frances, be helpful to our Leader."

"Aren't I always?"

"No."

"You're paranoid."

"That's my job." I felt his words land like an ice-pick on my departing back as I clattered on my high heels over the stone walkway past New Palace Yard.

When I reached the House of Commons Chamber, the place was already a churning cauldron of scuttlebutt. Not about the Prime Minister—any interest in her had long since evaporated. All the attention was on her likely successor. As I took my favourite place in the fourth row on the opposition benches, Gerald leaned over from the back row and wished me good luck.

It would be harder than usual to achieve any cut-through in the racket. There was only one person who would notice my question, so I figured I might as well make him happy. I mouthed my way through various forms of words, while all around me people bobbed up and down and heckled, and the Speaker struggled to control the mayhem. Finally, near the end of the session, he called out "Frances Quilter," and I stood up and launched into it.

"The Prime Minister says she wants to see more social cohesion," cue jeers from the other side, shouts from my own, "but when half her cabinet are property millionaires, how does she think that sits with my inner-city constituents who will be left homeless when the Cooper Estate is demolished this summer?"

Cheers from my side, finger-jabbing from the other, emollience from the PM, "Consultation.... Relocation.... Opportunities." Hugh turned round from the front bench and gave me a thumbs up. Job done. All that was left as the mob herded out of the Chamber afterwards was to do a quick radio interview en route to lunch.

· · · · ●·●· · · ·

I was due at a meeting on the Cooper Estate that afternoon to discuss the redevelopment plans with the tenants' group. I asked Stephanie to come with so she could see something of the people and place I represented.

As we walked from my office to the underground carpark beneath the cobbles of New Palace Yard, origins 1100-ish, I pointed out the landmarks: the fountain in the centre of the yard, replacing an earlier model dated 1445, said to run with wine for royal events; Westminster Hall, circa 1097, where Charles I was tried and President Obama spoke; Westminster Abbey, where royals have been crowned, married and buried since 1245. If they were lucky.

"Gee." She turned around, taking in all the sights with that acute interest Americans show in our history. "My folks came over from England way back when. All this would have been here centuries before they left."

"Apart from Big Ben. A newbie. 1859."

My car is usually my quiet place. But as I drove down the Old Kent Road that afternoon, Stephanie filled it with chatter about her family. "They were so excited for me to get this internship. It's the first time any of us have come back. My mother's a great admirer of your Queen."

"You're lucky to know your family's roots."

"My Gramps researched it. He says one of our ancestors helped cut off a king's head back in the day."

"Best not mention that this afternoon." I laughed. But if I'd been concentrating on Steph and not the traffic and what might lie ahead at the estate and whether Hugh would be nicer now I'd asked the question he wanted, I might have wondered if it was just naivety I heard in her voice, and how it would land in our difficult times.

Donna Collins had the welcome mat out for us at the entrance to the Cooper Community Centre. It sat in the middle of the estate, in a barren expanse of grey concrete which the estate's architects described as a piazza. The council's housing department called it piazza del hell. On one side of the piazza were three dreary tower blocks that threw long shadows over the estate. They already looked half empty, windows pepper-potted with signs of life; tattered curtains in one, another plastered with newspaper, Millwall flags hanging from several. On the opposite side of the piazza was a jumble of low-rise maisonettes where Donna and most of her friends lived.

The estate was scheduled to get millions in government funding, but only once all the residents had been moved out and their homes and memories obliterated.

"You're late," Donna's words shot out from her red-lipsticked mouth, her arms folded, summer dress tight across her hips. Her disapproval filled the doorway. I had reason to tread with care. As well as being the chair of the tenants group and caretaker at the community centre, Donna was where local opinion started and often ended with the gossip she picked up in the offices she cleaned and relayed around the shops and clubs, wherever she went with her sharp eyes and sharper tongue.

"I'm sorry," I said. "We got held up."

Her attention had already shifted to Steph.

"Who're you?"

Donna's eyes could peel through conceit like paint stripper. But Stephanie didn't flinch.

"I'm Stephanie Gardiner, Ms Quilter's intern. I'm over from the US for the summer. It's so exciting to meet you."

"Hmm." She looked Stephanie up and down. "I hope she's paying you proper; these people can be stingy buggers. Well, we'll let you off this time, seeing as you've come all the way from America just to see us." Then she switched back to me. "I've given them inside tea to keep them quiet, but they're not happy, especially now you're all over the radio talking about what should happen to their homes."

With that, she led us into the main hall. It was full, mostly of women, mostly older, with worn out hair and knowing faces, sitting on plastic chairs around vinyl-topped tables, all the feisty diversity of south London. Their chatter died down as we came in. Some greeted me, others smiled.

A girl in a yellow dress standing by the door with a baby on her hip came up to me. She looked a troubled soul, skin drawn tight over high cheekbones and a red bandana wrapped around her curls. Donna brushed her off with a "Not now, love." The girl retreated, clutching her child; her wild eyes spoke of torment.

The women watched our every move as we followed Donna to the front of the hall, where there was a table with two teacups, saucers set on top, and two chairs. Donna motioned for us to take them and then skedaddled off to sit at the side with her mates. I sat down and took a mouthful of tea. It was tepid. Stephanie took the saucer off her cup, but didn't drink any of it, and I prayed she wouldn't take a water bottle out of her handbag and swig at it instead. The girl with the baby radiated desperation from the back of the hall.

Then the women let rip. What did I think I was doing, letting the government pull down their homes? The low rise might be crumbling, and the tower blocks were full of mould, but they were theirs; their homes where they'd been plonked by the council, which their children had endured, from which their men had buggered off, and which they were now to be chucked out of to make way for... what?

"Not people like us." The woman sitting at a table near the back didn't need a megaphone. Her voice could fill the entire London sprawl inside the M25.

When they paused for breath, I said there was a chance that, even at this eleventh hour, the bulldozers could be stopped, but...

"There's always a but isn't there?" shouted a male voice.

I was explaining that regeneration could bring investment, new housing, more jobs, and I would support them in getting whatever they wanted out of the process, when a woman stood up in the middle of the audience. I'd seen her at community events before and she'd started popping up at political meetings. Her name was Laurelle, and she was wearing the blue uniform of a nurse or care worker. Her voice resonated with self-possession.

"And then you have the nerve to go on the radio and talk about social cohesion. What exactly do you think we don't know about getting on with each other?"

Donna leaned forward and stage-whispered, "I told you that radio interview was a mistake."

Before I could respond to her, or Laurelle, Stephanie jumped up. She'd taken off her suit jacket. There was a damp patch on the back of her silk blouse and a lock of her hair had escaped from its Alice band.

"I feel your pain." Whether it was her words, or her accent, or the emotion in her voice, people stopped their chuntering and listened to her. "I know what it means. My folks lost everything too, back in the day, when they lived in England. They lost their homes, their livelihoods, their families, even. They had to cross an ocean and start all over again."

There was some fidgeting in the audience. Laurelle pursed her lips and fanned her face with a leaflet. Donna folded her arms across her chest and cocked her head. Something in what Stephanie said must have struck a chord with the girl at the back, because she walked forward into the central aisle where she stood rocking her baby. I could see then how thin she was, bony shoulders sticking out of her yellow dress.

"They didn't have anyone to stand up for them," said Stephanie. "Not like your MP is doing. Most of the time, they were so hungry or sick they could hardly stand up at all. What kept them going was an abiding belief that somewhere they would find a new world which would be better than the one they had lost.

"And however many generations stand between them and me, I still hold fast to their dream of a better life. And I can tell from what you've said today that you do, too."

A trickle of sweat ran down the side of her face, which glowed. Heat or passion?

There was a split second of silence, and then Donna started clapping. Laurelle frowned. The girl with the baby gawked. I stood up and stepped in.

"Stephanie will be here for you," I said. "She'll listen to what you want, and make sure your voice is heard by the council, the developers, the government, and anyone else who needs to listen. She'll be yours for the summer."

Stephanie said it would be the honour of her life, which I thought was a bit gushy, but the people were won over.

Donna sent her friends into the kitchen to make some fresh tea, and then weaved her way around the hall, dispensing it out of the giant aluminium teapot, picking up the gossip at one table, depositing it at another, nodding her head in Stephanie's direction with an expression that said, "She's alright, that one."

Laurelle went into a huddle with a group of younger people in one corner of the hall and then pushed off. Before I could get to her, so did the woman in the yellow dress with the baby.

· · · ● · ● ● · · ·

On our way back to Westminster, I remarked to Stephanie that she'd scored a great hit.

"D'you think so?"

"Yes. You should do well on the Cooper over the summer." Stop-start, we went in the traffic trundling up the Old Kent Road.

"I'm glad." Steph took a bottle of water out of her bag and gulped down half of it, then screwed the top back on and tucked it away again.

"Especially when it's your first time even in the country." I took my eyes off the white van belching toxins in front of us to look at her.

"But I'm not really new, am I?" That certainty of hers. "At least I don't feel like I am. I feel like I belong here. Perhaps the past left some psychic imprint in my DNA. I feel like I understand where these people are coming from."

Sitting in the passenger seat of my car in her neat clothes, with her hands folded in her lap and her computer bag at her feet, she didn't strike me as the mystic type, just another American stressing about her roots.

"So it was true what you told people in the meeting?" I asked.

Her response was instant, her voice edged with hurt. "Of course. I wouldn't lie. My ancestors were market gardeners. That's where my name comes from, Gardiner. They had a farm in the country south of London, as it was then, and grew stuff to sell in the City."

A bus pulled out in front of me and as I braked, the driver stuck his hand out of the window and gave me a thumbs up. "That is so irritating."

Stephanie was unphased. "From what Gramps found out, it would have been somewhere round here. I guess it would be about where the Cooper Estate stands."

What else hadn't I known? "Is that why you were so keen to work for me?"

"Only partly. There are a few loose ends I'd like to tie up about what happened to the family over here. They disappeared from local records about the time of your civil war. All except one, who turned up in the States."

"And founded a dynasty."

It was only a throwaway remark. I was concentrating on the traffic. But Stephanie took it seriously. "I guess you could call it that, though if you're thinking founding father, you'd be wrong. More like founding mother."

"That's interesting. She must have been someone special."

"Yes. She was only a girl. Her name was Elizabeth."

Chapter 2
London: 18 April 1638

"My feet hurt Pa."

The girl tugged her father's arm. Around her, people jostled, pushed, shouted, careless to the child trapped among them. She clutched her wicker basket against her eight-year-old self, caught among the grinding bodies, squashed between rough clothes. Her coarse shirt and trousers were stiff with sweat and dirt, and her head itched under its scratchy cap.

But worst were her feet. She'd been walking since before dawn when she and her father had left their farm off the Kent road, south of the river, carrying baskets with the first pickings of their precious sparrow-grass, asparagus, to sell in the great City of London.

"Pa, Pa. My feet hurt."

All morning they'd walked, through Southwark, across London Bridge, past St Paul's to Fleet Street, laughing together at the ladies who wanted to buy from the "pretty boy." But now her father paid her no notice. He was shouting with the rest of the crowd, one hand cupping his mouth, the other waving his basket in the air, caught in the moment, part of the mob. His daughter squeezed round in front of him and hammered her fists on the front of his tunic. "Pa. Pa. Hear me."

She felt a blow on her arm. A man wearing a green hat over his long curly hair, hit her again with his cane and then poked her father.

"That lad of yours is cheeky."

Will Gardiner looked down and smiled.

"That's no lad. That's my Elizabeth." He squatted, so now she looked into his face, surrounded by its bush of ginger hair and beard. His eyes were as blue as hers were black, his frame as large as hers was slight, and his skin as ruddy as hers was pale like her mother's. She took off her itchy cap so her soft brown hair fell to her shoulders and she saw how his face lit up with a smile that she felt he kept for her alone. Then he pulled her up so that she could scramble onto his shoulders and rest her aching feet.

She shielded her eyes from the sun; unseasonal brightness for April. Its heat added to the boiling fury of the people. They spewed from alleyways and courtyards, climbed out of windows, became a human torrent pouring along the road from London City to Westminster.

Shops had shut, beggars given up, carriages and carts fled. Only pickpockets and dogs continued to work their sly way through the crowd, a purse stolen, a morsel snatched.

And then she saw what made the crowd shout.

Astride her father's shoulders, her wicker basket laid over his head, she followed the direction of the pointing fingers and saw a procession pushing along the road from the Fleet River. First a row of foot soldiers with pikestaffs clearing the way; then a group of men on horseback, sweeping hats with feathers, swords at their sides, and clothes of brilliant colours, reds, blues, golds, blinding white, even. They cut a slash of brightness through the grey-brown tide of people. Elizabeth had never seen such fine men before or horses with such gleaming coats that tossed their heads and snorted and danced, so it seemed to her.

Behind them came a body of soldiers marching in front of an ox-drawn cart. The men on their horses shouted at the soldiers to restrain the crowds, and the people roared their anger. As the cart drew nearer, the ox raised a long-suffering head and rolled its eyes at the mob.

A stream of stinking liquid flew past Elizabeth's head and landed on the foot soldiers. She twisted to look behind her to where a woman, hard lines around her pock-marked face, was leaning from an overhanging window, waving a chamber pot and shrieking laughter and abuse in equal measure. And then, around Elizabeth, people started chanting.

"Free John, Freeborn John, Freeborn John, free John."

Will's voice was louder than most. He pushed forward with the crowd and Elizabeth tightened her grip to stop from falling. A volley of stones shot over her head. She turned and saw a group of apprentice boys weaving a path below the overhang of the houses.

"Free John, Freeborn John," shouted the crowd.

"Make way, get back." The soldiers were brave behind their pikestaffs, the horses' hooves crackled on the cobbles, and the wooden wheels of the cart rumbled like thunder.

From her vantage point, she saw over the heads of the crowds to where a man stumbled behind the cart. Stripped to his waist, his pale skin was marked with blood, his hair was matted, but he held his head proud. His wrists were tied by a rope attached to the back of the cart, which jerked him along the road. Behind him walked a soldier with a flail of three ropes tied with knots at the end, which he swung and beat on the man's bare back.

"Free John. Free John. Freeborn John." The crowd called on God's heart, God's bollocks, every part of the almighty's anatomy and every pox known to his creation to descend on the soldiers as the flail lashed the man's back, his blood flowed, and his skin turned red. Elizabeth had seen men fight with their bare knuckles till their flesh turned to a pulp at the fairs on St George's Fields. She'd seen her father whip a stray dog and their neighbour beat his donkey. But for a man to be flogged in such a fashion was different. She thought this must be how Jesus had looked on his way to the cross. She twisted her hands in her father's hair.

"Ow, Lizzie, let go," her father laughed.

But this man didn't sigh or pray or bless people like Jesus did. And he didn't cower like her father's dog or drop dead like the neighbour's donkey. Instead, he drew himself up, threw out his chest, raised his arms and when the crowd roared, "Free him," he shook his tethered fists.

"Hallelujah. Brothers and sisters," he shouted. "I come before you, an innocent man. I've broken no law of the land or the heavens, I've lifted no hand against the King."

The lash fell again. The crowd screamed. Elizabeth marvelled.

"I go as blameless as Christ to the cross." The man staggered and nearly fell, but then recovered himself and shouted, "This is the doing of the bishops and their courts."

The whip cut again across his back, and he cried out in agony. Elizabeth clung to her father while he waved his basket and the people chanted, "Free John, freeborn John."

The cart trundled on, and another troop of foot soldiers held back the surging crowds, while Elizabeth watched in astonished wonder at the man disappearing up the road towards Whitehall.

Her father lifted her from his shoulders. "Come, Lizzie, we'll go and see what happens next. Hold tight." He took her hand and then set off with the crowd, pulling her along behind him.

"Who is he, Pa?" Elizabeth squeezed her father's hand, but he paid her no notice, so she dug her nails hard into his leathery palm. "Tell me!"

"Ow. Stop it." Will turned and shouted over his shoulder, "He's Freeborn John."

"Why do they beat him so?" Elizabeth struggled to follow her father. One arm ached from being dragged through the crowd, the other ached from clutching her wicker basket. Her wooden clogs clattered on the cobbles as she was swept with the throng into Charing Cross by Queen Eleanor's monument. Elizabeth slipped her father's hand and pulled on his jacket. "Why, Pa? Tell me, I want to know."

Will ducked into an alleyway, knelt down and pulled her so close she could hear the thumping of his excited heart. "His name is John Lilburne," Will said. "He's a common man, but he bows the knee to no-one—not the lords, nor the bishops. They throw him in prison, they beat him, but still he defies them. That's why they fear him, and why the people support him. And I support him too. There, Lizzie, now you know."

But it wasn't enough for Elizabeth. She put her small hands on Will's shoulders and looked into his shining eyes. "But why should they fear him, when they are so strong, and he is just one man? Tell me. Why?"

"Because he talks of freedom. And they are afraid of what that will do to people. Come. Take my hand so you don't get spirited away."

With that he set off again, and Elizabeth was pulled in his wake, buffeted by the crowd, skittering across the cobbles, clutching her wicker basket. She gaped at the royal palaces that lined Whitehall, and gasped as she was sucked into the majestic archway at the road's end, where she was deafened by the noise that echoed around the stone arches until she was spewed out into the wide cobbled courtyard of New Palace Yard.

There she stood dumbstruck. Golden stone buildings tow-ered overhead, glass windows glittered in the sun, and church spires soared so high she thought they must surely touch heaven. She felt giddy with the power of the place.

"See, Lizzie," said Will. "There's the cathedral, which is the power of the church." He whirled her around and pointed at another building. "And there's Parliament, which is our power, the power of the people. And you see that," he pointed to an elaborate canopied fountain in the middle of New Palace Yard. "That's the King's pissplace. When he was crowned, it's said that fountain ran with wine."

Elizabeth wondered how the wine got into the fountain, and whether it flowed faster than the wine in the inns in Southwark. A cart drew up to the fountain, and John Lilburne appeared, bound hand and foot, surrounded by soldiers who dragged him to a wooden platform at the far end of the yard.

"Come, Lizzie." Will pulled her through the crowd of people surging towards the platform.

"I can't see, Pa."

She pulled at her father's jacket, hammered on his back, but he was caught up in the excitement. So she wriggled her hand free, squatted down, and wormed her way forward, between people's legs, until she had a clear view of the platform. On it was the wooden pillory, towards which the soldiers were pulling their prisoner. But John broke free from them and ran to the front of the platform. He looked to Elizabeth like some martyred saint, his face wild, his body smeared with blood, open weals searing his shoulders and arms.

"I stand here, in this place of infamy and shame," he roared. Four guards rushed to pull him back while on the ground below the soldiers held out their pikestaffs to stop the crowds storming the platform. Elizabeth feared she'd be trampled underfoot.

"Pa," she screamed, and held her basket over her head for protection, "Save me." But her cries were lost as the guards wrestled with John and the people howled their anger.

She could just make out his words, "Innocent man .... Cruel burdens.... Free people..... Powers of the beast..." She peered out from under her basket and saw him dragged across the platform to the pillory. It was the place her father said was for punishing villains. But this man was no villain. He was a saint, or at the very least, a hero, not that he looked like one, at the mercy of the soldiers.

Then John broke away again from the guards. He lurched to the front of the platform, reached into the pockets of his trousers and pulled out a handful of leaflets, which he threw into the crowd.

Around Elizabeth there was uproar. A giant of a man leapt over her, waving his fists at the soldiers, while others pelted them with cobblestones, and on the platform, guards wrenched John back to the pillory and closed it around his head. Still, he shouted, so they forced open his jaws and thrust in a wooden gag so hard that the spittle that fell from his mouth turned blood red and his words were reduced to animal grunts.

Crouched on the ground, Elizabeth's attention was fixed on one of the leaflets that John had thrown. It had drifted down, a piece of cream paper that fluttered on the cobbles like an injured bird. Such a slight thing to cause so much trouble. Finally, it came to rest between the soldiers and the people.

She wanted that leaflet more than she'd ever wanted anything. Even more than the spinning top she'd begged her father to buy her at the fair on St George's fields. The soldiers were too busy to notice it. Just like, she thought, they wouldn't notice her if she darted out from the crowd, which she did, snatched up the leaflet, then dodged back and disappeared as fast as she'd come.

She tucked the leaflet into her shirt and twisted her way through the crowd until she felt someone grab her by the neck and lift her off her feet.

She screamed again.

"Found you." A man's voice. A smiling face. Her father. "I thought you were lost."

"I want to go now, Pa."

Will knelt and put his hands on Elizabeth's shoulders.

"Are you frightened, Lizzie?"

"No, Pa. I'm tired. I want to go home." She could feel the leaflet hidden in her shirt, as if every soldier in the courtyard must know it was there.

"Well, they've done their worst now. There'll be no more to see today. We must hurry if we're to get home before dark."

He lifted her onto his shoulders, and she turned to take a final look at the platform where John stood with the gag in his mouth and his head and hands sticking through the wooden pillory, as helpless as a trapped animal. He roared like an animal too—raw, wordless anger—and the people screamed back, at him, at the soldiers, at the injustice of it all.

Elizabeth's head spun with the noise and the heat, and she gripped her father's bushy red hair as he pushed through the crowd. She held her wicker basket close to her chest where the leaflet nestled and felt she was taking away the spirit of the day.

· · · · ·•·•· · ·

At the edge of the square, Will set her down, and they made the short walk from New Palace Yard to the riverfront, where small boats vied for passengers to ferry across the murky Thames. Will paid the boatman for a place on a boat already so weighed down and unsteady, that Elizabeth feared it would capsize and throw them into the filthy water. They clambered in behind a fat man in grey clothes. She squeezed herself into a seat between him and her father, and wedged her wicker basket at her side. With the tide going out, and a little effort from the tired oarsmen, the boat slipped downstream.

When they were clear of the quayside, she pulled the piece of paper from her shirt, unfolded it, and smoothed it out on her lap.

"What's that?" Will asked, leaning over his daughter.

"It's one of the leaflets Freeborn John threw into the crowd," Elizabeth said.

"Freeborn John?" The fat man bent so close to Elizabeth that his wheezing breath tickled her neck. "'An universal challenge to the whole world,'" he read over her shoulder. "That's what started all this trouble, Freeborn John and those leaflets. Put it away, boy, and don't open it out again where people can see. That or throw it in the river. Not that I don't agree with the words in it, you understand," he muttered.

"What does it say?" Elizabeth asked.

"It says things that will get you and your father sent to prison."

"A leaflet never hurt anyone," said Will.

Elizabeth looked from one to the other. At the fat man with his grey clothes and pasty face. At her father's open ruddiness and red hair. Then at the paper on her lap. "Can you read it to me, Pa?"

"Not with the boat jiggling around. Put it away like the man says and maybe your brother can read it to you when we get home."

In the afternoon sun, the boat glided past the luxurious gardens of Westminster's palaces, past the City Wall, past the awesome tower of St Paul's clustered around with mean houses.

Then the rowers pulled on their oars and the boat crossed to the south bank to where Lambeth marshes gave way to the raucous bear gardens and brothels, theatres and prisons that lined Bankside. It wove between a throng of vessels, to pull into the wooden landing jetty between the throbbing life of Borough Market and London Bridge, where the City's flotsam was trapped against the arches on the ebbing tide.

"Wotcher." A boy held the boat steady while Elizabeth climbed out. He was about her height and thinner than a river rat, with tangled hair and old eyes. Will tried to help her up the riverbank, but her attention was fixed on the boy, who dipped his hand into the fat man's pocket and then slithered away ratlike among the boats.

"Mind your step, Lizzie," Will said. "You don't want to fall in this muck."

The Borough's streets were steeped with the spoils of poverty, decayed and then baked by the sun into a noxious crust. Men rode past on horses that dropped yet more dirt, and women stood in doorways of the ramshackle buildings, cradling babies for whom survival would be success. Pigs nosed through the ordure and rattle-ribbed dogs skulked among the refuse from the market that bordered the great church of St Saviour, seat of learning, source of charity, upholder of order in the disordered Borough of Southwark.

Where Borough High Street met the long road to Kent, there lay a heap of filthy rags. As Elizabeth and Will drew nearer, the rags twitched, moved and then rose up as if alive, shook, parted and Elizabeth was confronted by a face covered with matted sooty hair, the skin so layered with grime that she could see no features, except for the white of one staring eye. Elizabeth froze, uncertain whether this was man or demon.

"Alms, boy." A voice came from the darkness.

"I haven't got anything," she said.

"For pity's sake, guv," the creature turned to Will, "if you don't give me something, I'll cuss you." A tear spilled from its staring eye and ran a silver thread down the blackened face. "For an old soldier."

The head swayed, its locks shook. Will delved into the bag around his neck and extracted a coin. A hand shot out from the rags and grabbed it, fingers with green-tinged nails like claws, more monster than human. Elizabeth hid behind her father.

"No god should inflict such suffering; no king should allow it." Will took Elizabeth's basket and put it in his own, then took her hand and they walked in silence.

Soon the wooden tenements gave way to stone houses set in gardens. Then came the shacks of the destitute and people newly arrived from the countryside. After they petered out, the road to Kent ran between open fields, their spring green fading with the day. Under the clear sky, the air soon chilled. For Elizabeth, it was a relief to be out of the choking city. The freshness revived her, and she felt her father's spirits lift too.

"What does 'freeborn' mean, Pa?" she asked.

"It means all people are born with god-given rights, that no power on earth can take away," Will's voice strengthened, and he quickened his pace until Elizabeth had to run to keep up with him. "Not the Church which oppresses us. Not even God's anointed king, who taxes us. Everyone is freeborn, so John Lilburne says, and I agree."

· · · ●·●·● · ·

Darkness threatened when they reached the ancient holly tree standing guard over the grey boulder that marked the boundary of their farm. But they needed no light to find their way. The spring grass was soft beneath Elizabeth's feet and she smelt the earthiness of newly tilled land. They crossed into a second field marked into long ridges, from which thrust purple-green shoots of asparagus. To Elizabeth, whose small hands tended and harvested these, the first and most precious of their crops, they looked like greedy fingers.

"Your sparrow-grass will be ready to pick again soon," said Will.

They followed the path through an orchard, under trees decked out in blossom, ghostly in the half-light. Beyond, in a carefully tended garden surrounded by a hedge of sweet rosemary, nestled a cottage, a well by its front door, over which trailed a rose bush. Small, latticed windows glowed on either side and smoke curled from the chimney on the thatched roof. Behind it stood a barn, from which came the honking of geese, the lowing of a milk cow. Elizabeth breathed in the comforting scents; animals, lemon balm, and wood-smoke.

A full moon rose and hung over the cottage. From inside the snug building came a high-pitched song, a voice of such startling purity that it sounded to Elizabeth like music from another world. One with none of the hardships or sufferings she'd seen that day, if such a place could exist.

"Are we freeborn?" she asked her father.

"Of course."

"Will we get whipped too?"

Chapter 3
London: 10 June 2019

Monday morning sunshine blazed through the picture window of my flat on the hillside. I pulled on a silk wrap, slid open the window and went out onto the patio.

Below me, South London was blanketed in a heat haze. In the distance City towers pierced through the ghostly pallor. I knew every street that lay beneath the mist: from the gentrifying riverside, through the tough estates where I'd spent my earlier years, to the green politeness of the southern boundary where I now lived.

It wasn't yet 8 am. Soon it would be too hot to sit outside.

I went into the kitchen and made myself a coffee, instant, found a trickle of milk in the fridge and rummaged round for something to eat that wasn't past its use-by date. An apple, a coconut yoghurt. I piled them onto a plate with the coffee, balanced my mobile on top, and went out and sat myself down on one cast iron chair, feet up on the other. For background noise I put on the radio and listened to the news while I scrolled through my daytime schedule. Check in at the office, meeting, meeting, reception, dip into the Chamber, afternoon committee, clear inbox—ha ha—quick drink, maybe, with Gerald. Switch to evening schedule.

The sun beat down. Five seconds of uninterrupted bliss while I got my caffeine hit and a spoonful of yoghurt. Then I took my first call.

"We promised to catch up."

Not a single one of Toby's words rang true.

"Did we?" I wondered if he was already in the office, or still in blissful domesticity with his wife in the suburbs.

"Yes. Don't you remember? When we met by the escalators. You were in a rush of course. Good question, by the way. Interesting."

Clang. I was surprised he was so obvious with his flattery. Perhaps not so sophisticated after all. But then I recalled he'd asked me about the Cooper Estate. I wondered who his client was and what he was up to.

"Coffee tomorrow morning?" I asked.

"Meal later?"

"Quick drink."

He suggested a bar on the South Bank, far enough from Westminster to be discreet, close enough to get back for votes. "We can always change it," he said.

There was a buzz on my phone, a call waiting from my mother's care home.

"Sorry, I've got to go." I just about heard him say, "See you tomorrow evening," before I switched calls.

"How is she?"

"Good morning Frances. It's Hanna speaking." The polite voice. The patience. It always left me feeling inadequate.

"She seemed alright when I visited at the weekend; if anything she was more focussed than usual."

"I'm told she had a bad night, and this morning she's very distressed. She won't eat."

"Oh dear." This was going to be difficult. I turned down the radio.

"She's calling out for you."

"Oh, god."

My relationship with my mother had always been one of unequals. Even when I sat in the reception of my primary school while the headteacher tried to find someone who might know where my wayward Mum was, I loved her besottedly. My toddler hands had wiped the hair from her face and had taken off her shoes whenever she crashed out on the settee.

"Tired Mummy."

"Yes, Franny, Mummy tired."

I'd heated up the ready meals, which she didn't eat, bundled up our washing and taken it to the laundrette. After an altercation, the man in the corner shop let me collect her alcohol.

It wasn't till I left for uni that the pendulum started to swing. Even then, I would never have found the emotional strength to disentangle myself from her clinging arms—"Who'll care for me now, Franny?"—if it hadn't been for my determined teacher-cum-mentor sitting outside our flat in her car with my pathetic holdall of belongings on the back seat.

"It's for the best." She made it sound like I was leaving some random stray at the Battersea Dogs Home. "Your Mum'll still be there when you get back."

She wasn't.

She moved down the inner-city chute of crap housing, while I found a job and a place to live in Stockport, then Birmingham, then finally back to London, where my tough upbringing became an inspiring backstory for a parliamentary selection. I tried to keep the guilt at bay by paying for her to go into the best care home I could find when alcohol finally overtook her brain function.

It didn't work. She still managed to wrong-foot me.

"I'll come," I told Hanna.

The sun's balm was shading into oppression. I dumped the ruins of my breakfast in the kitchen and was on my way to the shower when there was a ping on my phone.

A message from Donna. *Something's up. Call.*

I texted her that I would drop in later. I had to pass by the estate on my way into work. So I did a mental rejig of my schedule: first my mother, then the Cooper Estate, then Parliament; squeeze as much of the rest in before my afternoon committee meeting.

Midday. Don't be late again, she messaged back.

· · · ● ● ● ● ● · · ·

On the way to get my car in the parking area of my flats, I bumped into my nerdy neighbour at the recycling bins. An earnest man who worked in finance in the City, he'd only recently moved in and was still disposing of the packaging from his flatpack furniture.

"You're going to have an exciting summer then?" He looked at me, half condescension, half pity.

My mother was waiting. I didn't want a long discussion. "I guess so," I tried to sound friendly. "Watch this space, eh?"

"I will," he said and folded another expanse of his cardboard packaging into the smallest of small squares.

· · · ● ● ● ● ● · · ·

Down the green side of the hill in Kent, set in tranquil gardens, was the functional, white-washed building that was my mother's care home.

"She's perked up," said Hanna as she walked me through corridors that were the cleanest my mother had ever lived in. "We've sat her in the sunroom. Look, here she is. Mrs Garvey, here's your daughter come to see you."

Hanna stroked my mother's hair, like I used to as a child, and my mother smiled the way she used to do for me. She was dressed in a light voile gown I'd got her in Liberty's and the room was full of wicker furniture and golden cushions and sunlight. I wondered if, like me, she wished she could have had this earlier in life.

"You were only here yesterday," she said. "You checking up on me?"

"You were calling for me." I dumped my handbag on a chair.

"Was I?"

"I'll leave you together." Hanna patted my mother's shoulder. "It's nice to see your daughter, isn't it, Mrs Garvey?"

"Mostly."

I laughed. Mum was silent after Hanna left, silent but not peaceful. She moved her head from side to side and worked her lips. I leaned over and tried to hear what she was saying, but she raised a hand. In a previous lifetime she would have pushed me away.

"You're just like your father."

I didn't know what to say to that. Her emotional barbs caught me like fishhooks.

"He left me too. Like you did."

"But I came back for you, Mum."

She tossed and turned her head, her eyes glazed and her mind elsewhere. I'd never known how to deal with her demons. Now they overpowered her, capering around in the sunroom. I tried to escape into the garden, but the door was locked, so I had no choice but to sit and watch her do battle with whatever it was that had been tormenting her for as long as I could remember. Eventually her eyes registered me.

"You again."

"I've been here all the time."

"Have you?"

Hanna walked me out. "This hot weather is hard on our residents. You mother is coping better than most of them."

"She's very determined."

"She's lucky to have you." Hanna rubbed my arm with just the right amount of pressure to show her sympathy without actually making me cry. "Is there no-one else?"

"There's a father somewhere. That's who she's talking about. But I can't remember him. Garvey was my stepdad's name. Her own family has long since disappeared."

"That's tough."

I shrugged.

"We'll let you know how things go."

"Thanks."

I checked my phone when I got into my car. There was a message from Donna from an hour ago. *Stephanie's here. Where are you?*

"Shit," I muttered. Nothing I could do about it. I swiped the message away and set off back over the hill.

· · · · ● · ● · · ·

There was a ding-dong going on when I arrived at the estate.

"You can't just give up." A woman's voice blasted out of the office in the community centre.

"Don't bleeding give me 'give up'," said a voice I recognised as Donna's.

She was sitting behind the shabby desk. Laurelle, in her nurse's uniform, was standing opposite with her back to me, one clenched fist on her hips, the other hand holding a little girl wearing only a pair of frilly knickers and pink headphones with cat's ears on them.

"How can I help?" My voice dropped into the aggravation. Laurelle spun round. She looked exhausted.

"Help? You must be joking. Causing all the trouble, and now you wander in as if you've got any of the answers." Her voice ricocheted around the office like a squash ball.

There were footsteps behind me and Stephanie came in carrying a tray. She had traded down her grey suit for tan slacks and a white cotton blouse. "Here, I've made us all some tea so we can talk things over."

"Tea? Who's got the time? Come on, Sherine, let's get you home." Saying which Laurelle snatched up her daughter like any of it was her fault, pushed past Stephanie and left, the little girl's cat's ears bobbing over her mother's shoulders. "You people should try working for a living." A parting shot.

Donna fumbled in her blouse, pulled out a tissue and wiped her forehead.

"Laurelle's well out of order," I said.

Stephanie put the tray on the table and handed Donna a cup of tea. "Thanks, love." Donna peered into the cup. "You're learning." Then she turned to me. "Laurelle's at her worst in the morning when she's just off night shift. Comes at me like a bat out of hell today saying she's organising resistance to the redevelopment. I told her the tenants have already talked about that and there's not the support. She says she's doing it anyway."

"She won't succeed." I didn't picture a frazzled night nurse as a riot leader.

But Donna knew her estate. "Perhaps not, but she's force-ful and she can cause a lot of trouble. For you 'n all." Her disquiet was worrying.

"Perhaps I can speak to her later, when she's had a sleep?" Stephanie's voice was so fresh. Both of us looked at her.

And then, behind her, I saw a flash of yellow pass the open door. The girl with the baby from last week's meeting.

"Hey," I hurried out after her, but she was racing across the litter-pocked piazza towards one of the tower blocks. As she pulled the door open, she stopped and turned. She was too far away and in the shade of the building for me to see the expression on her face—but her body language was enough. Panic. She held the door open with one foot, and stood poised for an instant, wary, coiled.

Then she stepped inside and the door slammed shut be-hind her.

· · · · •· • · · ·

By the time I arrived in Parliament, my schedule had concerti-naed into a blur of meetings, followed by a dip into a desert-ed Commons Chamber, followed by the reassuring tedium of the afternoon committee. It was a delegated legislation committee, which gave me a chance to sign off on casework and respond to diary invites in between running to and fro for votes in the chamber where all the gossip was about who would win the brutal race to become our new Prime Minister.

It was later, when I was sitting four rows back in the Chamber, waiting for the final vote and trying to remember if I'd drawn the curtains over the picture window at home or if my flat would be stifling when I got back, that my phone came alive.

A message from Donna. *Laurelle's plastered the estate with posters.*

Oh dear. I knew my reply wouldn't be enough, but she came right back at me.

It's serious.

Bit tied up just now. I'll drop in tmrw.

Next came a message from Gerald.

We need a new leader. Meeting in my office tomorrow 3 p.m.

I turned round to see if he was sitting in his usual place with the rebels in the back row, but he wasn't, so I texted him. *I'll be there.* I was going to add a smiling face emoji but thought that would be too glib, a crying one too pathetic, a being sick one too excessive. I put the flexed biceps one and pressed send.

Ping. A message from Hugh in the whip's office.

You're on the non domestic rating (preparation for digital services) bill committee. First meeting committee room 10, 2.30 p.m tomorrow. Don't be late.

This was non-negotiable or refusable; it wasn't even particularly answerable.

So I texted Gerald. *Who told Hugh about your meeting?*

Reply from Gerald. *Shit.*

Next a message from Joey. *Urgent emails, check your inbox.*

I was scrolling through them when he sent another message.

Toby Davis says can you bring drinks forward to lunchtime tomorrow.

It would be tight, but it would be doable. It might even be fun, or at the very least light relief in what was shaping up to be a grim day. I sent Joey a thumbs up.

Then came a message from Stephanie.

Miracle's here with her baby.

Who's Miracle?

The woman from the meeting. The one in the yellow dress.

Where?

The Cooper Estate.

The place where our fates would be played out. Where her family had their farm. I wondered whether all Stephanie saw there was grey concrete housing on the brink of destruction. Or whether, in her mind's eye, she saw past that to the brighter colours of a lost world.

CHAPTER 4
London: 13 June 1638

R adiant spring gave way to easy summer.

In the fields outside the little cottage, Elizabeth tended her crops under a beguiling sun. It caressed her bare arms and kissed her face as softly as a lark's breath. Butterflies hovered over hedgerows white with elderflowers, laced through with pink dog roses, thick with moss-lined nests cradling sparrows' blue eggs.

Around her the farm shimmered green with the promise of a good harvest. From the orchard floated music. Her older brother, Young Will, lay under an apple tree singing to their sister Mary, his pure voice like golden fairy dust carried through the air to bewitch them all.

Beyond the sweet-scented rosemary hedge, under its arch of budding roses, the cottage door opened, and a woman came out carrying a bundle wrapped in a woollen shawl, followed by a young girl, alike her in her grey clothes and earnest bearing.

"Mother," Elizabeth called to the woman and then ran to meet her in the orchard, where she'd stopped to talk to Young Will and Mary.

"I'm taking Little Tommy to church for St Anthony's day," said Rebecca. "To pray that the saint's fires will burn away his sickness."

"Can I come with you?" asked Elizabeth. She pulled back the woollen shawl to uncover the wan face of her youngest brother, whose eyes registered only pain.

"No, Sarah will come with me," said Rebecca. "You're needed here to help your father with the farm."

"I'll say a prayer for you, Lizzie," said Sarah.

"I could come and say prayers for us all," said Young Will.

"No, Young Will, I need you to mind Mary," Rebecca said. "You understand her best of all of us." She stroked Mary's golden head, her daughter, nearly a woman, but still as helpless as a child.

Elizabeth followed her mother and sister across the fields to where Will worked with Richard, a sturdy young boy as like his father in looks as in hot-headed temperament. She saw the gentleness with which her father kissed his frail baby in Rebecca's arms.

Hope shone in Rebecca's face, though whether for her baby's health or her husband's affections, Elizabeth couldn't tell. She'd seen tenderness between her parents once, before they'd started arguing about Young Will studying for the church instead of helping on the farm, or struggled with the burden of caring for Mary and then Little Tommy.

Now it was left to Richard to put his arms round his mother and say, "We'll miss you Ma." He stood on tiptoe and kissed his younger brother.

"You've made him all dirty." Sarah scolded Richard and wiped Little Tommy's face with a corner of his blanket.

But Rebecca gave Richard the special smile that Elizabeth noticed she reserved just for him, before she and Sarah made their measured way along the path that ran beside the field, and then turned left by the holly tree on the road to London.

· · · · ●·●· · · ·

At midday they broke off their work and went into the cottage.

Opposite the door was the hearth, empty now in summer, with a nursing chair in front and Little Tommy's crib beside it. In the centre of the main room was a table, set with a platter of bread and cheese and a jug of water from the well. Benches stood on either side of the table, and at one end was Will's stout wooden armchair. To the right of the hearth was an elaborately embossed dower chest. Rebecca had brought it by cart as a hopeful bride from her father's grand house in Kent, full of treasures she'd not needed in her husband's home, apart from the Bible, from which Young Will read each evening. Beyond the chest was the bed the parents shared.

After they'd eaten, and Will and Richard had gone back out to work, Elizabeth set Mary in the nursing chair by the hearth and gave her a bowl of beans to pod.

"Pod, pod," said Mary and nodded her sleepy face and smiled. Then Elizabeth went into a small side-room, reached under the bed she shared with her sisters and pulled out her box of treasures. She opened it, lifted up the folded dress inside and from underneath took out John Lilburne's leaflet.

She called Young Will to sit down at the table and put the leaflet in front of him. "I want you to read this to me." The leaflet was the weight of a wren's egg, the colour of fresh linen, indented with uneven black lettering. "I want to know what it says."

Young Will took the leaflet to the door and held it up to the light and squinted. "Where did you get this, Lizzie?"

"In Westminster, the day John Lilburne was flogged," Elizabeth said. "Read it, Young Will."

"It says 'In which there is an universal challenge to the whole world...'"

"Yes, I've heard that bit, read on, read on."

"'A full demonstration that the Bishops are enemies of Christ and his Kingdom and of the King's most excellent Majesty.'" He lowered the leaflet. "Lizzie, this is wrong. Mother would never allow it."

"She's not here."

"You can't believe this."

"Pa does and he can't be wrong. Read on, Young Will." Elizabeth shook her brother's arm.

He turned over the leaflet and screwed up his eyes to read. "'These affairs may displease the priests and that fraternity which indeed are the very polecats, stoats and weasels in the warren of church and state.' Lizzie, this is wicked. Stoats and weasels. If it wasn't for the bishops' charity, I wouldn't be able to read at all. It's a sin to talk like this about the Church."

"People say this leaflet is what's caused all the trouble in London," said Elizabeth. "I must know what it says. If you won't read it to me, then teach me how and I'll read it for myself."

"Alright," said Young Will. "I'll teach you to read the truth." And he took the family's bible off the dower chest and led Elizabeth outside. When Rebecca returned home with Sarah and Little Tommy, the baby no better for his blessing, Elizabeth was tracing G-E-N-E-S-I-S in the dust outside the front door.

• • • • •• • •• • •

So Elizabeth learned to read, the summer faded, the asparagus grew into a forest of feathery green ferns, two goslings were sent off squawking to market, and in the orchard, the trees were hung with autumn fruits.

On the first frosty morning of winter, when Elizabeth brought in the bucket of fresh milk from the barn, she found Rebecca crying over Little Tommy's crib. When she looked inside, her brother lay still, his grey face turned to the wooden crib-side that was his last sight of this world, hands curled together as if praying for a safe passage to the next. She touched his cold skin and felt fear that life could be so insubstantial, that it could pass so easily without anyone knowing quite when it had gone, and felt sadness that his death had been as unnoticed as his life had been.

She went out to call her father, and when they came back, Rebecca was feeding Mary at the table, the girl with her golden curls, sleepy eyes and pink skin, gurgling, "Ma, ma," with milk dribbling down her chin. Light from the window fell on them, a golden shaft that enveloped mother and child like a holy painting in church. But it did not extend to Elizabeth, or the crib.

Elizabeth wondered at the ease with which Rebecca had moved on from mourning her dead child to tending to the living and whether, if she were to die, it would be of such little consequence.

"The boy should have thrived." Will bent over the crib. "What happened?" He turned to his wife and Elizabeth saw how his eyes rested on Mary and his expression softened. And how his eyes then shifted to Rebecca, spooning porridge into the girl who should have been able to feed herself. And how his face hardened, and how he kissed Mary's head, but didn't kiss his wife, and went outside.

Only Sarah truly grieved for her lost brother. In bed that night, Elizabeth held Sarah as she sobbed about how she would rock her brother when he cried.

"I loved him more than any of us," she said. "I used to talk to him about how we'd play together when he grew stronger. And when one day he smiled at me, such a dear smile, I told Mother that Little Tommy would live after all. But Mother didn't answer. I don't think she liked to hope, or perhaps in her heart she knew different. He was mine, all mine, and now I've lost him."

And Elizabeth wondered if there was something wrong with herself that she couldn't cry as Sarah did. Or if her heart was made of stone that the tears didn't flow from her eyes, or if perhaps it was because she was older that she felt less, and whether, if this continued, she might end up feeling nothing at all when she was fully grown.

"He should have become another pair of hands to work on the land." Will lifted the box with his son's body to take for burial.

Elizabeth walked beside her father and talked to him about the laying up of winter stores. But he didn't reply, instead ran his free hand through his hair and muttered about the king and taxes and how would they manage. Elizabeth said they could lift some of her asparagus crowns and sell them at the fair on St George's Fields. But he talked about selling land and turned to tell Sarah, walking behind with Young Will, to stop crying because Little Tommy's death was a blessed relief.

In church, Rebecca paid the priest to deliver a mass for the soul of Little Tommy. Elizabeth lit a candle for her dead brother and watched its thin light reach heavenwards where perhaps the boy's soul had gone. Young Will sang as his brother's body was carried out of church. His voice unlocked Rebecca's tears, and she sobbed a storm as her youngest child was buried. Even Richard's face was sad, and he stroked his mother's hand, as solicitous as a grown man.

Elizabeth felt the chill of Little Tommy's death creep over them all.

· · · ● · ● · ● · · ·

Winter withered the asparagus fronds and stripped bare the branches of the orchard trees. Outside the barn the geese honked as Richard smashed the ice sheet on the water trough.

Inside the little cottage, Elizabeth feared that even the hottest fire could not melt her parents' frozen hearts.

· · · ● · ● · ● · · ·

Spring offered hope of a new beginning. Will went to London with eggs and herbs to sell. He returned with reports that people in the city had been struck by a shivering sickness, so Elizabeth could not take her precious sparrow-grass to market. When spring turned to summer, he returned home with stories of riots, and it was Rebecca who told Elizabeth she must stay at home.

"Rebellion at last," said Will. "The King wants to raise taxes for his war in Scotland. People are rising up against him and his bishops."

Elizabeth wondered if it was the summer sun, or his passion for rebellion, or the time spent in the taverns in Southwark that had made his face so red.

"It's against the divine will. No good will come of the people's defiance," said Rebecca.

That autumn brought torrential rain, rotting the turnips in their field, keeping the family indoors. Sarah went out to sell eggs from the chickens she'd reared in the barn, and came home soaked. Rebecca set the girl's wet clothes before the fire to dry, wrapped her in a soft wool shawl taken from her dower chest and tucked her into the bed that she and Will shared. Sarah sneezed and coughed and sank until Rebecca cried that she couldn't lose Sarah too.

By Christmas, Sarah had recovered enough to sit in front of the fire and hold her hands out to its warmth. Elizabeth thought she could see firelight through her sister's translucent fingers and wondered if they would ever be strong enough to collect the hens' eggs or milk the cow again.

Death hovered over the little cottage that winter, looking for an excuse to strike.

· · · · · ● · ● · · · ·

Another spring crept in. Elizabeth went out to find the purple shoots of her asparagus poking through the soil. Hollowed out by hunger, she felt as if they were fingers reaching out to grasp the life from her. She cut them down and went with Will to sell them in the city from where she bought a greyish stick of sugar for Sarah. Rebecca scolded at the waste of money but chipped the sugar into hot milk and smiled as her ailing daughter plumped out.

Summer balm followed and Elizabeth spent long days under the fruit trees with the sister she thought she'd lost.

"Sun, sun," said Mary, or was it, "Sing, sing." For a while Elizabeth sang, joined by Young Will, and Richard and then their parents, the family singing with relief at their survival. But then the sun grew too hot, the rains failed, the crops shrivelled, and the music stopped. Storms battered what was left of the harvest.

"It's God's will, his judgement on us for these rebellious times," said Rebecca.

With nothing to sell and talk of plague in London, even Will kept away. Mary grizzled, "Food, food," until Will shouted at her and Young Will shouted at him and then the father hit his namesake who'd never shouted before in his life.

In the ruined fields, Elizabeth, dull with hunger, watched the couple on the neighbouring farm pile their household goods onto a handcart and walk away, the man's hat pulled low across his face, his wife's head sunk into her shawl. Elizabeth raised her hand to wave, opened her mouth to wish them God speed. But her words died as her neighbours' land had done. She knew how it would end for them, a half-life in the hovels on the city's edge. One more failed harvest, she thought, just one more, and there will we be too. And she determined that failure would never come so long as she survived.

· · · · ●· ●· · · ·

Waking one winter morning to an unnatural silence, Elizabeth breathed on the window by her bed, scratched away the ice that crusted the inside of the glass and looked out to a white world. The trees stood hoary-coated, every branch and twig rimed with frost, each blade of grass bent under the icy weight of it. Across the fields, whiteness tipped the numbed furrows of brown earth. Still, still it was, no flick of foxes' brush in all the land, no twitch of bird's wing in the orchard, no bark or song to break the silence.

In the first days of the new year, Will took Elizabeth and Richard to see the frozen Thames. He paid a penny to the lighter-men who stood by useless boats drawn up on the quay side and Elizabeth climbed down the steps to the river. She stretched out a foot that slid away from her across the slippery glassiness. Richard took two steps and fell on the ice, his cheeks nipped red, his laughter turned to cloud in the cold air. The frost fair was as busy as Borough Market. Will took Elizabeth's hand, pulled Richard to his feet, and led them among the crowds of people to a tent pitched on the ice. Smoke curled out of the canvas and inside stood a firebox with a cauldron of bubbling liquid over it.

"Wine." Will tossed a coin at the woman swathed in shawls, huddled over the cauldron. "Here Lizzie, this will warm you."

Elizabeth put her hands round the pewter mug, felt the heat on her palms, sipped the wine, felt a dizziness in her head. "What spell was cooked in that cauldron?" she asked her father.

"You can wonder," the woman hobbled out of her tent. Her shawl slipped back to reveal a face more wizened by age and malice than any Elizabeth had ever seen. "But there's no spell can save you."

Will laughed at the old woman. "Humbug," he said and turned his back.

Richard gulped the rest of the wine down and sicked it up red all over the white frost.

· · · • • • • • · ·

Spring came late that year. Will took Elizabeth to London to sell her first asparagus harvest. On the way home they turned into a courtyard close to St Saviour's Church, surrounded on three sides by the galleried buildings of St George's Inn. Will opened a door and pushed Elizabeth in front of him, and they stood, father and daughter, breathing in choking tobacco smoke that stung their eyes, hearing a cacophony of laughter, fights, and the scraping of stools on the wooden floors.

"That's a pretty boy you've got, Will." A woman with a jug of ale and a fistful of tankards sashayed towards them. "You are a boy, aren't you?" The woman bent to peer into Elizabeth's face, and the girl smelt her sour breath and caught a glimpse of soft breasts. "Cheeky sod," The woman stood up and mouthed a kiss at Will.

"Come, Will. Leave Kate alone." A young man in rough grey clothes called out from a smoky corner of the tavern.

"Oliver." Will took a tankard from Kate and joined his friend in a group sitting at a table. Elizabeth stood behind her father, rested her chin on his shoulder, and stared at the men who crowded around.

"My brother's set sail for America," said Oliver. "He says there's nothing left for him here. Our father's land is lost, our money's eaten up by taxes."

"He should stay and fight," said Will.

An older man, with a thin face made longer by his straggly beard, shook his head and waved a finger at Will. "You'll get us all hanged."

"You know that's how things will end with this King," said Will. "With his wars and his foreign wife and his calling of Parliament and then dismissing it. And now he's left London. Abandoned our city. If ever he tries to come back, we must fight him."

"We can't fight our own King. That's treasonous talk," the old man said.

"And what you say isn't true, Will." The speaker was a young man in a black velvet jacket with a ring in one ear, from which hung a pearl that jiggled while he talked. "What's happening is not the King's fault, it's the bishops'. Even Freeborn John says so."

"Our hero." Oliver held up his tankard. His reddened eyes fixed on Kate, hovering around the group with her jug of ale.

She smirked and filled his tankard until the ale slopped onto the floor.

"It's not the bishops who tax us. It's the King," said Will. "There's been a tyranny from him these many years."

"You go too far, Will. Besides, your wife's Catholic isn't she?" The man with the pearl earring might have said more, but Kate bent and whispered into his ear and refilled his tankard.

"My children are brought up good Protestants."

Elizabeth heard a new emotion in her father's voice. Fear.

When they finished their drinks, Will grasped Oliver's outstretched hand, and slapped the back of the man with the earring so the pearl jiggled till Elizabeth thought it would break loose. He reached a sly hand behind Kate and Elizabeth saw her start and heard the men laugh. They left the inn and walked along the wide road that led south.

"We won't tell your mother about where we've been or what's been said, shall we?" Will said, leaning on Elizabeth to steady himself.

That summer, the rain beat down and Will spent nights away. He'd return days later saying the road from London was impassable. Elizabeth wondered how hard he'd tried, and whether it was Oliver or Kate who had kept him in town. She got on with the planting, and harvesting, with Richard to help her in the fields and Sarah to manage the animals in the barn.

At the year's end Rebecca counted out their savings. "You see, you respect the natural order of things and you reap your reward."

· · · · ● · ● · · ·

The next year they all forgot their hunger. On the farm the crops grew, the animals multiplied. Outwardly, Elizabeth was little changed: taller, slimmer, still dressed like a boy and mistaken for one. But inside she felt herself to be a different person. She knew that her family had only survived the hard years on the farm because of her. That her father, who she loved dearly, so dearly, had failed them.

That blithe summer kindled in Elizabeth memories of summers past, recollections from a childhood she'd left behind. Looking up from hoeing in her fields, she saw her parents embrace under a tree in the orchard, a longing shine in her mother's eyes, her father's hand around Rebecca's back, pulling her to him, a kiss, a smile, a promise, perhaps. An instant, and then he returned to his fields and she to her cottage. And then in the evening, through the bedroom door, Elizabeth heard their whisperings, their moans and the creaking of their bed.

· · · ●· ●· · · ·

Autumn settled. There was a stillness on the farm. Dank air hung heavy over sodden earth. The summer birds had long since flown. In the orchard, the cow munched the ruins of the fruit. Only the chickens, pecking around the cottage, disturbed the peace.

Elizabeth smiled as she worked. Wearing rough trousers and smock, her hair was twisted away from her face, she cut back the season's dead growth, content that before the year ended, she would be ready for whatever the new one brought. Richard, dressed in his father's old clothes cut down and refashioned by his mother, appeared with a pitchfork to carry away the cuttings. Behind him waddled the geese, which careered off, necks and wings outstretched, honking at a figure walking along the path past the turnip field.

"Look, Lizzie," said Richard.

Elizabeth turned to inspect their visitor; a young man, dressed in grey clothes and heavy boots, a pack on his back. Over his shoulder he carried a gun, and swaggered with the power of it, although she doubted this particular man would ever have the courage to use it.

"That's Oliver. He's Pa's friend. What have you come for, Oliver?"

"I've come for your father."

"Are you going to fight?" Richard planted himself in front of Oliver, forcing him to stop. "Can I come too?"

"Pa didn't say he was expecting you." Elizabeth's fear worried at her like a yapping dog.

The cottage door opened and Will appeared. His ginger hair was flecked with grey, the freshness of his face was gone, and his eyes had narrowed. But he still filled the doorway with his broad frame which was dressed for travel.

"It's time," Oliver called.

"And I'm ready," Will replied. "Come in and keep out the cold while I say my farewells."

Her parents had been arguing again; Elizabeth sensed it as soon as she stepped over the threshold. Her father stood by the table, her mother was at the fireside where Mary, rounder but only a little taller, sat on the nursing chair. Her parents' anger filled the space between them.

"You shouldn't go, Will," said Rebecca. "There'll be no one to look after us." Mary's feet were curled on the floor, her face red, her mouth clenched, and she rocked back and forth.

"Lizzie can look after the land till I get back, can't you?" He raised his eyes to Elizabeth, and she realised with surprise that he wanted her approval. "And you've got Richard to help now."

"Look at her, Will," Rebecca put her arm around Mary. "She's your daughter. She's helpless. There'll be wild men everywhere if there's a war. Who will defend her?"

Elizabeth wished he would say something that would chase away the fear that skulked around the room, or at least provide the family with some comfort.

"What about your oldest lad?" asked Oliver. "He must be big enough to take care of the women."

"He can't see, let alone fight. All he'd do is run off to church to pray for both sides in any battle, which is what he's doing now." Will laughed scornfully.

Mary roused herself at her father's laughter. Her face pinkened and her mouth puckered; she laughed and then rocked even harder.

Rebecca put a hand on Will's shoulder as he bent over his pack. "I don't know how we'll manage if you go."

"And I don't know how we'll manage if I stay." Will shrugged her off. "In the bad years we can't grow enough to feed ourselves. And when we have food to sell, sickness keeps us out of the city. We can't pay the taxes for the king's wars, we're always in debt. We'll lose what's left of our land unless something changes. Don't you see, Rebecca? Our old life has gone, and we won't get it back. We have to fight for something new."

"And what if you don't come back?" Rebecca asked.

Her mother gave voice to the fear Elizabeth felt. Her father had talked to her about his dreams of freedom for as long as she could remember, and she had shared them. But now he was trading the certainty of their present life, however hard, to pursue something that, even if it did happen, would at best bring suffering for him, and at worst destroy them all. For once, Elizabeth understood her mother and sided with her. Her father shouldn't go.

Oliver shifted the gun on his shoulders. "You can't listen to this woman; you must come, Will. The call is out for every man in London to take up arms. The King's troops overran Parliament's Army on the road from Oxford. They beat us again at Brentford and captured Freeborn John. If we don't fight, the King will enter the city tomorrow and our cause will be lost."

Will swung his pack onto his back. "You can't be surprised, Rebecca. I've always said I would fight for our freedom. Up till now it's been all talk. Now the King's marching on London, I have to go."

"I'll go with you if you let me, Father," said Richard.

"I know, boy. But you're too young, you must stay here," Will ruffled his son's hair.

"What about me?" Elizabeth asked.

"You're a girl," said Will.

"We may never see you again." Elizabeth's words hung in the air like a spell until Oliver broke it.

"If you won't come with me now, I'll go alone."

Elizabeth knew then that she'd lost her father. He would be too proud to let his friend leave alone, too ashamed to be stopped by his wife, much less his daughter, too driven by the hope of achieving the freedom he'd talked about all her life.

"You'll need to be back before summer. There'll be another baby then." Rebecca was holding Mary, and the girl put her arms around her mother's stomach, cradling also the unborn child. Sourness flooded Elizabeth's mouth: the taste of fear. She swallowed. Oliver went to the door and lifted the latch.

"I'll be outside Will."

"I'm coming." Will lifted his pack. "Goodbye, Richard, Sarah, Mary." He slapped Richard on the back, caressed Sarah, lingered with Mary. "Lizzie. Take care of them." Elizabeth put her head against his chest, heard his beating heart, felt his arms around her, smelt his smoky earthiness and wished things could remain just so. Then he pulled away from her and turned to Rebecca. "I'll return before summer, I promise." He stroked her hair and kissed her, and Elizabeth saw a remnant of affection—or was it remorse?

"Wait a moment." Rebecca pulled away from Will and went to the dower chest. She opened its doors and took out a box, burrowed to the bottom of it and pulled out a package which she kissed and pressed into her husband's hand.

"What's this?" Will opened his hand and Elizabeth saw, lying in it, a yellow metal locket on a chain.

"It has a piece of our Lord's cross inside," said Rebecca. "My mother got it from her mother who had it from her grandmother who got it from a monastery in Kent. It will keep you safe."

Will lifted the locket to inspect it. For a moment Elizabeth thought he would throw it into the fire.

"Keep it with you, Will. For my sake if not your own," said Rebecca.

Will recovered himself and tucked the locket into his pocket. "Say goodbye to Young Will for me. Tell him to pray to all his blessed angels for victory, or if he can't do that, at least pray for my soul, such as it is."

Elizabeth felt the life go out of the cottage with her father. The latch on the front door clattered down behind him. For a moment the space where he had been held his imprint. Then it melted into the air and all that remained was the sound of Sarah's sobs and Mary's grunts.

Elizabeth ran outside. The air had chilled; the light was sullen. The two men were walking fast, already past the orchard. Oliver turned and glowered at her, then pushed Will to walk faster. At the holly tree, Will stopped and put his pack on the boundary stone.

"You will come back to us Pa, won't you?" Elizabeth had run out barefoot, and the winter wetness chilled her feet.

"If I can. God willing, although I don't think God will have much to do with what happens."

"How will we manage without you?" asked Elizabeth. There was so much more she wanted to ask him. Why the bonds that had tied him to his family had become so weak that he could choose to leave them and whether it was their freedom that he was pursuing or his own. Whether he still loved them, at all, a little, as much as she loved him. But close as they were, she couldn't ask. Or perhaps she dared not, in case he gave the wrong answer.

"You'll know what to do Lizzie. You'll cope; you always do," her father said. He looked sad and Elizabeth felt unworthy, as if in this final moment she'd let him down.

"Come, Will," said Oliver. "We must hurry, the light's fading."

Will picked up his pack. He held Elizabeth's arms and kissed her head, and she thought she heard him whisper something about love. She wished she was still small enough to climb onto his shoulders and be carried away with him. Instead, she had to stand in the cold evening and watch him walk off towards London.

A mist was falling. It obscured the road and muffled all sound, and soon its swirling whiteness claimed the two men. Before he disappeared into it, Elizabeth thought that Will turned and waved. But perhaps it was just a twist of the dying light. She'd have to ask him when he came home.

CHAPTER 5

London: morning 11 June 2019

*N*ame: Miracle James

Date of Birth: 01/01/2000

Address: 85 Speedwell House, Cooper Estate (temporary)

Sierra Leone citizen. Arrived Heathrow June 2015. Worked as carer for elderly British gentleman. Croydon. Exact address unclear. He died December 2018. Blessing (girl) born 8 November 2018. British. Since then lived in B&Bs etc in Croydon, Lewisham, Lambeth, Southwark. Now in single room in Speedwell House. Shared apartment. Informal arrangement.

Immigration status: Unclear. Home Office letter refers.

Wants: Visa. Work. 2 bedroomed house with garden for self and child. Failing that any place to live. Anywhere.

Smiley face emoji. smiley face emoji.

I re-read Stephanie's note and sighed.

"This is the woman with the baby?" I was sitting in the easy chair in the cool of my office in Portcullis House, my laptop on my lap, the desk behind me piled with publications and reports, tranches of paper that kept on coming however much I recycled. Stephanie was perched on a hardback seat opposite. She had spent a week on the Cooper Estate taking down in minute detail every resident's preferred outcome to the redevelopment.

Which Joey entered into a spreadsheet and generated zillions of emails for me to sign off.

His appearance had taken an upturn since Stephanie's arrival, and he sat at his desk in a pair of skinny trousers and a black shirt—both new—and with his hair trimmed. She had taken to dressing in a more casual style; light slacks and a loose top, although clothes that were so simple and looked so good were usually expensive. She still wore her Alice band.

"Yes, that's the person," she said. "Miracle hung around the community centre a few times but only plucked up the courage to come in yesterday afternoon, once everyone else had left."

"There's not much here. With other people you've got their whole life story and everything they want apart from the colour of their front door."

"She said a lot, but I couldn't quite catch all the details. It would be good if you could see her sometime."

"And she's only 19."

"She said her mother told her she was the first baby born in Freetown in the new millennium. So I've put 01/01/2000."

"She doesn't have a passport?" It was a question, but I knew the answer.

"She wasn't clear about that. I guess it got lost. She showed me a letter from the Home Office dated January but it's just an acknowledgement. I took a picture of it—see."

I looked at her phone. The address on the letter was in New Cross, and NRPF was stamped across the top. No recourse to public funds. Five words that kept her out of our welfare state. I sighed again. So many lost souls in my patch of south London. The only thing of use on the letter was a reference number. "Joey can email the Home Office and we'll put her on the Cooper Estate list for rehousing, but I don't fancy her chances until we get her immigration status sorted."

"The thing is, Frances, she's stressed out." A line appeared in Stephanie's smooth forehead. "I mean, like, completely. She can't sit still for five seconds and her eyes wander off all over the place as if she's scared someone's going to get her. She didn't exactly say what had happened, but you only have to look at the dates."

"Did she have the baby with her?"

"Blessing? Yes. She's real cute and Miracle is beyond devoted. She'll do anything for her little girl. I guess it goes with being a mother."

I winced. "Joey can give things an extra push with the Home Office, he's good at that."

The phone buzzed. Joey answered it while I scrawled, "Trafficked? Raped?" across the top of Miracle's notes. "I'll try to see her next time I'm on the estate."

"That would be great. She didn't say much about what happened in Croydon, and I didn't like to ask. You know, it's not something I'm competent to deal with. But I can tell she's terrified. Like someone that's drowning. She'll grab hold of anything."

Joey put his phone down. "Donna says can you drop in on your way home tonight. And Hugh called earlier to remind you about a committee meeting this afternoon. And you're overdue for your drink with that Toby Davis character."

· · · · · • · • · · · ·

When I went along the corridor to get the lift down to the atrium, I found Gerald slouched in uncharacteristic gloom.

"Shafted," he said. "Poison locally, bedlam nationally and Hugh's done a complete hatchet job on my efforts at a coup.

For the first time in my life, I've looked at our colleagues who've jumped ship and thought, 'good call'."

"Can't you ride it out?" The lift arrived, and we got in.

"When does riding it out become collaboration?"

"Come on, Gerald, it's not that bad."

"It is when your wife says you're a class traitor for even thinking of rebelling against our Leader and buggers off."

"Oh no."

"With the kids. The middle one's done a blog on it." Everything about him was hangdog; his face, his shoulders, even his trousers sagged.

When the lift doors opened on the ground floor, they delivered us into the snake-eyed gaze of Hugh on his way to the coffee bar. He didn't have to say anything. We all knew our choice of company was clocked.

· · · ● ● ● ● · · ·

Toby was waiting when I arrived at the bar in The Cut. He was sitting at a table far enough from the door to be discreet, but not so far as to be ignored. He'd taken off his jacket, loosened his tie and undone the top button of his shirt to create an aura of casual rakishness. In this light his hair which I'd previously thought was faded blonde, looked distinguished grey. Not so bad after all.

"Good of you to make space in your schedule. I know how busy you are." The table had chairs on two sides at right angles to each other. Toby stood up and held back the other chair, and when I slipped in, he sat down again, so close I could smell his after shave and see that, for all his composure, he had pinpricks of sweat on his forehead.

"It's about the Cooper Estate, isn't it?" I asked.

"Yes."

"Are you involved with the developers?"

"Now, Frances, don't go getting the wrong end of the stick." He only had to twitch a finger, and the waiter was there to take his order. "It's not quite like that. Not at all. The Loverage people aren't monsters. They're just the contractors caught in the middle of things."

"Just. And I suppose they're doing it for charity. I'm not stupid." Our drinks arrived. Diet cola for me, sparkling water for him. "By the way, these are on me."

"For goodness' sake, they're not even proper drinks. Look, it's not the contractors' fault. I mean, everyone's approved it. The government. The banks. The council even."

All the institutions which, over the years, had done down the likes of my mother. Not to mention the people on the Cooper. "But not the people who live there."

Toby blinked. The pinpricks of sweat on his brow turned to beads.

"Come on, Frances, you know the estate can't continue. You've seen the structural surveys, the financial projections for even the most basic repairs, let alone the kind of improvements that would future-proof it. Those tower blocks are a disaster waiting to happen. That's before you even get onto the need for more investment in the area. Shops, jobs. I mean, it's bang on the main road out of London."

"It's people's homes."

"And they can have new ones, better ones. I bet most of the residents would give their eyes' teeth for a move."

He had me there. I thought of all the transfer requests I'd sent to the council over the years. All for people wanting to get off the Cooper. None to get on.

"But they've got no inkling of what they'll be offered, or where. For all anyone knows they could be forced to move miles away. I mean, the council's been shunting people way up north. You know, Milton Keynes. How can people get to work from there?"

He put his head in his hands. "Your geography was always terrible." If it was faux-despair, it was still convincing. I had to laugh.

He brightened up at that. "Perhaps I could set up a meeting with my clients?"

"As in, do I want to commit political suicide?"

"You can put your people's point of view."

I laughed again. A different laugh this time, less funny-ha-ha, more funny-you-must-be-joking. Toby picked up on the edge in it. He leaned forward, serious.

"We've heard there's trouble brewing."

"And who started it?"

"Honestly, that's not going to help your constituents. It won't get them homes, or save the estate, and people could get hurt."

"And who's going to hurt them?" I gulped down what was left of my cola.

"Oh, really, Frances." He took a slow sip of his sparkling water. "My clients are only developers providing homes, not an invading army. It's not a war. Just regeneration. Much-needed, as you well know. You've made enough speeches complaining about the state of housing in your constituency. There's always some residents who hold out against projects like this; all we need is to find out what they want and make sure they're kept happy."

On he went with his "trust me, I'm a PR man" patter chipping away at my defences. My phone pinged. A message from Hanna.

"Affairs of state?" asked Toby.

I shook my head. "My mother."

"Is she alright? She has health issues, doesn't she?" Gimlet eyes.

"How did you know?"

"The one time you got less than perfect marks in our politics course, it was because your mother was unwell."

"You remember that?"

He smiled.

In some corner of my teflon-coated heart a little bird sang.

"OK. One short meeting, no notes."

Silly bird.

He was right—it wasn't war. But I didn't think the Cooper would go down without a fight. I knew whose side I was on even if the odds were stacked against them. I was due there soon. And then I thought of Stephanie, and how her family had disappeared in a real war.

CHAPTER 6

London: 16 November 1642

Elizabeth kept her terror at bay, hemmed into a corner of her mind like the fox that her father once trapped with his pitchfork in a corner of the barn. Man and beast sizing each other up for a kill.

It was three days since Will had left. During which time the sun hadn't shown its face and now had given up trying. Elizabeth was outside lifting turnips in the drizzle with her brother Richard to help her pile them into a basket and carry them to the barn to store for winter.

There was a flapping of wings and the geese rushed past towards the road, necks outstretched, honking. She stopped digging and saw a ghostly shape turn off the Kent road. As she leaned on her spade and strained to see, the shape turned into a figure with a pack on his back and a gun over his shoulder.

"Father," Richard shouted and threw down the turnips and ran across the field.

But the man who came back through the half-light wasn't their father.

"Oliver," said Elizabeth. The man who'd taken her father away, whose claims on her father's loyalty, if not his affections, had outweighed hers. And now here he was, returning alone.

It was as if the fox had escaped the pitchfork and was running riot round the barn.

"Where's Pa?" she asked.

Oliver stopped, one arm around Richard, and turned his stony face towards her.

The cottage door opened; Rebecca ran out and across the garden. "Where is he?" Her voice was more desolate than the winter fields.

"You abandoned him." Elizabeth grabbed Oliver's arm as if she could pull him down to her level, force him to look her in the face and admit his guilt. He shook her off, and walked on towards the cottage.

"You took him from us," Elizabeth ran after him. "You shamed him into it. And now you've left him to die somewhere."

Oliver rounded on her, "No," and then turned to Rebecca who was standing with one hand on her belly where the coming child lay.

"Is he dead?" Rebecca asked.

"I thought I might find him here," Oliver said.

"How should Will be here?" Rebecca led him into the cottage. "We weren't expecting him for weeks, months even."

"Why won't you answer my question?" Elizabeth followed him inside.

Oliver sat down in Will's chair at the head of the table, took off his pack and set it on the floor. Elizabeth felt Rebecca rest an arm across her shoulders, felt the weight of her mother's desperation bear down on her. The latch sounded at the front door: Rebecca gasped and Elizabeth turned, as if it might be her father returned. But it was only Sarah with a bowl of eggs stepping into the silence. The three women stood around the table. Richard climbed onto one of the benches.

"Pa is coming home, isn't he?" The brightness in his face had been replaced by blank dismay.

"Yes, he will come home," Oliver laid his gun on the table as slowly as an offering placed on an altar. "But I can't say when."

"Then how can you be so sure he will come?" the boy asked.

Elizabeth noted that although Oliver's boots were muddy and his clothes were wet, they were all as undamaged as the man: no bloodstains, no bandages, no sign of injury. His gun was as polished as it had been when he was last there, so recently that there'd scarcely been time for him to get to the City and back.

"You did go to the battle, didn't you?" she asked.

"Oh yes, we went to battle," Oliver took off his jacket and hung it over the chair with such deliberation that Elizabeth wanted to grab it from him and shout, "What did you do with him?" But she knew that if she did, he'd tell them even less, even more slowly. So she waited, they all waited, so quietly she could hear the crackle of the fire in the hearth, the hiss of the kettle sitting over it. Outside, a crow cawed. Sarah jumped, but Richard, disbelief hardening on his face, never took his eyes off their guest.

Finally, Oliver spoke. "We walked to London, and the mist thickened until it was so heavy we could scarce see. Men joined us along the way, appearing like ghosts out of the shadows. By the time we reached the river, we were already an army. At Bankside Will and I got into a boat crowded with men and it rowed off upstream.

"The water and the air became one in the fog and we hung in the whiteness. All we could see were the lanterns of the lookout boys at the front of the boats, all we could hear was the clang of their bells, sounding like tocsins. It was as if we were crossing the River Styx into another world, and I feared we were going to hell."

Oliver stretched out a hand as if to draw the scene before them. Richard and Sarah watched entranced; Rebecca with more caution. But to Elizabeth the gesture had the practiced manner of a storyteller in a tavern.

"It grew colder and darker," Oliver went on. "We huddled together for warmth and in this manner, we travelled up the river to Chelsea. It was late when we reached the fields where our forces were gathering. We found a place to put down our packs at the edge of the camp, but we didn't get much sleep. All night more men arrived until, when morning broke and the mist cleared, we saw the massed men of London, ready to defend our City against the King."

"And then you fought?" Richard leaned over the table to Oliver, but the man turned away and started tugging at one of his boots.

"Not directly." Oliver struggled with his boot until Elizabeth wanted to pull it off and hit him over the head with it.

"What happened to our father, Oliver?" she asked.

He got the boot off and rubbed his foot.

"You must tell us."

Instead, he started struggling with the other boot until Sarah ran around the table and yanked it off for him. Oliver flexed his foot, and kneaded it, and finally resumed his story.

"Carts arrived, sent by the merchants of London, piled high with food prepared by the wives of the City for their men. Some of the women came to cheer on their husbands in the battle. Will looked for you among them," he said to Rebecca.

"How would I have been there?" Rebecca protested.

"A lot of women were. And not all of them were wives." He chuckled.

"What's so funny about that?" Sarah asked.

"It was the women that held us back."

"Oh, it was the women's fault then?" said Elizabeth.

Oliver scowled at her.

"So you didn't fight after all?" Richard asked.

"Oh yes, of course we fought. A bit. Not much. The King's army fled before I could get to them. Some said they were hungry, and that when they saw us feasting, they lost their stomach for the fight. Some said the King didn't like to fight the people of London, especially when his soldiers were so outnumbered. His troops fired some shots, but we could see their hearts weren't in it and when daylight left us, they turned tail with their flags and fine horses and ran away."

"So what happened to our father?" Elizabeth wondered what Will had ever seen in this man who was like a rooster, puffing out his chest and crowing until the fox came too close.

There was a silence in the cottage. "I don't rightly know." Oliver's words hung in the air.

"You were with him. You must have seen." Rebecca cradled her stomach.

"He wasn't killed, if that's what you fear. No-one on our side died in the battle, not that I know of." Oliver's eyes flitted around the cottage, from the dower chest, to the bed, to the hearth; anything other than focusing on the desperate woman and her children. Sarah started weeping.

"When I saw how things were falling out, I tried to hold Will back. 'Don't go,' I said to him, 'it will all be over soon, and we can return home.' But he said, 'I've come to fight,' and pushed through the lines of men, joined the body of soldiers moving forward and was lost to my sight. I looked for him among the injured afterwards, but he wasn't there. So I thought he must have left already and perhaps I would find him here. He was very brave. I saw him with my own eyes pull one of the King's men off his horse and kill him. Small wonder they ran away."

"But you said there was no need to fight." The sharpness in Richard's voice pierced the storyteller's pretence: it was a new tone that spoke to Elizabeth of the hard man her brother would become.

Oliver thumped the table. "Why do you try to trick me? There was some fighting, and your father was at the front of it. You should be proud. It was a great victory we won against the King."

"It makes no difference to me who won or lost." There were tears in Rebecca's eyes and Elizabeth wondered whether they were for the missing father or the children he'd abandoned. "The only difference is that my husband hasn't come home. What does it matter if we win one battle more or one battle less, if Will's not here to work his land and protect his family? Without him, we're lost."

They had all been so intent on Oliver and his story that they'd forgotten Mary. Perhaps it was the fear in her mother's voice that unsettled her. Perhaps it was Sarah's sobs, although that was a familiar sound. Or perhaps it was just that she hadn't eaten since breakfast and was hungry.

Whatever it was, she rose from the nursing chair by the fire, lumbered across the room to the table and climbed onto the bench nearest Oliver. She spread her hands out on the table and leaned towards him and shouted, "Lost, lost," then screwed her face up with such venom that he recoiled.

"Is she cursing me?" he asked.

"Cuss, cuss." Mary stretched across the table.

"Shush," Elizabeth pulled her sister back, and then said to Oliver. "It's only Mary."

"She looks evil." Oliver crossed himself.

"She's not evil," Richard laughed. "She's just simple."

"She means no harm," said Sarah.

But Oliver wasn't to be placated. While Rebecca settled Mary back in her chair by the fire, he got up and put on his jacket and boots, lifted up his pack and slung his gun over his shoulder. "I must hurry if I'm to be home before dark."

Elizabeth followed him out of the cottage.

"Did he send no message for us?" Elizabeth searched Oliver's face for any sign of regret or understanding.

"What?" Oliver wouldn't even look at her.

"You heard me," Elizabeth said. "Did he give you any words of comfort to pass onto us?"

"No." Oliver glanced at her and then looked away. "He only talked of the battle and how we would defeat the King."

"He spoke nothing of us?"

She stepped so close she could see the nervous flicker of his eyelids and how his pointed tongue licked his lips as he opened his mouth to speak. And then she knew she didn't want to hear another lie from him.

"No matter," she said. "You'll tell us if you get any word of him, won't you?"

"Yes, of course." He spoke too quickly. She knew he wouldn't. This man who'd taken her father into battle and returned alone and without fighting would turn his back on the family he'd betrayed. She opened the garden gate, and he went out. Along the footpath she saw Young Will walking home from church, the oldest son, the family's provider and protector now her father had disappeared.

"Where was it you last saw my Father?" she called after Oliver.

"At a village called Turnham Green." He walked away, but then turned and shouted over his shoulder, "If you want news of him, ask Kate at the George Inn. She knows everything."

Across the bare fields Elizabeth saw a fox run off, a chicken clutched between its jaws.

CHAPTER 7

London: evening 11 June 2019

S corching day had mellowed into sweltering evening by the time I got to the Cooper Estate.

Boys were riding round the piazza on BMX bikes, jeans hanging halfway down their backsides. Above them soared the three inscrutable tower blocks. I'd been up and down them often enough, knocking on doors. But finding people in or getting them to open up was a different story. Judging by Stephanie's notes, it seemed that she'd been more successful, either because of her age, or her foreignness—or because the word had gone out that she wanted to talk to them about something that really mattered. One of the tower blocks was now completely empty, with the front entrance barricaded. One of the others was Speedwell House, where Miracle lived.

In the low-rise flats, windows and doors were open and kids hyped up by long hot days staying indoors out of the sun were running up and down the landings, laughing and shouting.

Donna's flat was on the ground floor, closest to the community centre. She opened her front door wearing a sleeveless top and loose cotton trousers, looking like she was about to melt. "You're late again." She led me into her sitting room, plonked herself down on the sofa and picked up the remote control to turn down the volume on her television.

"Come on, Donna, it's not a crime." I sat on a chair facing her.

"You've changed."

"I've grown up, Donna. I went away and made good. What's different is that I came back."

"It's not done you any harm, has it? Got you a cushy job 'n all."

"I've worked hard for it."

"Call that work?" She picked up a packet of cigarettes, took one out, then must have thought better of it because she put it away again. "Look, all I'm wanting is a place for me and the kid. A chance for him. Like life gave you."

"You've still got a child at home?"

Donna laughed, a deep-throated chuckle that made her face relax. "Don't be daft. He's my grandson. Dylan. Stella's boy."

Stella, Donna's daughter, the girl most of the others at school wanted to be. I was a few years ahead of her, so hadn't been around to see her spectacular fall from grace and only heard much later about her death from a drug overdose.

"Didn't you know about her son? He's out there now with his mates. Sometimes he lives with me, sometimes with them. I want to get him away from here before he gets into serious trouble."

"Where would you go?"

"You mean I have a choice?" Stella laughed, funny-bitter. "Wherever I can get. I've got a sister in Canvey Island. If I could get somewhere there, I'd think I'd died and gone to heaven."

"And you think you could get a move if the estate comes down."

"When. When. There's plenty others who want out. Trouble is, Laurelle and her crew are dead against it. I can understand where she's coming from, mind. They all work round here. They've got friends and they can manage. Like as not they'll get on and get out one day. And then there's some as don't want the council to know they're here in the first place. They don't want the place pulled down either. But some of us are stuck."

There was something I was missing in all of this. "You asked me to come round for something?"

Donna lit a cigarette. She avoided my eyes.

"I need your help to get a transfer." This time she took out a cigarette and lit it, blew out cigarette smoke, coughed, and only then did she look me in the face. "It's for the boy's sake, you understand. I need a two-bedroomed place." She took another drag on her cigarette. "Please."

I'd never known Donna ask for help. It must have cost her.

"Whatever you want, Donna."

"I don't need your pity." She could spot condescension a mile away. "I'm entitled."

I didn't know how to repair her battered pride. "Of course," I said.

She nodded. My signal to go. She came to the door with me. In the piazza the little kids had disappeared. Only the older boys were left, circling on their bikes in the sultry half-light, antsy, pretending laid-back but watching like hawks. A man's face appeared leaning over the walkway of one of the flats above. He spoke on his phone and then disappeared indoors. One of the boys laughed. Not at me. They weren't bothered about me.

A young woman in a yellow dress carrying a baby appeared from behind the community centre with a boy following her on his bike. The others started circling, closing in on her, and she screamed at them to go away.

"Miracle," said Donna.

"Oi, you, bugger off," I shouted at the boys.

They laughed. "Wotcher," one called back, but then to my surprise they cycled away.

"They're not bad really," Donna said. "That's my grandson over there." She pointed at a lanky young man slouching by one of the tower blocks. Whatever role he was finding in life looked no more promising than his mother's.

"And Miracle's off on one as usual. It's not drugs or anything, she's just not right. She's a good mother, mind. That child's always spotless."

"How does she manage?"

"She does childcare. You'd think social services would have something to say about that, but who's going to complain, so no-one bothers."

Miracle was shaking when I went over to her.

"Stephanie told me about you." I touched her arm; she started and pulled it away as if my hand was scalding. "Can we talk?"

She looked me up and down and then said, "Come."

Moisture cut black streaks down the grey concrete on the outside of Speedwell House. Some windows were broken, some were in darkness, a few were hung with net curtains. Miracle pulled the door open. There was no sign of the entry phone working. The hallway by the lifts was fly posted. "Refugees welcome," and "Hands off our homes," and, "Developers dream of your eviction," with a picture of a man in a smart suit rubbing his hands. He looked uncannily like Toby. Over everything plain white posters were plastered with the word "Occupy" emblazoned in red. Those must be Laurelle's.

The lift groaned upwards, then jerked to a halt not quite on a level with the top floor. Miracle clambered up and out, carrying the baby. I followed. The landing was silent. A light flickered

overhead. Metal frames covered the doors of three flats. Water
seeped out of an overflow from one of them and trickled down
the stairwell. Outside the fourth flat the vinyl floor had recently
been washed. There was a poster proclaiming "No Evictions,"
neatly sellotaped in the middle of the door and above it a picture
of a white man with long hair, a beard and folded hands, and
"Jesus loves you" written across the bottom. The letterbox was
sealed with industrial-grade sticky tape.

Inside was a hallway, clean so far as I could see in the gloom.

Miracle unlocked a door, and I followed her into what I
guessed was once the main bedroom. She pulled aside a sheet
that was tacked across the window and then opened it to let
in some air. The room was immaculate, mostly because it was
almost completely empty. There was a mattress on the floor
against one wall and three stuffed bin bags lined along the other.
A teddy bear poked out of the top of one of them. Beside the
bags was a chair with a microwave on it and a packet of dis-
posable nappies below. In the corner furthest from the window
three plastic boxes were stacked up, with a packet of Crunchy
Nut on top.

Miracle laid her baby down on the mattress, then lifted the
microwave off the chair and pointed to me to sit down. She sat
on the mattress with her baby and started changing her. Blessing
was a pretty child; her dark curls were thick and shiny and she
smiled and cooed contentedly. Her mother's woes had not yet
been visited on her.

"Stephanie's very kind," Miracle said.

"She said you've had a hard time." I pulled the packet of
nappies out from under the chair and passed one to Miracle.

"She understands."

"You were very young when you came here."

"I came here to be safe."

"How much did you have to pay?" There was no point asking whether.

Miracle rolled up the soiled nappy and went out of the room with it. I heard another door unlock, and then a tap run and she came back shaking water off her hands.

"My mother paid a woman who said she could get me a job working for an elderly gentleman. I was taken to his house from the airport and I had to stay there. I don't know exactly where it was. I did everything for him for two years. But then he died."

"Was he the father of your baby?"

She pulled a baby grow out of one of the plastic bags and put it on her daughter.

"It would help if I knew. It would help Blessing."

She didn't say anything.

"You were too young."

"I had no choice."

"It would make things easier for you with the Home Office." I felt mean being so brutal about it. Miracle undid the front of her dress and lifted the baby to her breast. The room was silent and both of us were still, watching the baby sucking with an expression of total bliss on her little face. I couldn't see the expression on Miracle's face, she had her head bent. If she'd looked at mine, she'd probably have seen envy. One of those moments when I regretted I'd been so focussed on my career.

My phone pinged. A text message from my mother's care home. *Call.*

"Think about it at least," I said to Miracle.

She nodded.

"And keep talking to Stephanie."

She didn't look up. As I closed the door she was sitting on the mattress on the floor feeding her baby, the Madonna of the tower block, with her yellow dress open at the front and the baby relaxing into satisfied sleep in her arms. The last of the sunlight, streaming in the window, caught the teddy bear poking out of the top of the bin liner. I thought it smiled at me.

· · · • • · • • · ·

Outside, lights speckled the flats. Most of the boys had gone; only two were left prowling on their bikes. They followed me, circling round, talking loudly as if that was going to scare me. In the carpark there was a black car with its headlights on. I got into mine and phoned my mother's home.

"She's refusing to eat," Hanna said.

"Is she drinking?"

"Oh yes. But she says she wants you to come and feed her. She says you always used to feed her."

There was the sound of an engine starting and tyres doing a tight turn in the carpark. The black car took off at speed.

"Tell her if she eats for you, I'll come and see her at the weekend."

"You're a tough lady." Hanna's voice was controlled.

I wanted to scream, "No, I'm not. It's just I know my mother's telling stories. I've never fed her. She'd never eat the food I made her. And before you ask, she never fed me much either."

A knock on the window. A police officer. Double take. On the Cooper? Yes, a police officer. A young one. I wound down the window.

"Alright, love?"

"I'm fine."

"You don't look like you belong here. Best not hang about."

"I belong here," I told him. But I didn't hang about. I needed a heart-to-heart with Stephanie.

CHAPTER 8

London: December 1642

Young Will sang so sweetly in the church at Christmas, his thin body lifting to shape the sound, his voice soaring to the vaulted roof in place of incense. Elizabeth watched her mother shut her eyes and raise her chin and smile, fingering, all the while, the rosary beads hidden under her shawl.

It wasn't just the thickening of her mother's body that troubled Elizabeth, it was the way she was withdrawing to focus on the new life inside her. There was an unforgiving relentlessness about it. Already there was no father to protect the children. Richard fidgeted beside her; Sarah was left at home to mind Mary. Soon they might not have a mother either. On the road that ran past the cottage, people going to London to sell produce or look for work were joined by men signing up for war or returning injured. Men with nothing left to lose.

Elizabeth nursed her fears into a wet new year. As the rain poured down outside, she sat on the bed in the little room she shared with her sisters. Her working clothes hung on a peg behind the door, and she wore a rough grey skirt and a blouse wrapped around with a heavy shawl which she pulled up over her mouth and nose and felt her warm breath caught in its folds. Through the lattice panes of grey glass, she watched rain struggle against a bitter cold. Time soon enough for planting and she wondered what the new season would bring.

She remembered a past winter when she'd walked on a frozen pond of water and the ice had fractured, cracks running from her feet in all directions. She recalled her panic, not knowing which way to run or whether to stand still, and if she did, whether the ice would give way and she'd drown. She felt like that now. Except then her father had held out a branch to her and pulled her off the pond. Now he was gone, and she carried the weight of her family on her shoulders.

Young Will spent most of his time at church, or when at home sat by the window reading his Bible. Their mother said he had a calling. Mary was still as dependent as the day she was born, Sarah looked after the hens and the cow, which left only hothead Richard to help her on the land. There was the un-certainty of the new baby and whether it would survive, or her mother. Of one thing Elizabeth was certain; her father would not return.

She got off the bed and reached under it for her chest, opened it and pulled out John Lilburne's precious leaflet. The pages were worn around the edges, but the lettering was clear:

"In the first place I desire you to understand that I am a freeborn Englishman and have lived thereof all my days. And have always sided with Parliament itself in the preservation of the laws, liberties and fundamental freedoms of England and the peace and tranquillity of people."

She thought of the day she and her father had seen John Lilburne flogged through the streets of London, how much change she'd seen since and what more might lie ahead. Peace, she'd known, or at least an absence of war, but she wondered what tranquility might be like. Between her fingers, the leaflet was so fragile it could be blown away like gossamer. But not the words it contained that had driven her father to rebel—and that inspired her. He'd told her she was freeborn, and she still felt that.

Rain sounded on the window, and she looked out through bleared glass to the smudged browns and greens of the land. She knew every tree, every stone, every last blade of grass. Had worked it all her life. Soon the rain would stop, and she would go out and tend the fields. So that the green shoots of the new season weren't choked before they had a chance to grow.

· · · ·•·•· · · ·

It was a bright spring day, the sun shone in a clear sky and a lark sang overhead. Elizabeth and Richard were picking the first of the asparagus harvest, when Sarah ran out of the cottage in a panic.

"Lizzie, Lizzie, Mother says you're to go and get Ma Turner." Sarah twisted her hands in her apron and hopped from foot to foot.

Richard jumped up, "It's the baby."

But Elizabeth's heart sank. "There's no need for Ma Turner. I can help Mother. I've seen enough births."

"Please, Lizzie, Ma Turner always helps her with the babies and they always survive and so does she. Please, Lizzie, do as Mother asks,"

"I know where Ma Turner lives, I'll go," and Richard ran off before Elizabeth could stop him.

"Come on, Lizzie, why are you being so slow?" Sarah fidgeted, but Elizabeth lingered, fearing what the day might bring, or who it might take and how she would pay Ma Turner. She collected Richard's basket and set it with hers under an apple tree in the orchard.

"Why won't you come for Mother, what's wrong with you?" said Sarah.

"There's nothing wrong with me," Elizabeth said. "It's Ma."

Inside the cottage, Rebecca lay in bed moaning. The sound was picked up by Mary, who sat on the floor rocking to and fro, with Young Will crouched beside her. He had an arm round Mary, trying to comfort her. But there was terror on his face.

"Young Will, you shouldn't be in here," Elizabeth said. "Take Mary outside. There are baskets of sparrow-grass under the apple trees. You can bundle them up to go to market tomorrow. Go on, move. And you, Mary, go with Young Will."

Elizabeth's voice was harsher than she'd intended. Mary grabbed her mother's hand, and Sarah struggled to prise her fingers off. Mary screamed, Rebecca moaned, and Elizabeth scolded until Young Will bent and sang into Mary's ear. The girl's face lit up, she relaxed her hold and let herself be led out. Elizabeth turned to her mother, who lay on the bed, silent now, eyes shut, her rosary beads clutched between her hands. Her lips moved, shaping words, but no sound came out.

"It's alright, Mother, you can say your prayers aloud now father's not here."

"That's what I have to pray about."

Elizabeth sat on the bed. She felt fear at her mother's pain, the lined face, the drops of perspiration on her forehead, the mumbling mouth, the helplessness. This would be her lot in life too, not so distant now. It wasn't a fate she wanted—not yet, not for a long time, if ever. She got up and went outside, lowered a pail into the well, then washed her hands and splashed water on her face. In the orchard she saw that Young Will and Mary were sitting under a tree. Perhaps they were even bundling up the asparagus.

When she went inside, Sarah had pulled the nursing chair beside the bed, and sat resting her head on the pillow beside her mother.

"You will promise me one thing, won't you, Lizzie?" Rebecca's eyes were shut, her face was composed.

"What is it, Ma?" She wished she could be like Sarah and share her mother's suffering. Instead, she felt only foreboding about what lay ahead and flickerings of anger at her father for not being there.

"Don't be hard on me, Lizzie. It's not my fault your father left. It's our times that did it. They changed him." Rebecca moaned. Elizabeth couldn't feel her mother's birth pains, but shared her fear of what might be the outcome.

"If I die, Lizzie, you will look after your brothers and sisters, won't you?" Rebecca asked. "You will promise me that; you won't leave them, will you? You were always the strong one."

"You're not going to die, Ma. Your babies come easily. They live, you live, this one will be no different."

"You don't know that, Lizzie," said Rebecca. "Only God knows."

"God hasn't done much for us of late."

"You're as bad as your father." Rebecca put her arm across her head again and moaned. "Oh, where is she?"

Richard ran in past Elizabeth. "I've told Ma Turner, and she's coming." He stroked his mother's hand, and she raised her arm from her head and smiled at him, a warm circle around the three of them, Sarah, Rebecca, and Richard, but not, Elizabeth felt, herself.

"You can't stay in here, Richard. It's not a place for boys," Elizabeth said.

"He can stay awhile," Rebecca clasped her son's hand. "Please."

"He can cut wood for the fire. Go on, Richard. I'll call you when..." Elizabeth wasn't sure when she would call him and whether after a birth or a death, "when you're needed."

Elizabeth and Sarah sat by their mother, washed her face, held her hand as the pains came and went, and came again. They stoked up the fire, walked their mother round the room, staggering from the table to the dower chest, then back to her bed again to groan with an agony that Elizabeth feared no human frame could survive.

"It won't be long; where is she?" Rebecca cried.

Then Elizabeth heard the latch lift at the cottage door. Ma Turner entered, dressed all in black, with a basket under one arm and a birthing stool under the other.

Ever since Elizabeth could remember, Ma Turner had been old—judging by the age of the people she'd brought into the world, she was ancient. Her eyes were sharp, her tongue sharper. But she was sharpest in her cunning and never provided more help than she thought women could pay for. Which was why, Elizabeth knew, she had come to Rebecca so late, knowing that with five children and a missing husband, there would be little money in the house.

Ma Turner put down her basket and rounded on Elizabeth. "You shouldn't be in here, boy. Get out."

"I'm not a boy, I'm Elizabeth."

"Oh," Ma Turner took off her hat and shawl and put them on the table and then inspected Elizabeth. "I remember you. The girl born in her caul. The day you came, red berries appeared on the holly tree. In spring. Unnatural." Ma Turner leaned over Rebecca.

After a few minutes she grunted and said to Elizabeth. "Bring the table nearer."

Elizabeth dragged the table across the floor and Ma Turner put her wicker basket onto it and lifted out a pewter dish, a candle, and scissors.

"And you," Ma Turner's eyes shifted to Sarah, crouched by the bed, as small as she could make herself. "Where's the water and swaddling bands?"

"I'll fetch them." Sarah brought the pot of water from the fireside and the strips of linen she'd prepared for the baby. She bustled around, caught up in this women's business. Elizabeth, in her rough work clothes, felt displaced even by her younger sister.

"We'll need more water," Ma Turner said. "And fresh straw for the floor."

"I'll go." Elizabeth was glad of an excuse to escape the fetid darkness of the cottage for the sweetness outside. Richard sat on the bench against the front wall in the sunshine looking across to the orchard from where came the sound of Young Will singing.

"Look, they're dancing," he said.

Under the apple trees Young Will lifted his feet, kicked out his legs and swirled a hand in clumsy flourishes. And Mary laughed, clung to him, swayed to his timing.

"For someone who makes such sweet music, he dances like a bear," said Richard.

A zephyr's breath rustled the apple tree and shook its white blossom down onto the brother and sister.

"They should stop and bundle up the sparrow-grass, so we can take it to market, or how will we survive?" said Elizabeth. "We can't live by dancing."

"They're doing no harm," said Richard.

"Young Will's the oldest of us. He should help."

"He is helping. He's making us laugh."

Richard was right, she thought. Such moments were hard-won, flashes of light even on a bright day. So she laughed too, and called out to them and waved, and they waved back.

Inside the cottage, the hot air was heavy with sweat and wood-smoke, laced through with Rebecca's cries and Ma Turner's exhortations. Elizabeth sent Sarah out to get some herbs to put on the fire. The sisters helped lift Rebecca from her bed onto the birthing stool. Ma Turner knelt before her, and Sarah stood behind, held her hand, and whispered into her mother's ears.

But Elizabeth hesitated. She had seen this too often; the pain, the joy, then the waiting to see if Rebecca recovered and the baby survived. Her head spun, the pungent air clogged her lungs, her vision blurred, whites, reds and browns shimmered in waves of heat. She went to the window and opened it, stuck her head into the freshness. Young Will and Mary were still dancing together under the apple tree. Mary's round face beamed, and she threw back her head, and arched her body so that Young Will had to stop her from falling. Closing her eyes and opening her mouth wide, she gave herself over to great roaring laughter.

And then Elizabeth understood how her father had felt. She loved these two, her clever brother who could barely see and her simple sister who couldn't talk. They had an untouchable purity about them, and as they danced under the apple tree, Elizabeth saw an innocence. Like the picture in church of Adam and Eve in paradise before they ate the apple and all the trouble started. But she could understand now how they so vexed her father. Both of them were burdens and would remain so.

The asparagus that had to go to market the next day was still unbundled. Elizabeth could see the baskets lying in the open sun, where it would wilt. Sarah would have to help her with it later, once the baby was born and her mother settled.

A cry behind her, from inside the room. Elizabeth shut the window. A wail, a shout of, "That's done," and laughter. Elizabeth turned to see Ma Turner holding the baby, arms flailing, protesting the indignity of birth. Rebecca was smiling now, and the same glow lit up Sarah's face.

"It's a boy," said Ma Turner. "Healthy too. You've had luck."

"He's beautiful." Sarah held out her arms for the baby. "Can I hold him?"

Ma Turner cut the baby's cord, the sisters washed and swaddled him, then cleaned Rebecca, put her back in bed and laid her new son beside her. Ma Turner prodded the afterbirth, then put it on the fire, and all the perfume from Sarah's herbs could not drown out the stench. There was a thumping at the front door, which Sarah opened, and Richard ran in.

"Have you been sitting there all this time?" asked Ma Turner.

"Of course." Richard took his mother's hand and kissed it, then seized the baby and cradled him, walking round the cottage jiggling the little figure in its tight swaddling clothes as if it was a toy, humming and hopping from foot to foot while Rebecca laughed and Ma Turner tut-tutted.

"There's money in my chest for Ma Turner," said Rebecca. "Get it out, Lizzie, and pay her what she's owed."

"What are you going to call him, Mother?" Richard kissed the baby.

"Arthur, after my father," Rebecca said.

"Is that what Pa would want?" asked Elizabeth.

"He's not here."

Ma Turner packed up her belongings in her wicker bag, took up her birthing stool and bent over the bed, sharp eyes on the baby, sharp words for Rebecca. "You've been lucky with that one. If your luck holds you won't have any more in these wild times."

Elizabeth paid Ma Turner, counting out coins that could have been saved, and closed the door on her. A peace fell on the cottage. Richard stood by the fire with little Arthur, kissed him again, and stuck a finger in his mouth.

"He's just been born, you can't stick your dirty finger in his mouth," Sarah said.

"He's hungry, I can tell."

"Then give him to Mother. Here, I'll take him," and Sarah lifted the baby from Richard and laid him next to Rebecca.

Elizabeth watched as her mother put her newborn to her breast, Rebecca as tender with this baby as with her first, the two of them so vulnerable. Elizabeth felt the weight of another responsibility.

"Where's Young Will?" Rebecca lifted her eyes from the baby. "And Mary?"

"They're still outside," said Richard. "They're dancing."

Elizabeth opened the cottage door. The sun had arched through the sky and shone with a lesser heat. In the orchard, she could see the wicker baskets, but not Young Will or Mary. They must be lying down, exhausted from their dancing; perhaps Mary was asleep. Was that Young Will singing a lullaby?

She ran to fetch them in. But when she reached the orchard, all she found was grass trampled underfoot, not just where they'd been dancing, but everywhere. It was as if a herd of cattle had stampeded through. The wicker baskets were upright, but their contents were scattered about, dotted with blossom from the trees. A warbler sang unseen. But its song fell on emptiness. Mary and Young Will had disappeared.

CHAPTER 9
London: 24 July 2019

I t was the hottest day of the year. The day we got our new Prime Minister. The day I fell into the oldest elephant trap in history.

For five weeks the political infighting in Westminster had been nuclear. Ten men and women did battle to be Prime Minister. It was cataclysmic. It was poisonous. It was riveting. At home, my nerdy neighbour took every opportunity to ambush me by the recycling bins to grill me about events. His eyes would light up with whatever insider details I supplied. Or invented.

In the office, Stephanie fretted about the impact on the Cooper's residents as the days ticked by. "It's like everything's shut down for the duration," she said. "No-one's making any decisions. And summer's halfway over."

Toby struggled to arrange my meeting with his client. "You have to agree a date sometime," he said. "You did promise."

And then after weeks of inaction, in a single day everything changed.

At lunchtime the failed Prime Minister, dressed in royal blue, stepped up to a lectern placed for the occasion in Downing Street to say her goodbyes to an unimpressed nation and then left wobbly-lipped to hand in her resignation at Buckingham

Palace. Hours later her replacement, a man bursting out of his jacket, bounced in to adulation from his fans and delivered an up-yours message to his detractors. Banner-waving protestors dodged, as best they could, police outriders escorting black cars to and from the Palace where our nonagenarian Queen counted in her fourteenth Prime Minister. Reflecting, perhaps, that the political world might have lost its head, but she was keeping hers.

And we MPs—elected by the people to our great mother of parliaments—watched, gossiped and tweeted. As hopeful men and women went into Downing Street and came out ministers. As the sacked and defeated licked their wounds in front of television cameras on College Green. As rioters added smoke, sweat and booming music to the torrid heat shimmering from the streets.

Until the police ended the gaiety with a lockdown, and I went for my dinner date with Toby and his boss, or as Toby put it, "my client." The man who was destroying, or as Toby put it, "regenerating," the Cooper Estate.

Discreetly fashionable off the South Bank, Toby had finessed his choice of venue. The restaurant was at the high end of haute cuisine, without being ostentatious. Our table was in one of the side cubicles, and the two men rose in unison as the maître d' ushered me in.

"Frances, how lovely to see you." Toby was wearing a light grey suit that more or less matched his hair, and a pale blue tie that more or less matched his eyes, which crinkled as he smiled. He stepped out from behind the table and stood beside me, one hand under my elbow: half familiarity, half possession. "Can I introduce Derek Rawlings?"

Derek's mid-blue suit wasn't as well-fitting as Toby's. His pink shirt clashed with his flushed face, which had the openness of an honest man. His handshake was firm. I took him to be someone whose background was in building, not finance or law or asset-grabbing. Toby was right; he wasn't a typical monster.

"Hello Frances. Nice to meet you." His voice was gravelly and tinged with estuary.

I took the seat beside him, with my back against the wall, and Toby slipped into the seat beside me, opposite Derek. A mistake that, because it meant I was trapped.

"Heard you on the radio talking about social cohesion. Couldn't agree with you more. It's what we're all looking for." Not bad for an opening gambit. Toby had briefed him well.

Toby raised a finger. The waiter materialised. Toby ordered steak. Derek and I ordered fish, and we made small talk while our food came. Toby remarked on the heat and said the roses at home were suffering. Derek asked after Toby's wife, "Veronica, isn'it? Lovely girl." I winced—at the "girl," not the wife bit. Derek laughed, "I s'pose I shouldn't say that nowadays."

Toby's steak arrived looking like it had barely seen a grill. The fish came with a smear of a greenish sauce on the side and five strands of samphire. Derek asked for a side of thick chips.

The conversation moved up a notch. Derek said Parliament had become a playpen. I speculated on how long it would take the new PM to throw all his toys out of the pram. At which point Toby concentrated on his food. Derek asked about the state of the opposition. Toby speared a cherry tomato with his fork and gave the half-smile of an insider who knows the answer. Derek looked at me with the curiosity of an outsider looking for an exclusive insight into the world of politics. When the truth was our ship of state was adrift on an ocean of no-one's choosing headed to an unknown destination with a narcissistic man-child at the helm. Saying which might not take the conversation forward.

"Well, we are where we are, and we have to make Brexit work." I trotted out the official line.

"That's not good enough. You're a south Londoner like I am, even if you haven't kept your accent. I expect plain speaking. You know it's a disaster."

"Yes, but..."

"What?"

"There's not a lot we can do about it."

"If you can't do anything about the biggest problem facing our country, why are you in politics? What's the point of you?" Derek was eating his chips with his fingers. He didn't give the impression of trying to be clever or vicious. But he had just managed to kick right on my sorest spot.

"Perhaps we should talk about things that are in our control." Toby had reorganised the food on his plate without eating much of it. "Frances is well plugged into the community on the Cooper Estate, aren't you, Frances?"

"So you know Donna Collins?" Derek asked.

"Of course."

"Well?"

"I was at school briefly with her daughter. She died some years ago of a drug overdose."

"I didn't know that," Toby said.

Derek shook his head, sighed and gave me a look that told me he'd been there. It touched another nerve in me.

"I'd long since moved away," I said. "I've never talked to Donna about it, but Stella was her only child. Ever since I've known Donna, she's been trying to turn the estate around. Stella's death must have been a denial of everything she'd worked for. When I came back to London, she was still there, still fighting, but she wasn't the same. In her heart of hearts, I think she knew it was no good."

Derek had put down his knife and fork. "I lived on an estate like that once." The estuary in his voice was stronger.

"I lived in worse."

"But you got out of it," Toby said.

"I got lucky."

"What would luck look like to Donna?" Derek asked.

That was my next mistake. It wasn't the food or the ambience that did it. And I can't blame the wine; I wasn't drinking. It was that here was someone who'd been on the same journey as me, and however far our paths had diverged, and however different our trajectories, he carried his roots with him.

"It would look like a home for herself and her grandson, close to where her sister lives on Canvey Island."

"What are Donna's feelings about the occupation?"

"You'd have to ask her." I'd already said too much.

"I hear your researcher's involved." Derek ate his final chip. For the first time that evening, there was a sharpness in his voice. "An American girl."

We locked eyes. Neither of us was going to blink. He spoke first. "It's half past midnight for that estate. The only issue is making sure the residents are kept happy. We're not looking for any trouble."

The greenish sauce had an acidic aftertaste. This conversation wasn't headed anywhere I wanted to go.

Toby steered us onto safer ground. "Let's run through how things might work." He gestured to the waiter, got pudding menus, noted our headshakes, got the waiter back and ordered coffees, all the while talking process. The tower blocks would soon be empty. They'd come down first. The low-rise would follow. Derek mellowed and talked about eco-friendly flats and a green space that would replace the concrete piazza.

It was a class act. But I'd heard enough and stood up to go.

Derek said, "I think we understand each other."

Toby insisted on walking me out to make sure I got the cab he'd ordered, despite my reassuring him that this was one of the safer street corners I'd hung out on.

"You've got a long journey home," I said.

"I've got a flat in town." He was looking up and down the road for the taxi.

"It must be hard on Veronica." I wasn't particularly sympathetic, but it was something to say, though his eyebrows raised. "I mean you having to work such long hours."

He shrugged. "It goes with the territory. She's got the family, she likes the lifestyle. You know the big house in the suburbs, the second home in Italy."

This close I could smell the wine on his breath, the perfume on his neck, feel the sexy squeeze on my arm as he helped me into the cab, and hear the sultriness in his voice as he said, "New Palace Yard, on account," to the taxi driver.

"You could come to mine," I said.

It was as casual and clichéd as that.

"I'll have to get rid of Derek first."

I scribbled my street address on the back of a card and he stuffed it in his pocket, shut the cab door behind me, and waved as the cabbie did the tightest of tight U-turns.

"It's always on account with you lot, innit?" the cabbie said. "Mind you, I wouldn't go to Westminster tonight, bit lively now the new PM's in charge." He didn't need much asking to do another tight U-turn and head south.

· · · ● · ● · · · ·

My entry phone rang at the same time as my phone pinged. It would be Toby on the doorstep, I wasn't bothered about my phone. He wasn't bothered about his either. We both knew what we wanted. We turned our phones off.

I was wondering what he'd look like in the morning, and whether I had enough coffee for two. But when we'd quite finished and murmured the kind of sweet nothings appropriate for a finite relationship, he got up and showered and started getting dressed.

"Oh?" I sat up in bed.

He moved round my bedroom in the gloaming that passes for darkness in London, leaned over the bed and gave me a kiss. Not quite lingering but not fleeting either. "Needs must. Veronica Face-times me in the morning when I'm away."

"Doesn't she trust you?"

"Well, she does have a point." He peered at himself in the mirror. I could see his face too. Bland innocence. He turned and fiddled with his phone; an Uber, I supposed. Then he sat on the edge of the bed and kissed me again and stroked my face and I thought I read something in his smile. More than the affection of a limited encounter, perhaps. "You're wonderful." He kissed me. "We must do this again."

"Oh yes." He'd left his wet towel on the bed, so I wrapped it around me and padded behind him, contented, drowsy, to see him out.

"Very soon." A final kiss at the door and he was gone.

· · · · ●· ● · · ·

I'd known our liaison wasn't going to be a change-your-life moment. But when I woke up next morning after the soundest of sound sleeps, I was sorry there wasn't more than the indentation of Toby's body beside me in bed. I'd neglected my emotional life for so long that sometimes I thought I'd forgotten how to feel.

Toby had left little sign of his presence in my flat: a rumpled shower mat, a black comb by the washbasin, a half-drunk glass of water. Perhaps there could be more between us than a casual affair. Or perhaps it would only ever be a bit of escapism, making up for missed opportunities in our student days when life was simpler and everything was possible. Either way, it was a chance to flex my withered heartstrings.

Meanwhile, it was time to return to turbulent reality. My car was still in the underground carpark in Westminster, so I had to get a cab into town. As I got into the back seat, I switched on my phone. Cue message dump.

One this morning from Hanna in Mum's care home.

Mother a bit better. Slept well last night. Asking for you.

And one from Gerald. *Missed you yesterday evening. Catch-up today?*

Before that, from last night, at times when only the mad, bad or impossibly lonely were on their phones, a string of messages from colleagues, ending with, *Where are you?* from Gerald in the small hours.

Earlier yesterday evening there was one from the local radio station asking for an interview. Damn. Missed it.

Two messages from friends. One of them political, the other from Birmingham.

Before that from someone unknown. *This is Leigh. CALL.*

And before that one from Joey. *Just leaving the office. Things a bit manic. Trouble on the patch. Two stabbings, one serious. Be in late tomorrow. Sorreee.*

While I was scrolling through the rest, a missed call from Gerald, ditto from Donna, ditto from Stephanie, a new message pinged up.

Great evening!! Spoken to Derek Rawlings. The Loverage man. Very happy with the discussions. Reckons he can help with project Canvey Island. Toby.

As the taxi careered through the streets towards Parliament, I sat back and wondered what Derek wanted in return.

CHAPTER 10

London: April 1643

"Young Will, Mary, where are you?" Elizabeth's voice dissolved into aching silence. Along the footpath, near the road, lay a white mound. Elizabeth ran over and found the geese; wings outstretched and broken, twisted necks, glassy eyes. She felt a spasm of relief. It was only the geese.

And then Young Will appeared, running past the holly tree. He stumbled, fell, got up and ran again, that clumsy gait that marked out her brother.

"William," Elizabeth's fear powered her feet across the field, "William, where's Mary, what have you done with her?"

Young Will stopped and sobbed. "Lizzie, Lizzie, I don't know where they took her. Oh don't be angry Lizzie, it wasn't my fault. We were only playing."

Her brother was a wretched sight. He staggered like the men did when they came out of the inns on Bankside. What she first thought was dirt on his face, she now saw was blood from a scratch on his forehead. His clothes were dirty from where he'd fallen. Apart from that there was no mark on him. And no sign of the sister left in his care. He covered his face with his hands and doubled over, his shoulders heaving, spit, snot and tears dribbling onto the ground.

"Stop it, Young Will, stop it." Elizabeth pulled him to standing and then wrenched his hands from his face. He swayed, turning one way, then the other, whimpering like a baby. She swung back her right arm and hit him hard across the face.

"What have you done with her?"

The blow stilled him. His sobs subsided.

"Where is she?" Elizabeth shook him.

"I don't know. I couldn't see." Young Will started weeping again, tears interspersed with words. "We were singing and dancing. And then some men came and took Mary. They surrounded us and jested and laughed and then they dragged her away like she was an animal."

"And what did you do?" Elizabeth didn't feel pity for her brother. If it had been her, she'd have fought them to the death; she'd have clung to the men like a bedbug in winter rather than let them spirit her sister away.

"They said she was a witch. Oh Lizzie, what will happen to us now?"

Elizabeth felt sick, spat bile onto the grass, wiped her hand across her mouth.

"Think, Young Will, think. What happened from the beginning? You were playing, and some men came. How did they speak, what did they say?"

"They said terrible things." Young Will hung his head. "They said it was unnatural for us to be dancing like that, brother and sister, dancing together. And then Mary looked at them, you know how she does sometimes, those looks of hers. And one of the men said she'd given him the evil eye and then another of them said she cussed them, which proved that she's a witch. Oh Lizzie," Young Will sobbed so hard he could barely speak. "What if they come back?"

Elizabeth wondered whether he wept for Mary or himself. "You have to stop crying, Young Will. Go and wash your face at the well and then go inside and kiss Ma and the new baby. Say I'm bringing Mary. Make whatever excuse you can, go up to your attic if you must, but don't tell Ma what's happened until I come back and we know what's become of Mary."

Young Will was absorbed in his misery. "You must despise me." He was weak, he could never protect them, her father's heir, who could sing like a skylark, the clever one who'd taught her to read, the brother whom she loved. Elizabeth understood the frustration her father must have felt.

"No, Young Will, it wasn't your fault." Elizabeth inspected the forlorn figure, dishevelled, pitiful, but whole at least. "Which way did the men go?"

"Up the road towards London. Oh Lizzie, if they think Mary's a witch, what will they do to her? Or to us?"

Elizabeth didn't answer. She wouldn't let words give substance to her terror, so she left his question hanging in the air for the sun to shrivel and the breeze to blow away across the fields where it couldn't hurt either of them.

The land felt hostile as Elizabeth ran onto the London road, crawled under hedgerows, waded into ditches, stopped travellers to ask after her sister.

"Have you seen a girl? With some men?" But the man leading the cow on a rope with the calf trotting behind, shook his head and hurried past.

"Have you seen a girl? With some men?" But the riders on horseback laughed, "A girl and some men," and winked and rode on.

She came to her neighbour's abandoned farm. The track to their cottage was overgrown with nettles. When she pushed the cottage door, it groaned open. Water pooled on the floor, thatch hung from the rafters. Cold ash littered the fireplace in which a roasting jack idled. Dank emptiness. She backed out.

Behind the cottage was a pigsty. Rough wood, sunken roof, rancid smell, as if, the pigs having gone, something worse had moved in. A putrid mound of rotting plants, bones, fur, and feathers. And beyond it, in the corner, a dim shape, a mound, a body. Elizabeth felt her chest tighten. She waded through the muck.

Her body, Mary, lying on her side, facing the wall, curled like grey Little Tommy. Her dress was torn away from her shoulders and rode up her hips, their round whiteness marked by bruises and smears of blood. Elizabeth sank to her knees. Her sister. Of the golden curls and helpless innocence. How Mary must have suffered in her last moments. What would Elizabeth tell their mother?

But then the body moved. She was breathing.

"Mary?"

Elizabeth touched her sister's arm. But it was as if she had lightning in her hand. Mary clenched herself into a ball.

"What have they done to you?"

The closer Elizabeth moved, the more Mary drew away. The more Elizabeth reached out, the more her sister struggled. And then she thought of how Young Will would calm Mary. She leaned over her and started to sing. Her voice didn't have the sweetness of her brother's, but she knew the words. "I saw my lady weep," she crooned until Mary relaxed, unwound, and turned her face towards Elizabeth. Her cheeks were speckled with grime, her hair threaded with straw.

"Mary," Elizabeth stroked her face, plucked the mess out of her hair, pulled down her rumpled dress. Mary made no sound, gave no recognition. Elizabeth put her arm under her sister's shoulder and tried to lift her, but Mary stiffened.

"Let me see." Elizabeth tore the bottom of her shirt and dabbed at the blood on her sister's legs. At her touch, Mary erupted. She clutched her crotch with both hands, kicked her feet, shook her head and screamed, a sound worse than anything Elizabeth had heard, worse than a vixen in the dead of night, worse even than the screaming of their mother in childbirth. It was all that Mary would ever tell of what had happened.

"Shush, shush, Mary. Let's go home now. Come." Elizabeth put her face directly in front of Mary's to fill the space with a presence she hoped would reassure. Mary's eyes were baby blue. But there was no recognition in their blankness. And then her face twisted into one of its sidelong looks of venom.

"Oh, what are we going to do with you?" Elizabeth pulled her sister to her feet, winding an arm around her shoulders, propping her up while she arranged her torn skirt.

"Come Mary, we're going home to Mother." She started singing again and coaxed her sister out of the pigsty. They staggered in the waning light, through the landscape that had shaped their lives but was now utterly changed. Elizabeth knew there would be no more peace for them here.

·· • • • •·• • •· ··

Her mother knew it too. That night, Elizabeth went out to salvage what she could of her asparagus to take to market. She sat on the bench in front of the cottage and worked by the light of a full moon until her fingers felt like blocks of wood and she was uncertain whether she waked or slept. She lifted the latch to the cottage, leaned on the door, listened to the sounds of breathing from the bedroom where her sisters slept, the creaking rafters where her brothers shifted in their loft, the sullen embers sparking in the fireplace.

"Lizzie."

Moonlight fell across the cottage to where her mother had risen in bed, leaning on one arm over the little Arthur lying beside her. Rebecca's face glowed with maternity, and she smelt of blood and milk and childbirth. Elizabeth was torn between love for them and fury at the cruelty of it all. She went and sat beside her mother. "He's a beautiful baby."

Rebecca rocked the swaddled figure. "Lizzie, you know we won't be safe here any longer. Not if they say Mary is a witch. We'll have to go away. I'll be up soon and once I'm churched, we can go to my father's house in Kent. He'll shelter us."

Elizabeth couldn't think beyond her tiredness and how she would get to market in the morning. She wondered at her mother, nursing her newest baby, finding the strength to plan the future for the entire family. It was like when she was a small child, stretching for the mother who was always just beyond her reach.

"What when Father comes back and finds us gone?"

"If he comes back, Lizzie. If."

Moonlight isn't kind. It might not be as bright as the sun, but it throws long shadows even in the darkness of night. And it's cold, like the fear that lodged itself inside Elizabeth's heart.

"You look tired, Lizzie," Rebecca stroked her daughter's hair. "Go and sleep now, we'll talk tomorrow. Take Sarah with you to market, but don't tell her what we've spoken of; she'll only cry."

· · · · · ● · ● · · · ·

Next morning, Elizabeth and Sarah walked through the grey dawn. To the world they looked like a boy and his younger sister, he with a cap, she with a kerchief, wicker baskets on their backs, going to sell the produce from their farm.

"I want to see the shops and palaces and rich people in the City," said Sarah. "I want to see the ladies and their silk dresses and the men with their bright cloaks and how they bow with their hats like this." And she twirled a hand in the air and laughed.

"They're not there any longer," Elizabeth said. "They've either fled to Oxford with the King, or else they're in hiding."

"D'you think I might have a silk dress one day?"

"Is that what you want?" Elizabeth had never known her timid sister want anything.

"Sometimes. Mother used to wear fine clothes, you know, when she was a girl at her father's house. She talks about it to me when no one else is there. I think she misses that life, however much she says she loves us all. I know I would. Miss it, that is. I'd like to be rich."

Elizabeth shifted the basket on her back. Her younger sister had always seemed a paler version of her mother, content with the boundaries of her life, no thoughts beyond her hens and the cow. Now Elizabeth wondered what else she'd misunderstood.

Soon the road ran through hovels that squatted among dirt, smoke filtering from blackened roofs. Next came ramshackle houses where doors opened and dishevelled people tumbled into another day. Then Elizabeth felt herself sucked into the Borough's life, she and her sister, two small figures, hand in hand, baskets on their backs, bobbing along the road in all its hustling, thieving, suffering tide. In front of them walked a man with a monkey crouched on his shoulder, the animal baring its teeth and screeching in terror. Two servants dressed in black jackets weighed down by a sedan chair, tripped and tipped their passenger into the dirt. A small boy turned round and round and screamed, whether lost or discarded none in the throng that surged past him knew or cared.

From every courtyard came more people, drunk from inns, roused from whorehouses, until, where the flow of people pouring north towards the river met those spilling southwards across London Bridge, they stopped. They eddied. They swirled. Elizabeth and Sarah were caught in the vortex and spun around until, disorientated, they were released from the crowd to land by the gates of the hospital of St Thomas.

Here, where the sick dragged themselves to be treated, there now crowded men returned from the war, limbs missing, clothes bloodied, propped up on crutches or resting on dead or dying comrades. Elizabeth stepped over a prone body to inspect the face of a man with red hair, then lifted a hat that looked familiar off another's head. And then, seeing that they all looked the same, half-dead, demented creatures, she waited for one to recognise her, to call, "Lizzie, is that you?" She hoped, then dreaded that one of these ruins might prove to be what was left of her father come back to her.

"He's not there is he?" asked Sarah.

"No." She was uncertain whether to feel relief or sorrow.

They crossed the road to where Borough Market squatted below St Saviour's church. From the first stall hung a row of dead chickens, blood dripping off their dangling heads, the woman behind ignoring the flies that congregated and chasing away lurking dogs, the man beside her counting out his money then wrapping it in a rag and tucking it inside his shirt. A cleaver rose, flashed and thudded into a pig split open on the next stall, where a woman pointed at the exact piece she would buy, and the butcher breathed his irritation.

"Milk below," came a cry, and Elizabeth and Sarah stood aside to let a woman pass, a yoke across her shoulders from which hung two pails, overfull, spilling milk onto the already stinking path.

"Oysters, fresh oysters," and a man pushed past with a squeaking wooden barrow covered with shells that glistened with water thrown over to make them look newly pulled from the Thames.

"Sparrow-grass, best sparrow-grass," cried Elizabeth, and haggled over prices while Sarah handed over the green spears of asparagus and smiled to charm an extra penny from the buyer. They worked their way along the river front, past the prison, past the bear garden until they reached the theatre, closed now by order of Parliament.

Elizabeth felt the sky was closing in on her; the air of the City weighed her down, or perhaps it was her tiredness and hunger. Her basket was empty, the money bag around her neck was heavy with their earnings. She took Sarah's hand, and they walked to the alley that led to St George's courtyard and the inn and sat outside it at an upturned keg.

"It's Will's girl, isn't it?" Kate had grown fuller, her face heavier. The hair that before billowed around her face was tucked into a dull cap and the fleshy bosom that once over-flowed her bodice was buttoned into a high-collared grey dress. Lines of disappointment cut from her mouth down to her chin. She eased herself into the chair beside Elizabeth, put two tankards of ale on the table and wiped her hands on a grimy apron.

"Is this your sister?" Kate pointed to Sarah, who sat as still as a rabbit caught in firelight. "But of course it is, you can see the likeness. So, there's three of you for your ma to fend for: girls I mean." Kate talked over Elizabeth's attempt to correct her. "Boys are different. It's girls that have the problems. That's why Will always had you dressed as a boy, wasn't it? That and to make up for the disappointment of your brother, the one who hangs around the church."

Elizabeth tried to protest, but Kate carried on regardless. "Oh yes, I've seen him, and the priests he goes with. I see all of life in this place. Most of it has a drink and a smoke and, if it's lucky, a fuck, and passes on. Sometimes there's a little keepsake left behind." She nodded her head at a round-cheeked, blond-haired girl, who turned and in her laughing blue eyes Elizabeth saw her brother Richard.

"Have you heard news of my Father?" she asked.

"I heard he was captured at Oxford at Christmas. It's said he was unhurt."

Kate reached under her apron and pulled out a clay pipe, then fumbled again and pulled out some flakes of tobacco, which she stuffed into its bowl and lit, puffing out a cloud of acrid smoke. Sarah coughed and sidled away. "Don't you wriggle away from me; it won't be long before you'll be thanking the virgin or God or whatever it is you pray to these days that you met me.

"Will always talked about his three girls. You." Kate took her pipe out of her mouth and prodded the stem of it in Elizabeth's chest. "His favourite child. The mouse." Kate pointed her pipe at Sarah.

"And the witch." Kate put her pipe back in her mouth and clenched it between her teeth.

Elizabeth choked on her ale. "Father never said that."

"There's plenty that do."

"Who?" asked Elizabeth.

"It doesn't matter who. They say it and words are enough." Kate took another pull on her pipe. "It was Oliver that started it."

"He was father's friend; he wouldn't do us harm."

"Wouldn't he? Guilty heart, lying tongue. He said she put an evil eye on him and spoke words that could have no meaning to any but the devil. Then he took sick and died which proved it, people said. And then his sister took sick and his parents, so the whole house was left to die. The witch-hunters will come for your sister now your father isn't there, and even if he was, they would probably still come for her. And you too as like."

Kate inspected her pipe and tucked it under her apron. "I'll set meself on fire one day." She leaned on Elizabeth's shoulder and heaved herself out of her seat. "Pay me for the ale." She held out her hand for Elizabeth's coins, then picked up their empty tankards. "Go away somewhere, anywhere, if you want to live. But don't say I told you. I can't be helping witches."

Elizabeth felt every eye on them, heard every tongue talking about them. Sisters of the witch.

She looked for the men who had drunk with her father before he went to war. But she saw no familiar faces among those dressed all alike in their dark clothes and squat hats, the pious, the wanton, the careless and the vicious who would come for her sister. Apart from one, a bearded young man seated among a crowd, reading aloud from a pamphlet. "On Tuesday morning they set fire in diverse places of the town, and have burnt near a hundred dwellings." She looked over his shoulder and saw a picture of an armoured cavalier beside a blazing town with the name "Brimidgham". The young man caught her eye and held it for a moment. The pearl earring that used to jiggle in his ear had gone.

"You'll have to hope your father's not there," he said.

•••••••••••

The road home is always shorter, or feels so, and Elizabeth was glad. The clouds had darkened, and the cloying air wrapped itself around the girls. The green fields beyond the City brought no relief from the sticky closeness of the day. When they reached the holly tree, Elizabeth slowed her pace. Home. Safety. Soon she could lift the latch at the cottage door, stumble inside, hand over her takings to her mother and then stretch out on the bed and sleep. Every aching footstep held the promise of relief.

But from the direction of the cottage came voices. Not of her mother or Richard, not of Young Will singing. These were hard-edged sounds of trouble. Past the orchard, Richard was standing at the garden gate, pitchfork in hand, confronting a group of four boys dressed all in black.

"Bring out your witch, bring out your witch." The boys ran at Richard, taunting him, demon shadows against the land's spring green.

"Go away." Richard lunged at them with his pitchfork. "Leave us alone." He jabbed the pitchfork and swung it round, his back against the garden gate. The boys kept out of reach.

"Hang the witch, dunk the witch, roast the witch," they chanted.

One of the boys put his arm like a hangman's noose round his friend's neck who stuck his tongue out and rolled his eyes as if on a gibbet. Their faces were flushed, their eyes merry with intended cruelty. Another boy broke away from the group and ran towards the cottage: Elizabeth heard the sound of breaking glass.

"Burn them out, burn them out," the boys chorused.

Richard screamed and charged at them with his pitchfork. Elizabeth ran along the path, shouting, Sarah close behind her, as if the two girls were a whole army on the move.

The boys turned towards them. "Witch's bitches," they shouted, and then they ran away, laughing, through the orchard.

Richard was shaking, her brave brother. He bent forward and leaned on his pitchfork, wheezing to get his breath. Elizabeth touched him and felt his fear travel along her own arm and grip her heart.

"D'you think they'll come back?" Sarah had crept up behind them and now stood with an expression so innocent that Elizabeth could cry at the unfairness of it. Fear trickled in the sweat down Richard's face.

This land was theirs and their father's and his before, back as far as anyone could tell. But Elizabeth knew it could no longer be their home. She nodded. "The only question is when. And where we go."

CHAPTER 11

London: 25 July 2019

There's a pub called the Mayflower by the Thames in Rotherhithe. It's my favourite place to take Americans in London, so I thought it would be a good place to have a heart-to-heart with Stephanie.

Sandwiched between gentrified wharf buildings and smart new flats, it's a quaint, timbered building with hanging baskets of petunias at the front and a wooden jetty at the back that juts out over the river. Nowadays, the boats that ply these tidal waters are unassuming tugs pulling industrial barges, river taxis, more often leisure boats.

Once this place was the centre of the maritime world. Tall ships cast off from here to sail oceans, known and unknown, returning with cargoes of unimaginable riches and tales of more to be discovered. Redriff was a village at the edge of London, caught between desolate marshes to the east and the destitute squalor of lives eked out on tidal mudflats to the west. People fleeing the poverty of their times converged on the quayside at Rotherhithe, packing whatever bags they had and crowding the jetties to board ships bound for the Americas.

Forget the heroic images of the Pilgrim Fathers in their pointy hats at Plymouth, wives and children clustered around worldly possessions, eyes lifted to the western horizon where they would find their religious freedom. Here in Rotherhithe was where the journey actually started for many of them, desperate people taking their chances against the elements in their only hope of escaping destitution. Reckoning that either the high seas or poverty would kill them, but death at home would be sooner and more certain.

I thought Stephanie would like to see a part of the city that had played such a role in her country's story. And I might be able to work out what kind of trouble she was bringing into my life. As in whether she was, as Derek Rawlings said, involved in causing mischief on the Cooper Estate.

· · · ● · ● · · · ·

But before that, the hand of history, in the shape of our new Prime Minister, was preparing to whack us all around the head again.

As the taxi sped me through the streets of south London, a message from Hugh appeared on my phone.

Reminder. Statement from the Prime Minister. Chamber midday today. All colleagues are asked to attend. It wasn't an ask. It was an order from the man charged with whipping us all into line.

This was our first chance to question the new PM. It would also be our last chance until the autumn. Our exhausted Parliament was due to totter to a close that day for the summer. We wouldn't meet again till September.

I didn't want to pass up the chance to mark the new Prime Minister's card. I scrolled through the messages on my phone. There was the one from Joey the previous evening about the stabbings. That was it, I thought. I'd asked the PM about what he intended to do about knife crime in London.

Joey and Stephanie arrived in the office soon after I did. Together. I should have appreciated the significance. Instead, I only stopped to get Joey's briefing on the stabbings, including that one of the victims, as yet unnamed, had died, before I scuttled off to the Chamber. The only way to guarantee a seat on the hard green benches, is to turn up and occupy one. Even going over early, I had to bum shuffle my way in beside a fellow London MP and then endure an excruciating question and answer session with a newly appointed minister.

At last, the minister's boss, our nemesis, the people's servant, billowed in on a cloud of hubris.

We MPs all knew our new Prime Minister for what he was, even if the nation hadn't found him out yet. He lived up or down to everyone's expectations. He savaged the faint-hearts in his own party and eviscerated ours. His jibes hit every jangling political nerve and a good number of personal ones. Both sides screamed at each other. Mr Speaker, struggling to control the ruckus, added to it. The Prime Minister was in his element. It was like watching a bear pit, where the bear ran amok and destroyed every last dog.

Gerald bellowed from the row behind me. Mr Reasonable no more. His heckling was undiluted, visceral hatred. Plus, he had the advantage of an ear-splitting voice. I spent two hours being deafened, bobbing up and down from my seat to catch the Speaker's rattled attention. By the time he called out, "Frances Quilter," most people had snuck off for lunch.

"Would the Prime Minister's mission for government," I gesticulated extravagant quote-marks, "Include more police in my left-behind constituency with tougher powers to end the epidemic of knife crime, which has so tragically claimed the life of yet another of my young constituents?"

"Hear, hears," from my colleagues. Muttering from my opponents, who couldn't actually heckle the announcement of a death. A bemused look from the Prime Minister at a question about real life, followed by a glib expression of sympathy and a form of words that meant, "Yes, but don't hold me to it."

My tiny pebble thrown into the duck-pond of history. Plop. Sunk without a ripple. I could almost hear Hugh roll his eyes at the wasted opportunity to score a more political point.

· · · · ●●·●●· · ·

I had an afternoon appointment at the local police station, a red-brick building in need of an update, where I got the latest word on the stabbings. They were the result of a turf war between rival drug gangs over control of the Cooper. Depressingly familiar. A young woman in civilian clothes came in and handed the police inspector a piece of paper. He grimaced. "We can release the name of the boy who died. You probably know him. Dylan Stafford, Donna Collins' grandson."

An asteroid might as well have landed. The gangly boy hanging about in the piazza. Donna's only reminder of her daughter, Stella, also a casualty of drugs. If only Donna had been able to get her daughter or grandson away, things might have been different. Perhaps it was the estate's fault. Through my numbness at Donna's family tragedies, I heard the police inspector's clipped voice.

"Sorry, what was that you were saying?" I asked.

"There's been a fresh wave of flyposting about a sit-in," he replied. "But this time tempers are fraying. Someone might get hurt. If you know about any of the people involved, you should tell them to desist."

I wondered if he'd heard something about Stephanie.

· · · ● ● ● ● ● · ·

When I reached Donna's flat, the day's blistering heat had settled into scorching. The estate was quiet, the air heavy with collective sorrow over a life lost. Bouquets of flowers in giant cellophane wrappers decorated with extravagant ribbons and sympathy cards lay at Donna's front door. I was glad I'd stopped to pick up a bouquet at the petrol station, although mine—tightly closed lilies with green foliage and white babies' breath—looked stingy in comparison.

A woman, who I guessed must be the sister from Canvey Island, opened the door. She was a younger, gum-chewing version of Donna. Her face twisted with undisguised venom, and she chewed on her gum double-quick time before launching into an outburst.

"You've got a fucking nerve coming here like this, you cunt."

Beyond her, in the living room, was Donna. Her blonde hair was unkempt, her face puffy, her eyes hidden behind big sunglasses. She was sitting on the settee clutching a picture frame, which I guessed contained a photograph of the dead boy. Opposite her was a man I'd not seen before, who looked like he must be Dylan's father. There was a likeness, but the father's face was marked by 20 years of disappointment his son would never know.

"Let her come in, Leigh," Donna said. "I want her to understand what she's done, if that's possible."

Leigh's eyes bored a hole through my back as she followed me into the room. She sat down beside her sister. There was one easy chair left. "You can't sit there," she said, "that's his chair." So I stood in the corner. My flowers were redundant.

"You used my grandson." Donna spat the words out.

Of all things, I wasn't expecting this. "Donna, I'm truly sorry for your loss."

"Sorry my arse, I'll make you sorry," she said. "There's him dead, murdered, not even in his grave yet, not even cold, and there's you running around bigging yourself up like you're some kind of saint."

Leigh held up the evening paper so I could see the headline. "MP wins pledge on knife crime."

"It's not quite how it looks," I said.

"Looks, fuck looks," said Donna. "Looks don't come into it. We're talking about my boy, my Stella's boy. All I've got left of her. Had." Tears appeared on her cheeks, rolling from under her sunglasses, and plopped off onto her chest.

"Now you've gone and upset her all over again." Leigh put an arm round her sister. Dylan's father leaned forward, like he wanted to get up and run out of the flat.

"You'll never know what it's like, will you?" Donna's mood switched from sorrow back to anger. "What it's like to lose your child. Let me tell you. It's like you've had your whole life taken away from you. Torn out. When Stella went, at least I still had Dylan. Now there's nothing."

Her body shook with huge sobs. She bent over and lost herself to her grief. Normally, in such a situation I'd put my arm around a person, or at least touch their hand, but given the turn of events, I didn't think it would be welcome. I wished the flowers in my hands would vaporise.

"Ain't you got no shame?" The sister jumped into my uncertainty. "She trusted you, and you let her down."

There was something I wasn't getting. "Sorry?"

"You'll be sorry enough when I've finished. She was always there for you. Frances this, Frances that, Frances let me climb right up your arse. And where was you when she needed you? Canoodling with that cowboy who's going to knock her precious home down. As if she hasn't lost enough already.

"Oh you can look surprised," she continued. "I suppose you thought no-one would find out. That's how you people operate, isn't it. But Donna heard. Of course she did. How d'you think she felt knowing you were out wining and dining with that bastard when her grandson was bleeding his guts out on the pavement?"

I could handle the sister's fury. If Saint Theresa had wandered in she'd have been bundled into a handcart and pushed off to hell. And though Dylan's father glowered at me, he didn't have much of a leg to stand on, having failed to show up between his son's conception and his death.

But when Donna lifted her head and took off her sunglasses, I understood. I finally got it. Her ravaged face held the accumulated grief of years of pain. The sharp tongue, the belligerence, what I always took to be her fighting spirit was, in reality, a cover-up for a soul pulverised by life.

I floundered. "It's a terrible thing that happened." They glared at me, the three of them.

"I'm so sorry."

Still that silence.

I can handle noise. Usually, I'm surrounded by it. I thrive on it. When I'm driving, I'll put the radio on so loud people at traffic lights turn to see whose car is making all the racket. But silence—no, that I can't take. This one went on. And on. Until...

"It wasn't my fault." The crass words floated into the air from some disembodied voice. My voice.

"You bitch. Now I've heard it all," Leigh said. "Why don't you just bugger off instead of hanging round upsetting everyone?"

"Perhaps another time," I gathered together what was left of my dignity. Donna levered herself up from the settee.

"It's alright, I'll see her out," Leigh said.

But Donna straightened herself up. "You sit down Leigh. I've got something to say to her. In private." She followed me out, shutting the living room door behind her.

And that's when she did it, when the two of us were alone by the front door. There was a rumble from somewhere deep inside her, a growl that started in her chest and rose into her throat, and then she opened her mouth and out it came. A big gobbet of gunk shot past my left shoulder.

"Missed," she said. "But I'll get you. You watch me."

On the way to my car I squashed the bouquet among the pizza boxes and beer cans in one of the litter bins on the piazza.

· · · ●· ●●●· ·

By the time I picked up Stephanie and Joey outside Southwark tube station, I'd got my disordered feelings under what would pass for control. Joey concertinaed his long legs into the back seat, and Stephanie, best grey suit on for the occasion, sat up front with me.

"Ready?" I asked her.

She nodded, "I'm real excited." She smoothed down her already smooth hair and laid her hands one on top of the other in her lap.

"This is about your history." I drove us across Bermondsey and down the bumpy cobbles of Rotherhithe Street, and found a parking spot close to the council estate that clung on defiantly amid the stylish warehouse conversions. We clambered out and walked to the churchyard of St Mary the Virgin across the road from the Mayflower pub.

Evening was a relief. The sun was lower, and this close to the river, the air was cooler. There was even some birdsong in the churchyard, and it lifted my spirits. Joey read out the inscription on the blue commemorative plaque on the church wall:

"In 1620 the Mayflower sailed from Rotherhithe on the first stage of its epic voyage to America. In command was Captain Christopher Jones of Rotherhithe."

"So you see," I said, "All that stuff about the Mayflower setting sail from Plymouth isn't strictly true. Where she actually started her voyage was here."

Stephanie studied the plaque carefully. Such a composed figure in her trademark grey suit, her expression completely inscrutable. Then she took out her phone and photographed the plaque and the church and the churchyard and everything else in sight.

"That's so awesome," she came out with finally. "I had no idea. Was he buried here?"

"I believe so."

We searched the parched grass in the graveyard for a memorial. But there were only a few headstones from which time and weather had eroded all details. So we crossed the road to the pub and plunged into the antique chic and busy chatter inside.

"You can imagine it four hundred years ago, people crammed into this little place waiting to get on their boat," I said. "You can imagine the jostling and the dirt and the noise and the smell. It must have been such an event for them, leaving here to sail to America."

Stephanie looked around and perhaps she could smell the past because she wrinkled her nose.

Joey was sceptical. "It can't have been the same building."

"Perhaps not, but it would have been very similar: tiny rooms, low beams, river at the back. It would have been full of tobacco smoke back then."

I got a Pimms for Steph, a pint for Joey, a tonic water for myself and ordered burgers all round, and then we took our drinks out to the jetty where we found an empty table.

Steph put her drink down and went to the edge of the jetty and peered over. The tide was going out, and the Thames beaches were visible below—greyish sand and pebbles—and beyond that the brown water of the river.

I'm not superstitious, but I could see crowded around her those poor people from the past, maybe with a bag each, rough clothes, standing on the jetty with the tide underneath, getting into the lighters, the small boats that would take them out to the ships anchored in deeper water. I could see their faces, perhaps bright with unfamiliar hope, perhaps fearful of the journey or sad at whatever they were leaving behind. I could hear the sailors shout curses at them to hurry aboard, the cries of fear, children's laughter, the lapping of the water and then the slapping of the oars as they were rowed away from everything they'd ever known, however bad.

Stephanie looked out to where the boats would have been in the middle of the river and then turned round and leaned against the jetty railings. "My folks say one of our ancestors sailed over to America with the Mayflower."

"Really?" I'd always thought that if every such claim was accurate, the ship must have been the size of the Titanic. But I was prepared to give Stephanie the benefit of the doubt; she was always so exact. A man came out and offloaded our burgers and a barrage of chatter.

"Yes," Stephanie was still standing by the railings in her bubble. "The one I told you about, Elizabeth Gardiner. Some of them claim she was actually a passenger on the Mayflower. But Gramps says Elizabeth sailed later. I always assumed she set out from Plymouth. But she must have set sail from here."

With that she turned round again and looked out over the water, joining the ghosts, her grey suit blending in with their drab clothes, her face with its timeless quality merging with their shadows, as if her ancestors were reclaiming her.

A seagull landed on the table and stepped towards her neglected plate.

"Hey Steph, come and eat your food before the seagulls get it." Joey pricked her bubble, and she laughed, photographed the river, then came and sat next to him. He handed her some sachets of ketchup with the certainty of someone who knows a partner's eating habits.

"Is this why you feel so involved with the place?" I asked.

"I wouldn't say involved," Stephanie took a careful bite out of her burger. "Apart from with Miracle, and it's hard not to feel involved with her."

"How about Laurelle and her occupation?"

Stephanie laughed. "Laurelle's a dynamo. She doesn't need my involvement, though she did ask for help with the flyposting in Speedwell House."

"When I said to help the tenants get whatever they wanted, it didn't include flyposting."

"Come on, Frances." Joey had finished his burger and was eyeing Stephanie's chips. "Did you never do any flyposting? Not once in your misspent youth?"

He was right, of course. Flyposting was the least of it. But I was irritated and pulled rank. "It's not helping in the negotiations with the developers."

"I'm sorry," said Stephanie. "I didn't mean to cause trouble." She wiped her fingers one by one on her serviette and then scrunched it up on her plate.

Would someone so finickity mess up my constituency? As far as I could tell, Stephanie was just one more American interning in London whilst digging up her family roots. Bad luck for me that they ran through my constituency. In our febrile times, I didn't need any complications, however innocent.

Joey got us back on track. "Just think, you could be cousins to the nth degree."

Stephanie laughed. I asked if she'd finished researching her family tree.

"Pretty much. There's one more thing I have to check out. If it's OK with you, I'll take a few days off in September."

· · · ●·●·· · ·

The waiter came out with a card machine, and then Joey announced that they were going on to a club in Greenwich where he was doing a session as a stand-up. He tried to make it sound casual, but the words came out with asterisks around them and a couple of heart emojis after. They made an unlikely couple, her with her neat suit and precise mannerisms, him with his sweeping gestures and skinny jeans. I noticed he had on another new shirt. I hoped he wouldn't get hurt. Then I wondered if that would be before or after she went home and felt a twinge of sadness for his future heartbreak. I thought of my half-night with Toby. Neither of us was invested enough in our relationship to be able to get hurt, or so I thought.

Joey jumped at my offer to take a picture of them together on the jetty. He stretched a dramatic arm towards the river, taking in the view, and, in the process, enveloping Stephanie. She let herself go, did a thumbs up and stood at an angle so that the picture caught the shaft of sunlight that fell on the river behind her, on the place from where, centuries before, her ancestor had set sail.

CHAPTER 12
London: April 1643

F ear prowled Elizabeth like a dog. It stalked her by day and lurked in her dreams by night.

If a lark sang, she stopped working in the fields, not to scan the blue sky for the songstress, but to search the land for who had disturbed her nest. If a cart rumbled along the road, she hid behind the holly tree to watch if it carried people, and if so, how many, and whether men or women and whether it would slow or stop. If a traveller turned into their farm, a migrant from the countryside, a soldier from the war, Elizabeth didn't ask if he wanted fresh water or a crust to eat, but chased him away from the cottage where her sister was hidden. Mary. The witch.

It was also where Rebecca rested and nursed baby Arthur. On the seventh day, she rose from her childbed, opened her dower chest and took out an exquisite shawl. Elizabeth loved the shawl, the softness of the silken fabric, its exotic reds and golds that glittered in the drab cottage and especially the happiness it signified: of survival, renewal, hope. It was what Rebecca wrapped her babies in to take them for their christening. But this time, Elizabeth sensed foreboding as her mother shook out the shawl.

"It's too soon for your churching, Ma," she said.

"It's time enough if we're to leave." Rebecca spread out the silk shawl on the table, placed the swaddled Arthur in the centre of it, and wrapped him around.

"Shall I come with you?" Sarah was feeding Mary pieces of bread softened in milk, rubbing her cheeks and throat to make her swallow. "I would so like to."

"No. I'm taking Young Will. He can sing the mass for us. Put on your Sunday clothes, Young Will." The boy stumbled up the ladder into the loft he shared with Richard while Rebecca put on her bonnet, wrapped a shawl around her, and then went from child to child to kiss each of them goodbye. Richard threw his arms around his mother's neck and wouldn't let her go. Sarah held her face up to be kissed. "Will you pray to the saints for Mary, too?" she asked.

"There's no saint can help Mary," said Rebecca. "There's only us."

When her turn came, it seemed to Elizabeth that her mother's mind was elsewhere, and her kiss felt as insubstantial as a butterfly's wing brushing her forehead before fluttering off to something sweeter.

Young Will clambered down the ladder, dressed in dark breeches and stockings with a white square collar over his black jacket. He went outside to wash his face, and then reappeared with a black hat pushed low on his forehead, blinking his weak eyes.

"You look like a cleric, not a farmer," said Elizabeth.

"It's what I am at heart."

"He looks perfect," said Rebecca. "Wait." She opened the dower chest again and reached deep into the back of it. "Take this, and perhaps one day you will be able to understand it."

She held out a book, a leather volume with gold on the front and sides. Young Will took it with the reverence of a priest holding the sacrament. He ran his fingers over the cover, smelled it, then carried the book to the window and opened it at a picture of an island shaped like a human head, covered with fine buildings, set in an ocean where a ship was moored with furled sails.

"What does it say?" Elizabeth pointed to unfamiliar words above the map.

"Utopiae figurae insula," Young Will read. "It's Latin. It means Utopia, map of the island. I've heard the priests talk about this book, but I never thought I could own a copy. It's about a world where people are equal and share all they have, where they want for nothing and live in perfect peace, like in the olden days. Where did you get this book from Ma?" Will squinted at the picture and stroked it, then closed the book and kissed it.

"My mother was given it by her father. He was a rich man of the old faith. I had to keep it hidden from your father. It will be safe with you. Bring it and let's go." Rebecca threw a woollen shawl around her shoulders and, carrying her youngest son and followed by her oldest, left the cottage.

· · · · • · • · · · ·

Elizabeth dug over the outer field, smashed clods of earth, tore out the brambles that grew behind the barn, while the dog of fear snapped around her ankles. The day faded. She was inside, lighting the fire, while Richard dozed in his father's chair and Sarah sang to Mary, when the latch sounded, the door opened and Rebecca bustled in.

Richard jumped up. But the smile on his face quickly disappeared.

Sarah's song died on her lips.

Rebecca had only one son with her. Arthur in his red and gold christening shawl.

"Where's Young Will?" asked Elizabeth.

"He's staying with the priests at the Bishop's Palace. He'll sing in the choir and help them say mass, and perhaps one day he'll be a priest himself."

"Is this the Church's doing?" Elizabeth asked.

Rebecca's face was like flint. "It will be good for Young Will. It's the life to which he was destined. Here, Sarah, take Arthur and put him into the crib."

"When will we see him again?" Tears rolled down Sarah's face. "We never said goodbye to him. Not properly." The baby in her arms, disturbed by the noise or perhaps his hunger, started to whimper.

"Don't cry, Sarah," Richard jumped up to comfort her, but knocked over his chair so it fell with a clatter, and the baby wailed in earnest.

"Look how you've upset him," Rebecca slapped Richard around the face.

"Ma," cried Sarah.

"What have you done?" asked Elizabeth.

"I've done what's best for all of us." Rebecca took off her shawl and bonnet and then placed a scroll of parchment on the table. "Here, Lizzie, Young Will taught you how to read. Read this." She stood opposite, touching her hair, then her face, then her chest as if that might still her heart.

Elizabeth lit a candle at the fire and set it in a candlestick on the table, then sat on the bench and unrolled the parchment. It was thick and cream-coloured, covered with heavy print interspersed by elaborate whirls of black handwriting. At the top was a heading, "This Indenture," and at the bottom was a red seal.

"'This bond is made the 29th day of April Anno Dominae 1643 in the ninth year of the reign of our Sovereign Lord by the grace of God King of England, Scotland, France and Ireland, defender of the faith, between Rebecca Gardiner of the Parish of Bermondsey in the County of Surrey, and Reverend Ezekiel Balhatchet, of Broome in the parish of Southwell in the County of Bedford.'"

"Who is he Mother?" asked Sarah. She'd settled Arthur in his crib and now climbed onto the bench beside Elizabeth and draped an arm around her waist.

"A godly man," Rebecca pursed her lips. "Very learned and with a fortune left to him by his late father. Read on, Lizzie"

"'Before witnesses the said Rebecca Gardiner hath bound over her son Richard.'"

"That's me," Richard sat down on the other side of Elizabeth and peered at the document. "Show me where it says my name."

"But it doesn't mean you, you're too young," Rebecca told her son. "It means Lizzie. Read on."

"'So that he, being of age, is become and doth agree of his own free will that he should remain and continue the Covenant servant of the said Reverend Ezekiel Balhatchet and his heirs.'"

"You're to be a servant, Lizzie, to the Reverend Ezekiel Balhatchet of Broome." Rebecca said.

"But I'm not a Richard; and I'm not a boy."

"There's plenty as think you are a boy. You dress like one, you work like one, your father treated you like one. Reverend Balhatchet wanted a boy to farm his land. Read on."

"'To be by the said Reverend Ezekiel Balhatchet or his heirs transported unto Jamestown in the country and land of Virginia, and to be by him or them employed there, for the space of seven years for the consideration herein after set out.'

"You're sending me away." Transported, to Virginia, for seven years. The words spun in front of Elizabeth's eyes. She put down the parchment. "To Virginia, Ma."

"Where's that?" asked Sarah.

"They say it's in America." Rebecca folded and refolded the christening shawl and put it in the dower chest.

"America. You're sending me to America," There was only a table between Elizabeth and her mother, but it seemed they were already a world apart. "Why are you doing that, Ma?"

"Reverend Balhatchet is travelling there with his wife and children. They're good people. You'll work their land, grow their crops, and when you're older, you'll get some land of your own. You can do well in Virginia."

Elizabeth felt the smooth parchment, touched the red hardness of the seal. What promises had been made to whom before her stony-faced mother, had given her away? The second child her mother had given away that day.

"You said a consideration," said Richard. "What's that? Does it say, Lizzie?"

Elizabeth ran her finger down the parchment. "It says here it's £5. Ma, you've sold me. For £5. How can you do that? I'm your daughter, your own daughter, how can you sell me like I'm one of our animals? How can you do it Ma?"

Rebecca went to the crib and picked up Arthur, shushed him, rocked him, anything Elizabeth felt to avoid accounting for what she'd done.

"Don't you hear me Ma, or don't you care? You can't sell me. I'm freeborn. Father told me so. What would he say if he was here?"

"If he was here, there'd be no need." Rebecca's tone told Elizabeth more than her words. Its iciness spoke of a frozen heart.

"What if I say no?" she asked.

"You have to go." Rebecca leaned across the table, clutching her baby. "Why are you always so difficult? I'm your mother. You must do as I say, and I say you're to go, and that paper says so, too. See, I've signed it."

She pointed a finger to where a shaky R was inscribed beneath the elaborate flourishes of Reverend Ezekiel Balhatchet's signature.

"I don't care what it says. I won't go."

"Don't you dare defy me, you wicked girl. The deal's done," Rebecca shouted the words across baby Arthur who wailed in her arms. "We need the money."

Elizabeth looked at the document: a signature, a seal, a consideration, her life stolen. By her mother. "Judas" she screamed. "You're a Judas. Your own flesh and blood and you sold me."

She ran to throw the parchment in the fire, but Rebecca moved faster and blocked her way, baby tucked under one arm.

"Lizzie! No!" Richard jumped up and wrestled the parchment from his sister's hand.

Rebecca swung her body back and raised her hand.

"No Ma," Sarah sprang from the bench, "don't hit her."

A wild scream split the cottage, not fear, barely human. Mary, sitting in her low chair by the fire, screamed again, clawed at the air, kicked her legs, shielded her head, then curled herself into a lump and howled. Elizabeth, Rebecca, Sarah and Richard were helpless in the face of her anguish. Baby Arthur whimpered unnoticed.

"She'll never recover, and if you don't go, she has no chance even to survive," said Rebecca once Mary was at last calm again. "Not now she's called a witch. The rest of us might not survive that, either. We have to leave. We can go to Kent. My father will shelter us and Mary's not known there. But she can't walk to

Kent. That's why I signed that paper. For £5 to buy a horse to carry Mary."

"You sold me for a horse?"

"I indentured you to a clergyman to save my family."

"When will we buy the horse?"

"Reverend Balhatchet is buying it for us. He'll bring it when he comes to collect you."

"And when is that?"

"Tomorrow."

"So soon." Elizabeth looked from her mother, now rocking the baby again, to her helpless sister curled on the chair, to Sarah comforting her, to her troubled brother. All their futures at risk. She had no choice.

· · · · ● · ● · · ·

Finally, it was done. The family's life reduced to a chest, crammed shut, roped around, on the floor in the middle of the cottage. Beside it were three blankets stuffed full and tied into bundles. One of them was Elizabeth's. The kettle still hung in the hearth where the remnants of a fire smouldered. The dower chest, locked with its treasures, and Will's chair, were moved into the girls' bedroom. In hope of a return, if hope there could be. Richard climbed alone to his loft, but soon came down again and climbed into bed with Sarah, unable, he said, to sleep alone.

Elizabeth went out into the barn. The chickens were roosting. Sarah would take her favourites and the rest would be let loose. The cow slept. Richard would lead her on the road to Kent. Perhaps her father would use the pitchforks and pails when he came back from the war. If. In the orchard, blossom was giving way to tiny fruits that she wouldn't see ripen. Dew weighed the meadow grass that she would never cut again. In the sky, the evening star twinkled.

From the cottage window, a dim light shone. Through it she saw Rebecca nursing Arthur beside the dying fire. Such peace, such tenderness was in her mother's face, the likes of which Elizabeth felt she had never known. Now she would have no chance. She went inside.

"Did you always hate me so much?"

Rebecca detached the baby from her breast and placed him in his cradle. "I bore you Lizzie, how could I ever hate you? Why would you think such a thing?"

"Then why did you sell me?"

"Don't be hard, Lizzie. Come and sit with me."

Elizabeth sat on the stone floor and put her head on her mother's lap. "Reverend Ezekiel is a fine man," Rebecca continued, "inspired by his belief in doing God's work to found a new world order. He needs a boy who can work the land and grow food for his family in America. His wife is a good woman, kindly, with five children and one expected. You'll be safe with them. And they say that there's great wealth in the new world for people like you."

"What kind of people are those, Ma?"

Rebecca stroked Elizabeth's hair. The gentleness of her touch took Lizzie back to a time before all their troubles started when she thought the sun would always shine, the birds would always sing, and home would always be her safe place.

"People who are clever and work hard and can make their way in life," Rebecca said. "Like I thought your father was, and perhaps he is, wherever he is now. Oh Lizzie, from when you first opened your eyes you looked like someone who would get on with life, and that's what you've done. You are what I would have wanted to be, if I'd dared. I never hated you."

Elizabeth felt her mother's body relax and heard her breathing slow. She lifted her head. Her mother's eyes were shut. Then she settled her head again in her mother's lap, looked into the fire as it guttered, and resolved to watch through these final hours. She swung between fear, sorrow, anger, love, then a fleeting hope that perhaps some divine act might yet rescue her. Perhaps it would not be the Reverend but her father who walked through the cottage door in the morning. She looked into the fire, and its redness became his red hair and laughing face, until the last glowing ember gave up its struggle and faded into blackness.

·········

"Lizzie, wake up, you need to get ready." Elizabeth heard her sister Sarah's voice, felt herself be shaken and found herself lying on her mother's bed with her sister holding a cup of fresh milk. "You fell asleep on Mother's lap. She put you to bed."

Elizabeth washed in the bucket of water Rebecca had set by the fire for her, then dressed in the trousers, jacket and cap laid on the bench by the table.

"This is for you." Rebecca held out the red and gold silk christening shawl. "I will have no more use of it, and you may need it one day, before you come back." Elizabeth unfolded the shawl which caught the light and glowed like fire. She held it against her face and felt it as soft as a newborn's skin.

"Take these." Richard held out a brown cloth bag. "You may have some use of them in the new world." He looked at his feet, his face as sullen as a winter sky. Elizabeth opened the bag and found pouches of seeds inside. "They're for planting when you get to America: turnips, carrots, beans and wheat. An asparagus crown wouldn't survive on a boat. You can think of us when you watch them grow. I'll miss you, Lizzie." He put his arms around her and then turned away.

"Put this in among your clothes, Lizzie." Sarah held out a small pouch made from the muslin she used in the dairy. "You'll never forget us then."

Elizabeth held the pouch to her nose and smelt rosemary inside. She shut her eyes and saw Sarah tending the garden, the blue flowers in the hedge around the cottage with its red and white roses twined over its front door. She untied her bundle and buried the pouch in the folds of her dress, the only one she had, that her mother had made for her after the last good harvest. She rolled the bag of seeds up in her work clothes, and folded the shawl and placed it on John Lilburne's leaflet, then she tied the bundle up again.

So little of her old life to take into the new.

"Sarah and Richard, take Mary into the barn and stay there with her until the Reverend has gone," said Rebecca.

And me, take me too, thought Elizabeth as she and Rebecca were left alone, mother and seeming son, sitting on either side of the hearth. Elizabeth willed the sun to stand still, for time to stop, for the next moment never to arrive. But then a hard rap sounded at the door and Rebecca opened it.

A dark shape blocked out the sunlight. Reverend Ezekiel Balhatchet had to stoop to enter the cottage. When he stood upright, Elizabeth got her first measure of her master. A lean man, dressed in black from his pointed hat to his buckled shoes, carrying an ebony cane with a silver handle, which he planted before him as if claiming the place for his own. He had shoulder-length black hair and when he removed his hat, revealed a silver streak that started from the hairline at the centre of his high forehead. It gave a wisdom to his face which was chiselled, with prominent cheekbones and a long, thin nose.

A gentleman's face, Elizabeth concluded, but without colour. His cheeks were pale, as were his lips, and his eyes, which swept around the room, were such a light blue they were almost white.

"Is this Richard?" His eyes rested on her, but to Elizabeth it seemed he was looking through rather than at her.

"Yes, your honour," said Rebecca, bobbing, hands now clutching her apron, now pushing Elizabeth to her feet. "This is my Richard."

"He's small."

"But he's strong. He works hard and has managed the farm since my husband departed. He has green fingers, everyone says so. He'll raise you a fine farm in America." Elizabeth feared her mother would fall on her knees and grovel to the man.

"Mmm." The Reverend looked around the room, his eyes passing over the packed bags and coming to rest on the crib. "And that's your new son."

Rebecca nodded and bobbed again.

"It will be a better world we'll take you to, boy." For the first time Ezekiel, directed his words, if not his attention, at her. "Come, we must away. Mistress Balhatchet waits at Rother-hithe with my children. We sail on the tide."

He turned and ducked out of the cottage, then walked ahead to the road, picking his way through the mud in his fine shoes, his cane held against his shoulder like a standard, Rebecca and Elizabeth following behind.

"Don't forget us," whispered Rebecca.

Elizabeth struggled with her bundle. She gazed around: at the blossom blowing in the orchard, at the asparagus spears reaching up to bid her farewell, at the green buds bursting in the hedgerows. She breathed the pure air, suffused with morning sweetness: listened to the hens clucking around the farmyard, to the birdsong overhead. She shut her eyes to capture the essence of it, imprint it in her mind and on her soul, so she could summon it up in whatever lay ahead.

A hackney carriage with two horses stood beside the holly tree. Its driver, a large, cruel-faced man, opened the door and bowed as Reverend Balhatchet jumped nimbly inside. The driver slammed the door and turned to Elizabeth. "Put your bundle on top, boy," he pointed to the roof of the carriage, "and climb up at the back. You'll stand beside me."

The carriage window opened and Reverend Balhatchet's head came out. "Take your horse." He pointed his cane at the rear of the carriage, where the animal was tied; a brown creature with a rough coat and bowed back.

"It's not much of a horse," Elizabeth muttered to her mother. "You could have got more for me. Will it even reach your father's house?"

"Small mercies," said Rebecca. She untied the horse, which plodded off with her and then put its head down to graze.

Elizabeth climbed up next to the driver. When she turned, Rebecca was standing by the road holding the horse with one hand, the other covering her face. Her shoulders were shaking, her body doubled over in grief. It was only then that Elizabeth realised how dearly the horse had cost her mother. She wanted to jump down and run to her and say not to worry, she would be fine in the new world, and one day she would come home again. But the driver whipped his horses, and all she could do was shout, "Don't cry, Ma," and hope her mother heard and understood.

As the carriage moved forward, two figures appeared from the cottage and streaked across the fields, one in trousers, the other with a skirt billowing behind. Elizabeth waved, and from the distance, Sarah and Richard waved back before the carriage went behind a hedge and they were lost from sight.

Elizabeth had never felt more alone.

The driver whipped up his horses and they clattered along the road, past the neighbours' abandoned farm, past the shacks where the destitute were starting their empty days. To Elizabeth he was the horseman of the apocalypse. He lashed the horses, cursed them, the rutted street, "And you, devil boy," swirled his whip again and the carriage spurted forward with such force that Elizabeth feared her bundle of belongings would fall off and she would lose what few possessions she had. The horses' hooves churned up choking dust and her teeth chattered less now from fear than from the roughness of the ride. She clung to the carriage and looked down into the despairing faces of the street beggars and wondered whether she might be reduced to such a life, and if so, where in the world that would be.

There was still the chance of escape. When the carriage rattled into the cobbled streets of Southwark, it slowed at the crossroads to turn towards Rotherhithe. She could jump down now, run down an alleyway, hide in the backstreets, find her way home.

"Don't even think of it, boy." The driver whipped his horses, and they were off again, down the uneven road to the riverfront. Where the carriage stopped and she climbed down, and the driver threw her bundle off the roof. She lifted it onto her shoulders and followed Reverend Balhatchet along the jetty, him striding ahead as if he expected the crowds to part for him, which they did, until he reached the rowboat that would take them to the ship which his wife and children had already boarded.

There he seated himself up front, while behind him huddled the desperate, the hopeful, the despairing. People who had sold everything they'd ever owned, borrowed every last penny from their families, indentured themselves to get a place on a ship to take them to a new life in America. Children rounded up off the streets, abandoned, lost, or inattentive. Scoundrels fleeing justice, adventurers seeking riches, idealists pursuing their dreams. And among them Elizabeth, clutching her meagre bundle of possessions. The oarsmen strained, heads down as they set out from the shore, the agitation of their human cargo drowned out by the squeaking of the oars in their rowlocks, the splash of water as the blades rose and fell.

As the boat approached midstream, the current grew stronger, and so did the noise of those on board. Cries of fear or excitement, curses, prayers. Elizabeth wondered where her family were, how many chickens Sarah had left behind, and whether Mary had managed to climb onto the pony. And then the images of the farm were driven out by the looming presence of the ship which would be her world until she reached the new one. It towered over her, three masts, a figurehead of a woman garlanded with flowers, and painted below her in elaborate white lettering the name "Speedwell".

Behind her, Elizabeth heard a dog bark. When she looked back, she saw it standing wild and dirty at the end of the jetty. It growled, howled, and slipped away.

CHAPTER 13

London: 1 August 2019

August is the cruellest month.

A seductive mirage of languid days, romantic nights. An escape from Westminster.

But that August, just below the surface, was turbulence.

Toby came calling on the first day of the month. We'd arranged to meet at my place and go for lunch, and exactly on time my buzzer went. He was a study of smart-casual, announcing he was going to whisk me away to the country.

"Today is for us," he said.

I blocked out that his real "us" was himself and Veronica, his wife in the suburbs, and the two daughters that he talked about as he drove us, his fantasy "us"—himself and me—down the green side of the hill from my flat. He was concentrating on the road as he described how one daughter was waiting for her A Level results, the other shifting to a sixth form college in September to reboot her flagging interest in education. His voice was carefully modulated, his hands firm on the steering wheel. I couldn't see his eyes; they were hidden behind sunglasses. But he couldn't control his face. It glowed with pride.

"My mother's in a home near here," I said.

"Oh."

"Like you said, she has health issues."

"I'm sorry."

"Are you?"

"Why?" Laughter. He turned, dark sunglasses, towards me. "Aren't you?"

"I'm not sure how I feel." Outside the car window, London suburbia in all its blandness slipped by. "She's been on a trajectory for a while," I said. "Now is probably her least destructive period."

"Mmm." His face was as non-committal as his voice.

"Did life never deal you a complete wild card?"

A hint of a pause. The slightest furrow creased his brow and disappeared behind his sunglasses.

"Not that I can think of."

"No real big fat bummer that upset everything?"

He smiled. "Veronica would never allow it."

He stopped at a place of chintzy cuteness off the A3, down a lane sunk so deep between wooded banks with trees closing so densely over the top that it was like going down a rabbit hole into another world, before bursting out into a clearing set with a duck-pond and flint cottages and a red post box on a wooden stake.

"How pretty," I said.

"It's one of my favourite places."

He parked where the lane turned into a footpath and I got out. The silence sang. Then, in the woods, so did a bird.

"A cuckoo." He turned his face to the sun and smiled with unaffected pleasure, then swung his jacket over his shoulder and came round the front of the car.

"Shall we go for a walk?" He held out a hand.

"I'm not dressed for it."

I avoided the hand. He didn't take offence.

"Only to the pub, then."

It was tucked behind the cottages at the other end of the lane, past the pond, which had genuine ducks being fed by two small children and their mother. The kids looked impossibly soft and round and white, with sunhats shading their faces and cotton shirts that covered their shoulders. Their mum was pointing to the ducks and talking in dulcet tones that rippled across the water. "Look Johnny, look Matty, that's a mallard, that's a moorhen."

"What is it about posh people and birds?"

Toby laughed. "Still the chip on your shoulder?"

"Come to that, how did you manage to skive off work for the day?"

"This is work. Client relations."

My turn to laugh. "You're shameless."

"It's true." Offended innocence behind the sunglasses. "Besides you're one of my oldest friends."

That felt comfortable. An anchoring. I put an arm through his.

It was a gastro pub, of course. Too late for lunch, too early for dinner, we sat in the artfully wild garden and nibbled on a series of exquisite, expensive dish-ettes. We didn't need wine. The conversation flowed from my slog to establish myself post-university.

"Gritty," he said.

"Character-building," I replied.

To his shimmy up the career ladder. We filled in the missing years and swapped scurrilous stories like a pair of dodgy card sharks. I never remembered him as a wit, but he made me laugh and his undisguised lust for me was gratifying. No, it wasn't lust. Attracting lust is easy in Westminster where the threshold is low. And it wasn't admiration, either. That is too undifferentiated:

admiration for cunning, for ruthlessness, occasionally even admiration for courage.

It was his affection that got to me. Here was someone who had known me for so long, must have carried some kind of a torch for part of that time, and was now letting it shine, so I thought. I should have asked him to remove his sunglasses.

We avoided the subjects that might upset our present applecart. My mother, his wife, where our relationship was headed. It was only once we finished up in our fantasyland and I'd gone and paid the bill before he did, to protests until I promised, "OK, next time it's on you," and he was driving us back into town, that he talked about the future. As in tomorrow.

"I'm going to Italy."

"Work?"

"No, holiday."

"'You' plural, as in you and Veronica and your girls." I lobbed a brick into the conversation. He didn't notice.

"We always go there for August. This will probably be our last chance *en famille*, what with our oldest going to university and the youngest being generally uncooperative."

"How difficult." I'd only once been on holiday with my Mum, for a weekend at a Butlins camp with one of a string of "uncles" in tow.

"I'm glad you understand."

He didn't take his eyes off the road.

We had sex before he left. It was good, better even than last time. We knew each other's bodies, and I knew that whatever the limitations of our relationship, there were at least some genuine feelings attached. If he wasn't looking for anything permanent, neither was I. But I felt a sense of loss that he would be gone a whole month, and wondered whether he would think of me at all.

He put on his sunglasses before he kissed me goodbye. It was the second time that day I should have told him to take them off. The sun had, after all, gone down.

· · · · ●·●· · · ·

In the days that followed, it was Donna's face that most often stared at me from my phone. South London online. Pictures of the grieving grandmother, the tragic Dylan. Long stories about his equally tragic Mum. Pictures of him on his first day at school, in his football strip, with his first bike. A good boy misled. Her voice blared from the local radio station, berating "them" for letting him down. "Them" including me.

Stephanie came with me to the funeral. She wore her grey suit with a black hat I loaned her for the occasion. The church was packed, ditto the community centre afterwards. The vicar asked me to come up front and shoved a microphone in my hand to say something. There were some nudges and ungenerous mutterings. It was my job to give expression to the collective sense of shock and the need for justice, but I had to dig deep to find suitable words.

"Dylan was a child of our times and our community. The third generation of his family to live on the Cooper. Someone whose roots were here, who should have been reaching for the stars in his adult years.

"Instead, his life was so tragically ended. The victim of yet another knife crime. And despite all the CCTV and the many people out and about on the estate that day, the police are still no further forward in bringing his killers to justice.

"We owe it to Dylan to do that.

"But more than that we owe it to Dylan to make sure that our times and our community are better for future generations." I looked at people's faces. Donna was in a daze, Leigh belligerent, Stephanie impressed. Laurelle was missing—at work I guessed. Others in the crowd nodded in agreement or shook their heads. Sorrow or anger? Each had their own idea of what "better" looked like. I wasn't going to stray into such difficult territory. "We all owe it to Dylan, especially those of us who have the power to make things happen. We owe it also to Dylan's devoted grandmother, Donna, to whom we all extend our most sincere condolences. Our hearts are with you Donna. Now and always."

Afterwards, Leigh put an exclusion zone around her sister. Stephanie breached it and embraced Donna. She was beyond registering what was happening, or who was there. I touched Leigh's arm. She pulled it away and glared at me. I decided to pay my respects to Donna later. Time would, I hoped, produce the killer, and that might take the edge off her grief. How little I understood.

As we walked across the piazza to my car, I saw that one tower block now had a security fence around it, and another had its front entrance barricaded. That only left Speedwell House in use. Stephanie asked if we could go and check out Miracle.

"I have to give her some bad news."

The entry phone was still broken. I guessed it would never be mended. The hallway smelt of abandonment, but the lift was still working, and jerked us up to the top floor. "The housing projects back home are bad, too," Stephanie observed. "At least there's not so many guns in your country."

Miracle's floor was as pristine as before. Stephanie texted from the doorstep of her flat and, when the door opened a crack, did one of those frenetic little hand waves.

A child's laughter came from inside. As we walked through the flat, I noticed the doors that had previously been closed were open, and it looked as if the rooms were empty. Whoever had been living there must have left. In Miracle's room, a toddler was playing on the floor with building blocks and Blessing sat on a mattress chewing a rusk. The toddler, a girl, was wearing pink headphones with cat's ears. Laurelle's child, Sherine.

I sat down on the only chair, again. Sherine came up and presented me with a building block, and I acted like I knew how to play with a two-year-old. Stephanie sat on the mattress and dandled Blessing while Miracle stood by the window and talked.

"It's not safe for my baby." Miracle took the wrap off her head and twisted it around in her hands. "Bad people broke in downstairs. I lock the door when she comes," she pointed at Sherine, "and I don't open it until Laurelle comes in the morning to collect her."

"Have you spoken to the council recently?" Stephanie's voice was even enough, although she didn't put down Blessing and didn't look at Miracle.

"They told me I'm not entitled to housing."

"Have you anywhere to go?" I asked.

"No." Miracle wound her wrap around her hands and wrenched it, as if she could break it instead of her heart.

"We'll keep on pressing them," said Stephanie. "They can't put you out on the streets. Not with the baby."

"They can take her away from me." Miracle was pulling the wrap so tight it must have hurt.

"There's no reason for that," said Stephanie. "You're such a great mom. Look what a lovely girl she is."

"How about you?" I asked. Miracle looked as if she didn't understand the question. "It must be hard on you. Are you alright?"

Miracle wiped her face with her headwrap. "There's nothing wrong with me. Apart from my heart keeps on beating. That's all. Sometimes I wish it would stop. Blessing would be better off without me. With someone who could give her a proper home. A kind person who would look after her."

"No-one could look after her better than you," said Stephanie.

I wondered whether, somehow, I could find someone who knew of a corner in this great city where there was space for a needy mother and child.

"Let's see what we can do."

Miracle took my hand and kissed it. I wondered if she'd heard some hope in my voice that I hadn't intended.

There was an extended thumping on the front door of the flat. Sherine ran out of the room, followed by Miracle. Then there was the sound of a woman's voice, "Hiya baba," then, "Sorry to be so late. I had to do an extra shift." A clatter and Laurelle came in wearing her nurse's uniform, with a tan shoulder bag over one arm, holding her daughter with one hand. With the other she was carrying a bulky black plastic bin liner which she dumped on the floor. It fell open and a stack of posters slid out.

"You." She said, and then, "Hello Stephanie."

"You use Miracle as a childminder," I said.

"Interesting choice of word, that. Use. How else is she supposed to live? Come on, Sherine, let's get your things together."

"I'll help you." Stephanie sat Blessing on the mattress and scooped up the building blocks. "OK if I put them in here?" and dropped them into the plastic bag with the posters. Laurelle went out and there was a banging around in the kitchen and she came back with a Tupperware which she also shoved into the bin liner. "Anything else?" She looked around the room, fatigue written all over her face, and then smiled at her daughter and said, "OK baba?" Sherine fixed her mother with big brown eyes and nodded. I recognised that look. Total adoration.

I stood up from the chair. There was nothing more I could do here. "Come on, Stephanie, I'll give you a lift into town."

On the way out I saw that a poster—fluorescent yellow—had been plastered over the front door with "Occupy" blazoned diagonally across in red lettering. It covered the bottom of the Jesus poster, the bit that said, "Jesus saves".

Stephanie was subdued going down in the lift. As we reached the ground floor, she pulled a tissue out of her bag, then caught my eye and looked embarrassed.

"It's allowed to be sad," I said.

It was a side of Stephanie I'd not seen before. She wiped under her eyes and blew her nose. "Back there, you talked about how all the people on the Cooper want is something better," she said. "That's so right. It's all Miracle wants for Blessing. And I guess it's what Elizabeth must have looked for in America."

CHAPTER 14

Ocracoke: June 1643

O n the horizon, a smudge of land. To ships that lost the ocean winds and currents and drifted south on endless waters, it offered hope. To those caught in the storms that crashed onto its unforgiving shores, it spelt death. To Elizabeth, standing on the deck of the Speedwell, watching the shadow turn from blue to grey, then beaches appear, catching the light and glowing yellow, it brought a chance of escape from the charnel house that the ship had become.

Of the people who had crowded aboard in Rotherhithe, just over half now lined the deck to wonder at the miracle of their arrival. The rest were below deck, even now drawing their final breaths, or had already been committed lifeless to the ocean.

Elizabeth watched land take definition before her, the sand seeming to rise in gentle dunes to greenery which took the shape of trees—wind-stunted, but trees at least—and then grass, brackish looking, but vegetation of some sort growing on what was at last solid ground. Above her, gulls wheeled and called, and around her the creaking of the ship's timbers, the rustling of her sails, mingled with the cries and laughter of people who'd survived. Thus far.

Whatever hopes she had of life in this new world, were tempered by the pain of her departure from the old.

"What's this?" Ezekiel's rage had shaken his family's cabin while the Speedwell was still at anchor in the Thames. Elizabeth cowered beside her bundle of belongings, which were spilled open on the floor. Poking through its contents with his ebony cane, he'd lifted out her dress which he waved over her like a flag of shame.

"I paid for a boy," he screamed.

"Shush," said his wife, Agnes. "The whole ship will hear you."

"You cheated me," Ezekiel shrieked. "You lied."

Elizabeth ducked and dodged as Ezekiel raged after her, wielding his cane, landing blows now on her back, now on her arms, now on his own children, who fell over each other to escape his fury in the cramped cabin.

"I can work harder than any boy," Elizabeth tripped over the family's fifth child, crawling across the floor to his mother who, pregnant with her sixth, stood big-bellied in the chaos.

"I'll have you stripped." Ezekiel's eyes burned with a fire that looked to Elizabeth more devilish than divine.

"No, you won't." Agnes pulled Elizabeth behind her for protection.

"At the very least I'll have her flogged."

Elizabeth curled into a ball on the floor. And then the ship lurched, and Ezekiel lost his footing, his howls drowned out by the singing of the sailors and the clatter of the anchor being hauled on board. And then the ship tilted as she turned to catch the tide, the sound of rippling water filled the cabin and Agnes staggered, groaning, onto a wooden bunkbed that ran along one side of it.

"The girl can help me. She can care for the children, and when the baby comes, she can tend to me." Agnes held her swollen stomach and moaned with a sickness that grew worse as the Speedwell's sails caught the wind, and she set out down the Thames.

Elizabeth watched London disappear, ramshackle buildings jostling for preference along the riverfront, small boats plying around the ships midstream. The city's clamour gave way to the silent desolation of the estuary marshes, tidal mudflats inhabited only by wading birds and the skeletal timbers of marooned shipwrecks.

When the Speedwell reached the open sea, she turned south and west. Past the white cliffs and busy ports of England's south coast. Past harbours thronged with merchant ships and fishing boats. Past sparkling beaches, pockets of yellow sand scalloped out of grey rock, light alternating with darkness. Until, finally, Elizabeth stood on deck and watched the black cliffs of England recede. Somewhere behind their darkness was her lost family, her rebel father, their abandoned farm. She hoped Young Will would be praying for them all. And then the cliffs disappeared, the last bond with her old life was broken, and she turned her face westwards to the unknowingness of the ocean.

Small wonder that the old world turned its back on the band of people leaving its shores. As the Speedwell was buffeted by storms, climbing the ocean's mountains, and sinking into what each person on board expected to be their grave, Elizabeth found herself in a world stripped first of kindness, and then of humanity.

Each passenger fought a daily battle for survival, pressed together in the groaning belly of the ship. From her place outside the Balhatchet family cabin, Elizabeth listened as the anger of winds above deck out-howled the agony of those below.

The first to lose the struggle to survive was Jasper, a pallid boy indentured to a tailor from Colchester. She found his body lodged cold and rigid under a cannon on the third morning out from England. When she held a candle to the dead boy's grey face, she saw his lips were drawn back in agony, or perhaps a final smile at his early release?

The boy's master sent Elizabeth to rouse the ship's surgeon to provide an explanation.

"What was it killed him? Will it kill us too?" he asked.

Whatever it is, thought Elizabeth, it won't get me.

But the ship's surgeon could find no cause for the death, other than a chronic nostalgia, and ordered the body to be wrapped in a blanket and given a blessing. After which the tailor and his fellows hauled it up the ladder and out onto the deck, where raging sky and sea swirled into a single watery mass, into which the boy's body was launched, un-mourned.

The men returned below deck and sat fearing, while outside the crew struggled to save the ship, inching along rain-slippery timbers in the driving torrent to furl the sails, then cut adrift a mast which split in the tumult.

When the storms eased, Elizabeth sneaked onto the open deck to watch the sea, the gulls, the sailors, anything to escape the filth, stench, and death below. Sometimes she took Ruth and Samuel, two of Ezekiel's children, to see the animals in their pens under the foredeck, pigs and goats and chickens, which, as their owners died, she tended. Or she would climb up on the front deck of the ship to scan the horizon ahead in the hope of seeing land. Or she would risk the irascible captain's wrath by scaling his navigation deck at the rear of the ship to ask him about its progress.

Other times, with Ezekiel's oldest son Malachi, she would descend to the depths of the ship. Past the crowded main deck, where the men and women who had staked their lives on this venture, gambled, prayed and wept as their hopes of the new world rose and fell with the pitching of the ship. Past the deck of the London street children, rounded up to work in the new world: children abandoned, orphaned or plain unlucky, all ignorant of their destiny or destination. Past the cargo and munitions, to the domain of the ship's cook, a giant whose voice bellowed louder than the clatter of his pans, shaved head gleaming in the heat, stumping around his little kingdom that smelt of blood and spice on a wooden pegleg for which he, Christopher Conquest, had earned the nickname Peggy.

"What happened to your leg, Peggy?" they'd ask him.

"A monster leapt out of the sea and bit it off when I left my home in Africa."

"No."

"The ship's surgeon sawed it off to save my life after a battle with Barbary pirates."

"No."

"I chopped it off myself to escape a British slaver."

"Tell us, tell us."

And then Peggy would reach for one of the cleavers that hung from the low ceiling and slam it down on a barrel of salt beef with such force that Elizabeth believed he could as easily chop off a person's head as his own leg. And he would throw them a scrap of meat as a reward for their audacity, and she would hear his laughter follow them as they ran up the ladder to daylight. If she woke early or late, she would go on deck and find Peggy alone, crouched on a mat, saying prayers.

Elizabeth comforted Ezekiel's children when their mother died. Agnes never left the family's cabin. She ruled it from her bunk bed, between bouts of sea sickness, organised her children and kept Ezekiel's vicious temper away from Elizabeth.

Ten days into the journey, in pitch darkness, Elizabeth was woken by the sound of Agnes screaming. Inside the cabin, she found the mother writhing, the younger children crying, their father praying. "It's too soon," Agnes cried. All day, Elizabeth tended the labouring woman, her husband and children banished to the main deck. Through the next night the agony continued until, at daybreak, Agnes clutched Elizabeth's hand, forced out a tormented, "Care for my children," and then between seasickness and birth pains, she and her unborn baby died.

Ezekiel seemed to need no comfort as he delivered a blessing on the soul of his dear departed wife, as her body with the unborn child inside was tipped overboard to find a watery passage to eternity. Elizabeth wondered what it would take to make this man feel, or whether he was incapable, and whether perhaps that was the only way to survive such sorrow.

Without their mother, Ezekiel's two youngest children, Naomi and Zachary, gave up their fragile hold on life. Elizabeth wondered at Ezekiel's composure as the Reverend consigned them to the waves. She moved her bundle of belongings into the family cabin to care for the surviving children, Samuel, who was muted by his grief, and Ruth, for whom she made a doll that the little girl cradled and talked to constantly. The oldest child, Malachi, left the family cabin to join the ship's crew.

"To avoid madness," Malachi said.

Then the ship lost its way and was becalmed. The wind died, and the sun grew hotter until those baking below deck prayed for another storm. The captain took to his cabin, and the crew grew restless. Elizabeth spent long, still days under Ezekiel's tutelage, reading the Bible and listening to him expound its prescription for a new world order. Which God had called him to establish, so he explained, the silver streak in his hair grown wider and more prophetic, on the land which He had promised. And Ezekiel lifted his pale eyes to the horizon, where the intense blue of the sky met the darker blue of the waters and they burnt with such a fervour of belief that more than once Elizabeth ran to the edge of the deck to peer over the railings and see whether perhaps a miracle had happened and there was land to be seen.

As the ship drifted further, and the despair on board became the more profound and the heat more intense, so the divine promises, it seemed to Elizabeth, became more extravagant, more founded, so it seemed to her, in Ezekiel's mind than on the printed words she read. Until they seemed to her so far-fetched, she doubted they were credible at all. And then she wondered whether the hardness of her heart that cushioned her from feeling was matched by a hardness of the soul that prevented her from believing this man who was, by common accord, the holiest on board.

"The most righteous and the cleverest. Inspired by God," said Annie Meadowsweet, a woman with wispy blond hair and thin shoulders that stuck through salt-stiff clothes. After her husband and son had died, she'd attached herself to Elizabeth. and hovered around Ezekiel like a disciple, devoted but ignored.

When at last the Speedwell caught a breeze, the ship made such sluggish progress that Elizabeth wondered whether she or those on board would survive till landfall. And when seagulls appeared, riding on winds of sweeter air, she wondered what land they were from, and where, when they reached it, if they reached it, they might find themselves to be.

· · · ●· ●● · · · ·

And now Annie Meadowsweet stood next to Elizabeth on the Speedwell's deck as landfall approached.

"I wish my Jack had lived to see this. And our lad." Annie lifted her apron to her face and wept. "It's paradise."

Elizabeth put an arm around her friend. "No Annie, it's not paradise," she said. "It's America."

Alongside the two women, the ship's first mate stood scanning the shoreline. A sinewy man, long on sealore, short on words, his grey beard was twisted into a plait tied at the end with a knot.

"It is America, isn't it?" Elizabeth asked him.

"It should be." The first mate twiddled the knot in his beard. "If the charts are right, and—for once—the captain."

"You see, we've arrived," Elizabeth turned to Annie, who had wiped away her tears, smoothed down her apron, and was looking at the seashore with a face on which relief fought with fear and won.

"Is this Jamestown?" Elizabeth asked the first mate.

"No."

"So where are we?"

"Ocracoke."

"Will we go ashore?"

"Now that's a question." The first mate twiddled the knot in his beard again. "To go ashore, we need a harbour. There is one here, of sorts, beyond the headland, but to reach it we have to sail through sandbanks and strong currents. A ship can be swept off course. She can go aground. Few dare sail there, apart from pirates."

"But we are saved, aren't we?" asked Elizabeth.

"Now that's another question."

CHAPTER 15

London: 14 August 2019

Gerald bounced down to London from his constituency up the M1 partway through August and we went for lunch at a restaurant behind Marsham Street. He was busy plotting a new rebellion, this time directed against the Prime Minister; trying to force him to end our parliamentary summer holidays and recall Parliament to debate the national crisis.

"Crisis, what crisis? No-one's told me about any crisis," I could hear the bluster from the Prime Ministerial home in Downing Street.

"At least you've got the right target this time," I said to Gerald. "Hugh should be happy."

"Hugh's never happy. It's not in his nature. Truth is, I'm better off in London. I've lost the support of my local party, and Phoebe's got the house. I'm squatting with a friend, but it's hard to keep focussed when you're living out of a plastic bag."

"You look like you're doing alright out of a plastic bag." He'd lost weight, was wearing new clothes and was picking at his food: grilled prawns, no sauce and a salad with a yoghurt dressing. Usually he was an industrial-scale eater, mostly of carbohydrates.

"Truth is, Franny—"

"Frances." Only my mother called me Franny. I didn't need reminding that, instead of visits, there'd been two weeks of text messages exchanged with Hanna from her care home.

"Sorry. Frances. This shambles can't continue much longer. I'm sorting out a life for myself afterwards."

"As in?"

"I don't know. Portfolio existence. Bit of academia. Couple of boards. Anything that will keep me afloat and pay the bills for my kids. You'll be alright, though. Whatever the political storm that's coming at us, you'll survive."

"As in that's what I do. Survive."

"It's not such a bad life skill."

He munched his last salad leaf, looked longingly at my fries, then checked his phone and fiddled with the cuffs of his shirt.

"OK," I said. "What is it?"

"I was wondering." He put his phone in his pocket, then took it out and put it on the table beside his plate. "The thing is Franny—"

I glared.

"—Sorry, Frances. I'm going on holiday, just a short one, and wondered, if you're not doing anything, if you might like to come with." He leaned forward on his seat and put his hands palm down on the table. "It's nothing special. Villa overlooking the Amalfi coast. With friends. He and I were at university. She's in health management. Plus their children."

"You mean *en famille*?"

"Well, I was supposed to be going there with Phoebe and the kids, but..."

"Honestly, Gerald. You know how to make a girl feel good."

"It's more like hop across to Europe while you still can without a visa. I can't promise no politics, but no strings attached. And no sex."

But there was my mother. I'd already left her too long. And Gerald wasn't Toby. I tried to imagine what it would be like to be *en famille* with him in Italy, and then thought I'd better not go there.

He picked up on my hesitation. "You've got someone."

"Not particularly." I attempted nonchalance.

"It's that PR bloke isn't it?" Gerald flushed. Anger, or was there something more to it, I wondered. "What's his name again? Toby Davis. Absolute dick."

"I'm not a kid, Gerald."

"I could give you his pedigree." He held up his hand to signal to the waiter.

"If you click your fingers at that waiter, I'll fucking walk out."

He put his hand down. "It's long and interesting."

"I can live without it."

"And he's married."

"And so are you."

"Only technically."

But I joined him for a long weekend. Stretched myself out by the infinity pool with a glass of Chianti and thought, "I could get used to being part of Europe just as we're leaving." It wasn't as hot as London, and Gerald's friends' kids were OK. Gerald was too. Undemanding, like-minded, I'd almost say a kindred spirit if it wasn't for my hankering after Toby. He kept his promise, and we had our separate bedrooms.

· · · · ● · ● · · · ·

Courtesy of someone's smartphone, a picture of the two of us lounging in Italian luxury popped up on my news feed the evening I arrived home. The local newspaper headlined it "PARTNERS IN PARADISE." Cue Twitter stormette. I

hadn't expected that, but it was August after all, and one of
us was still technically married.

It was enough to attract a text message from Hugh. *Hope
you had a good holiday*. Subtext: company noted.

And another from Toby.

?

Just that.

?

Did I detect a touch of jealousy, or was it discretion that
kept him from texting anything longer or more incriminat-
ing? It took two seconds to send him a heart emoji as I got on
the express train to London. He didn't respond. As I opened
my front door to a flat full of stuffy air, I wished I'd sent
something less flippant. I also wished I wasn't arriving home
alone.

I knew I could count on my mother to enjoy the story.
Scandal was her lifeblood, and she could never understand my
ability to keep out of trouble. She'd sigh and say, "You're such
a good girl, Franny," in a voice that told me goodness was the
last thing she wanted from me. I thought her eyes would light
up when I told her about my gentle flutter in her territory.

But the next day when I visited the Surrey care home,
Hanna stopped outside my mother's room and, one hand on
the door, turned to me and said, "You'll find her changed."
Her tone told me it was a professional understatement.

My mother lay under the smoothest of sheets, her arms by
her side, eyes closed, white hair spread out on her pillow like a
halo. She looked so peaceful that for an instant I thought she
had already died. But then I realised that if that had happened,
Hanna would have used a word other than changed, or my
mother's face would have been covered, or there would have
been some other sign to indicate that here lay someone who

had passed through the porous boundary between this life and whatever comes next.

"When did this happen?" I asked.

"Three days ago. She'd been asking for you every day, and when you didn't come, well..." Hanna leaned over my mother's bed, gave her bare hand a gentle stroke with her little finger and said, "Here you are, Mrs Garvey, here's your daughter come to visit you. Just like you wanted. Isn't that nice?"

Mum's hand twitched on the sheet.

"See, she knows you're here. Why don't you sit and talk to her?

"Will she be able to hear me?"

"They say hearing is the last sense to go."

So I pulled up a chair, sat down and leaned forwards until my mouth was on a level with her still apparently functioning ears. What did one say in these circumstances? *"Sorry I wasn't here earlier, Mum, I was on holiday with a married man."* She'd like that. The only thing she wouldn't understand was why there was no shagging. That would take a lot of explaining. Or how about, *"Sorry it's come to this, Mum, going out with a whimper alone in bed between clean white sheets in a Surrey nursing home, when you'd much rather have gone out on a bender banging some john with two fingers up to the world?"* The last thing to do was what I actually did, which was to whisper, "Is there anyone else I can get for you, Mum? Anyone you want to see?"

Nothing.

"Like my Dad?"

Her whole body started and her eyes sprang open. She couldn't turn her head, so I put my face in front of hers where she could see me. Her eyes drilled into mine.

"What's he got to do with anything?"

I didn't want to let the man who had upset her life upset her death as well, so I tried to smooth it over with, "I don't know, I just thought it might give you closure."

"What's closure when it's at home? I can't even remember what he looked like other than he wore a dog collar."

"He was a vicar?"

"Perhaps it made him feel good. How should I know? Anyway, why are you so interested in him all of a sudden? Wasn't I enough for you?"

"Of course you were, Mum."

She closed her eyes. I took her hand. She smiled. Possession.

A woman came round with a tea trolley, put a cup on my mother's bedside table, and gave one to me. I needed it. I felt as if I'd been through an emotional wringer. I sat down and drank it and then scrolled through my social media. The stormette had moved on from me. Hugh's grandson had been caught selling drugs at school. Actually, it was his daughter's partner's son from a previous relationship, but who's bothered? Then I checked on my emails and was busy replying to them when my phone went down.

I was scrabbling under the bed to find a socket and put it onto charge when Hanna came in to check on us. Mother's cheeks were pinker and her breathing was more determined. In, out, in, out, it went, fuck you, fuck you, holding on, holding on.

"She's not going anywhere," I said.

Hanna gave Mum's arm a rub, more expressive of her frustration than my mother's need for comfort. "Is there something unresolved in her life?"

"Her whole life is unresolved."

Hanna drew the curtains, turned on the lights and left.

My mother's lips moved. I leaned forward so I could hear what she said. I thought someone who'd been so close to death must weigh her words carefully.

"That woman drives me mad," she said.

"That's a bit unkind Mum."

"I don't care. It's true." She opened her eyes and gave me the kind of sweet smile that usually presaged trouble. "Can I have something to drink?"

There was a glass on her bedside table, and I went into her en suite and refilled it. I sat on the bed and lifted her up until she was resting against my shoulder. She snuggled her head into my neck. I smelled her faded sweetness mixed with disinfectant and urine. Our bodies fitted together. I tried to think of when I'd last felt so at peace with her. Mumsy comfort wasn't her thing, but cuddling her I felt all the tensions of the past weeks disappear. It was like being a snake or a newt or something, that sheds a skin or a tail. I felt I'd slewed off my most recent past and emerged as someone new, better. Mum lifted her head, and I thought how fine her bone structure was, how pretty she still looked. Then I held the glass to her mouth. She took a sip and pursed her lips.

"Water?"

"I've not got any gin."

She smiled.

"Don't you fucking ever abandon me again."

CHAPTER 16
Ocracoke: June 1643

Around Elizabeth, the open deck of the Speedwell was crowded with passengers; some cheering the land before them, some praying, some crying.

Alone on the foredeck stood Hywel Williams, a man with unkempt black hair and a shaggy beard who'd spent the voyage alternating fierce argument about the nature of God with morose silence that he said was prayer. Rich Josiah Carver strutted amidship with his wife Beatrix, he bursting out of his fine grey jacket, pointing with his cane and declaiming on the nature of the land ahead, she straining the seams of a fine silk dress unpacked for the occasion and with new ribbons in her bonnet. At the stern high on his navigation deck stood the captain, best uniform and wig on, spyglass in hand, commanding his ship again as she approached land.

"It's our new Jerusalem." Ezekiel appeared beside Elizabeth, clutching the railings with hands that were still soft and white. His face was lit up with an ecstasy that seemed to Elizabeth to be unrelated to what lay before them.

"There's nothing there."

"Perhaps your eyes have not yet been opened, but mine have." Ezekiel put one arm across her shoulders and held her with a vice-like grip, his flushed face almost touching hers. With his other hand he traced the outline of his dream. "'Build ye houses, and inhabit them, and plant ye orchards, and eat ye the fruit of them,' that's what God ordered, and it's what, by his grace, we'll do." And he tore off his black hat in an expansive sweep that took in the beach, the woods, the sky.

Elizabeth looked at the bare shore and the windswept trees. Hope of survival, she could feel now that land was before them. But that was all, though perhaps for now that was enough.

"Rejoice, Elizabeth," Ezekiel's fingers dug into her arm, and his speech became more agitated so that fine drops of spittle flew from his mouth. "This is my destiny. All my life I have listened to the voice of God calling me to some higher purpose. But after we set sail, as the storms raged and it seemed the ship would sink, and all would perish, I started to doubt. And then when Agnes died with her baby, and then Zachary and Naomi, it was as if He was punishing me for my doubts."

Ezekiel beat his chest with a clenched fist. "And when the tempest abated, and the wind left and we burned under the sun, I thought perhaps it was the devil I had listened to in leaving England." And he thumped his chest again. "But now, you see, the Lord has delivered us. We are the chosen, and here we will build our city on the hill."

Elizabeth wondered how the weakened survivors aboard the Speedwell could build a city, or where the hill might be in the flat emptiness to which, on a stiffer wind, they grew ever closer.

"Are you ready to land, Papa, Lizzie?" Malachi jumped from the riggings, as agile as a cat, and landed as quietly. He was sea-changed from the boy Elizabeth had first met in Rother-hithe, his scholar's tight clothes replaced with the loose trousers and looser bearing of the sailors. His bare top was now as brown as theirs.

"I thought landing here was too difficult," Elizabeth said.

"The captain says we must take stock of our damage before we travel on to Jamestown. We'll be here a few days." Malachi smiled at her before turning and frowning at his father. "Where are Ruth and Samuel? They should be here."

"I'll fetch them up." Elizabeth was glad to free herself from Ezekiel's grip.

Below deck, shafts of light from the gun-ports lit her path to the family's cabin. Above her head, the low beams trapped in air grown fetid from so many weeks of sea and sickness. Underfoot, the wooden planks were slippery with stains of suffering that no amount of scrubbing could ever purify. Inside the cabin, Ruth and Samuel were sitting in the gloom on the bed where their mother had died. Ruth, thinner from the voyage so that her dark clothes hung on her, was playing with the doll that Elizabeth had made for her. Samuel had his knees drawn up to his chest and his head buried between them.

"Say hello to Lizzie, Baby." Ruth waved her doll's hand. Samuel lifted his head to show a wan face that had frozen after his mother's death.

"We're near land. Your father says you're to come up on deck with me."

"Father told us we must stay here, didn't he, Dolly?" Ruth held her doll up in front of her. "He said we must be good little children and wait here until he comes for us."

"He didn't know then how close we were to shore. Come up with me and see America. Your new home." Elizabeth took a comb from the top of Ruth's chest to smooth the girl's blonde hair and then covered it with a grey cloth bonnet.

As they left the cabin, Elizabeth heard a rustling sound followed by giggling. She stopped and held a finger to her lips, a gesture which Ruth repeated to her doll. Another giggle, the sound coming from the Carvers' cabin, which was, apart from the captain's, the biggest on the ship, and the only other one to contain a bed. She put an ear to the cabin door and then opened it. A flash of red disappeared under the bed, while on it sat a small girl holding in her hands a gold crucifix set with green jewels. Her ragged dress hung off her soft pink-white shoulders, and her head, covered with red curls, was topped by a golden coronet that glinted in the sunlight that shone in through a porthole. She turned a heart-shaped face to Elizabeth and smiled.

"Are you going to be cross with me?"

"May, you will hang one day. Those are Mrs Carver's. Take them off. And Barty come out from under there." Elizabeth knelt down and reached under the bed. "And don't bite." She pulled out a small boy, red-haired like his sister, wearing only a torn pair of trousers that bulged at either side.

"Empty your pockets," said Elizabeth.

"Will you beat me?" Barty asked.

"No, but Mr Carver will do worse than that if he discovers you've been in his cabin again. Put everything back and come up on deck."

May climbed off the bed, sighed, and put the coronet into an embossed jewel box on a table under the porthole. Her brother emptied coins, a pair of spectacles and a small book from his pockets and dodged round the cabin replacing them in boxes, on shelves, and in a money-bag hidden under the mattress of the bed. Then the two ran out of the door and Elizabeth heard their bare feet patter across the wooden decking. Ruth and Samuel followed hand-in-hand.

Elizabeth was at the foot of the ladder when she heard a voice.

"Are we at America?" A boy lying in the shadows at the far end of the deck propped himself up with one hand and, with the other, scratched at his matted hair.

"It seems so, Haz."

"What's it like?"

"Well..." Elizabeth tried to find a way to describe the empty land they'd reached without causing the boy to give up all hope. "It's hard to describe exactly. Why don't you come up and see?"

"I'm not sure I can. I'm too sick. Me gums is bleeding and what's left of me teeth's all wobbly." Haz pulled a bug from his hair and squashed it between his fingers. "What will happen to me in America?"

Elizabeth knew the answer. She'd heard it many times from the planters and merchants aboard the Speedwell. And Haz knew it too. He flicked the dead bug across the deck and continued. "I suppose I'll have to be sold as a labourer to pay for my crossing, but who'll want a sick boy like me? I should've stayed in London. Either way I'll be dead, but this way I've had to go to hell and back first." He fell back on his blanket. "D'you think we can sleep somewhere steady tonight, somewhere that doesn't move around all the time, somewhere we can go outside and piss?"

Elizabeth didn't like to tell him of the reality before them. "Come and see for yourself."

"I'll try. Honest."

From the open deck, over the nerve-jangling creaks of the Speedwell's straining timbers, the orders of the ship's officers, the shouts of the crew, Elizabeth heard a hum like the sound of a swarm of bees. She emerged onto the open deck to find the passengers kneeling in prayer. Ezekiel stood erect above them on the foredeck, Bible in hand, face raised to the sky, his eyes firmly shut to the chaos as the ship's crew struggled to prevent the vessel from running aground. Hywel's brooding figure stood behind him, and Annie sat at his feet. The shore was now so close that Elizabeth feared that at any minute a wave would land them on the beach.

"This is the hour of our deliverance," Ezekiel roared and the passengers cried, "Amen," and then, at Ezekiel's bidding and following Hywel's melodic lead, started to sing. "The waters saw You, O God; The waters saw You, they were afraid." Elizabeth calculated that, given the frailty of the ship and the disorganisation of her captain, it was the people and not the waters that should be afraid.

Around her the sailors heaved on their ropes, and the captain yelled from his vantage point for men to go aloft and let out more sail. The mariners climbed up the ship's rigging like monkeys and their shanties rivalled the psalms rising from the passengers. The sails billowed out, catching a gust of wind, making the ship lurch, causing the passengers to holler and a man to fall from the main mast.

"Save me." His final wail seared the air before he hit the water and disappeared.

"God save us all," screamed Annie.

Elizabeth felt arms clutch her waist. Samuel and Ruth clung to her with the desperation of souls already drowning. Ruth called, between sobs, for her mother. Samuel shed his tears in silence. The Speedwell heeled onto one side, her timbers groaning against wind and tide. The land, so welcome when it first appeared on the horizon, now looked hostile. Relentless waves crashed onto the pitiless beach, which grew ever closer. Elizabeth's legs trembled and the spray of ocean water stung her face. For once she agreed with Mrs Carver, who shouted at the captain, "For God's sake, do something."

And then over the hubbub she heard Ezekiel's voice. "Lo."
He stood on the foredeck, one hand outstretched with his
ebony cane, the other holding aloft his black hat, his hair blowing in the wind. "The Lord has caused the sea to be divided.
Behold the hand of God parting the waters."

Elizabeth strained to see what lay ahead, but it appeared to
her as if it was the endless beach, and not the waters, that were
parted. A channel had opened up, towards which the ship was
headed.

Hywel's voice rang out, "A Moses, so he is," and Elizabeth
tried to remember whether in the Bible story it was strictly
Moses' or God's hand that had parted the waters of the Red Sea,
and which of the two Ezekiel thought he was.

"You'll capsize us," the captain yelled from his navigation
deck at the rear of the ship. "Passengers below deck." He bran-
dished his spyglass at Ezekiel. "You there, get down."

But Ezekiel took no notice and roared above the crashing
of the ocean waves, the people's screams and the sailors' songs.
"The Lord breathed on the waters and the Red Sea was parted.
For us, yes, for us."

"Papa will save us, Dolly. He will, won't he, Lizzie?" Ruth's
face was covered with tears. Samuel looked too scared even to
cry.

"Passengers below now." The captain waved his arms at the
people who were only slightly more panicked than he was.
"You'll be the death of us all. Ship's crew stand by."

"It's the Lord who will lead us through these troubled waters." Ezekiel was as a man possessed, one hand raised heavenwards, the other pointing his ebony cane towards the channel
where, before the people's awestruck eyes, beyond the headland
an expanse of calmer water appeared. Cries of "America" alternated with cries of "Moses."

The Speedwell tilted again and, over the side of the ship
swirled choppy water, breaking waves that did indeed now part
to reveal, rising above the surf, a bank of yellow sand.

The captain climbed down from the rear deck, pushed
through the passengers and stood by Elizabeth. He peered at the
sandbank. His jowls sagged, his mouth dropped open. He was
a man cursed.

Ezekiel, meanwhile, radiated confidence. He told his flock to
stand firm. "Have faith. God will guide us to shore." Kneeling
at his feet, Annie gazed up at him in burning devotion. She
looked, thought Elizabeth, like Mary Magdalene gazing at the
risen Christ in the paintings in St Saviour's church at home.

"Hard to port," the captain shouted.

The ship lurched again, then swung around and Elizabeth
fell against the deck with Ruth and Samuel. From below, rever-
berating through the ship's timbers, came the rasping of wood
grating on sand, a deadening sound as if the land, having risen
up, was saying to the ship and those aboard her, "No further."

The Speedwell shuddered to a halt.

For an instant there was silence. Elizabeth sat up. And then
the madness returned, shouts, screams, footsteps hammering
the deck, the captain, bellowing in quick order for sails to be
furled, the anchor dropped, rowboats readied, the ship abandoned. He strode the deck, thumping his chest, hat askew, kicking any mariner who crossed his path, peering overboard, muttering to himself, then climbing back onto his navigation deck,
wrestling with the now-useless wheel and raising his eyeglass to
confirm the obvious. The ship was aground.

Ezekiel walked among the terrified passengers, wielding his
Bible. "Fear not. We will enter into the land that the Lord our
God has given us, a land flowing with milk and honey, his word
says so, and I hear it now Lord; I hear it."

Over the side of the Speedwell, Elizabeth saw a channel of fierce-flowing water which pushed the stricken ship further onto the deadly sandbank. Then from below came a rumbling sound and her friend appeared, the giant cook Christopher Conquest, nickname Peggy. He hauled himself up onto the deck by his brawny arms and thundered along it on his wooden pegleg; he launched rowboats single-handed, ordered passengers aboard in his chosen order.

So it was that Elizabeth, carrying Ruth, dragging Samuel, found herself on the first rowboat to the island, with Ezekiel bundled aboard by Peggy to get him out of the captain's way. The clergyman sat erect in the bows of the crowded boat, like some giant figurehead. Elizabeth, sitting in the middle with Ruth and Samuel under either arm, wondered what was going through his mind. When he turned, she thought there was a flicker of fear in his eyes, even as he exhorted the terror-struck passengers, "Trust me." Samuel leaned over the side of the boat watching the swirling current, and Ruth alternated between asking Elizabeth, "Will we have proper beds in our new home?" to relaying to her doll, "Lizzie says we have to build our new house," and then, screwing up her face, and asking, "Which of us exactly is going to build it?"

The oarsman facing them laughed. There were four of them, pulling against the current, inching across the channel, the boat so overfull and so low in the water that Samuel, stretching down, trailed his fingers in it.

Just as it seemed to Elizabeth that the tide would sweep them past the headland and out to sea, the oarsmen gave a final, desperate lunge. The boat moved out of the current, towards the shore, and the rowers heaved again until finally two of them set down their oars, jumped overboard and dragged the boat into the shallows of the beach off Ocracoke.

Looking back, Elizabeth couldn't remember their disembarking.

Were they pulled out by the oarsmen, did they climb out, or did they fall? All she could remember was the shock of cold water, then wading through it—heaving Ruth, screaming, under one arm, towing Samuel behind her with the other—Ezekiel striding ahead clutching his hat to his head, holding his Bible and cane aloft. Waves swirled around her legs and tugged at her clothes as if to reclaim her for the ocean; the sand moved under her bare feet, the waves receding and leaving her beached, then surging forward and crashing around her, until finally there was no more water and she was on dry land where she let Samuel go, set Ruth down and fell into the sand. She turned onto her back, felt the sun on her face, heard the gulls calling and the rhythmic swishing of the waves. But no more the creak of the ship's timbers, or the slap of her sails, no more the constant shifting and rolling. Beneath her was unmoving land, something she had feared at times she might never feel again.

She took a handful of hot sand and let it run out through her fingers.

And then she heard someone call her.

"Lizzie."

CHAPTER 17
London: 22 August 2019

P^{*ing.*}

I should have turned my phone off.

Stephanie was talking me through the results of her survey of residents of the Cooper Estate over a coffee in the deserted atrium of Portcullis House. Everyone else might be on holiday, but she was powering on, conscious that her internship in Parliament was coming to an end. She'd done a complicated computer presentation with diagrams of what the Cooper residents wanted. For most of them, it was a two-bedroomed house with a garden in a street that wasn't cratered with potholes or racked by crime. Failing that, another flat would do. One they wouldn't be evicted from again.

She'd just reached the slide that set out the logic of who was best-placed to deliver what, council, developer or government, and I was thinking, *"logical isn't a political term,"* when my phone sounded.

"Hang on a minute." It was a message from Toby.

We were thinking of this for the Cooper, followed by a smiling face emoji with sunglasses on.

He'd attached a video of three huge cooling towers at a power station being blown up. The towers collapsed into neat piles of

rubble, and then the video played in reverse so the cooling towers resurrected themselves out of the rubble and then collapsed
again—complete with superhero sound effects and silly stickers.

"Oh, honestly."

"What's happened?" asked Stephanie.

I was already texting back to Toby. *The sun's got to you.* I could
imagine him lying on a lounger on an Italian beach playing the
little video on a loop like it was some kind of game.

"Look." I showed the video to Steph.

"That was on the news last week," she said. "It was in a
place called the Midlands. Things went wrong and the local
community had their power cut off."

"No."

"Yes, a bit of one of those towers hit a pylon on the way down
and it exploded. There was a huge fuss. You must have seen it."

"It's what the developers are thinking of doing to the Cooper
Estate."

"No." She was all wide-eyed innocence. At least that's what it
seemed, if only because wide eyes are supposed to signify a clear
conscience.

· · · ● ● · · ● ● · ·

I was putting out my rubbish that evening when my nerdy
neighbour collared me.

"I see you're blowing up that housing estate." He emptied a
bin liner full of wine bottles into recycling. Not such a nerd after
all.

"Not me. Not personally," I said. "That looks like it was a
good party."

"Yes, it was. You must come to the next one." Three champagne flagons went into the recycling bin, followed by a blue

glass carafe that looked too expensive to throw away. "Seriously, though, you should check out what's being said about you on social media. They're definitely saying you want to blow up a housing estate. There's even a video of it."

"Any idea who 'they' are?"

He laughed and wiped his hands on the back of his designer jeans. "Come on, how would I know? I'm only a banker. It's one of those agit prop accounts. I hate to say it, but they're really clever. Make you look a proper villain."

He was right. When I got into my flat, I checked my phone. There was a torrent of notifications. #Fight4Cooper. I traced them back to a new account @CooperFightback that described me as the collaborator, colluder, conspirator in the secret plan to blow up the Cooper Estate. Complete with a video, the same one in Toby's message, and a quote from resistance leader Laurelle Miller

I texted Toby. *We need to talk when you get back.*

His reply was immediate. *Looking forward to it.*

I felt gratified. He must care. A bit at least.

· · · • • · • • · · ·

London held its breath the weekend Toby came home. Sunlight refracted from the city's glass towers, and in the concrete wastelands beyond, heat radiated into the already scorching air. Grasses wilted along walls and around lime trees and foxes slinked into underground shadows in cellars and carparks. Cars idling along sticky roads discharged their toxins into a stagnant atmosphere. Above their engines came the sound of children's laughter. It was the hottest August bank holiday on record.

My entry phone buzzed early Sunday morning when I was lounging on my patio. Once, twice, and then a continuous earworm of a racket. I hoped for Toby. Instead, on camera was a woman: plump face, helmet hair, careful make up, but not enough to conceal her flushed fury. It had to be Veronica. The wife. The wronged wife, less glamourous than I'd expected, older and more worn, and spitting teeth all over the entrance to my block of flats. I buzzed her in and went onto the landing to wait for her at the lift.

"Not even dressed yet?" Her voice matched her face. "Alright for some."

I was wearing a beach wrap Gerald had bought me in Italy. She was wearing jeans and a striped cotton shirt and gardening shoes.

"Would you like to come in?" I looked around the landing. It was an instinct, no more, but she picked up on it straight away, planted her stolid feet and raised her voice.

"What? Embarrassed, are we, at being caught out?"

All the muscles in her face were pulling in different directions. Even if I'd wanted her understanding, there wasn't going to be any.

"You can stay here if you like; I'm going inside." Her footsteps beat a warpath behind me. She managed to make it sound as if she was taking three steps to my one and her breath came in loud, angry bursts. When I waved her into my flat, her eyes went round the pristine living space, the minimalist furniture, TV set against one wall, the coffee cup on the table beside the laptop.

"So this is where it all happened." She was looking now through the open bedroom door at the double bed, covered with a silky red throw and scatter cushions. There were the dregs of a wine bottle and two glasses on the floor. Both mine. One from last night, the other from the night before.

"That's my bedroom." I closed the door on it. When I turned around, she was waving a bit of white cardboard at me.

"You had to put it in his pocket for me to find, didn't you? Rub my face in it. You tart."

"What are you talking about?"

"Your card, your bloody card. Everything I might want to know about the woman who'd waylaid my husband."

The blotched anger on her face had subsided, but the effort to contain it had left her struggling for breath. I thought she might turn weepy, but instead she had a curious glint in her eyes. She folded her arms. There was a silence, while we took the measure of each other. She looked perfect for her role in this drama: the indomitable meek, a woman who would extract a lifetime of submission for her husband's infidelity, hide the emptiness of their marriage behind their suburban respectability. And I was—well, she'd found her voice, so she told me.

"I gave him the choice," she said. "Keep it up with you if he wants, but he'll find all his belongings outside the front door, and that will be the end of it. Although he'll still have to pay of course, for the house here, and the one in Italy, and for the girls. There'd be no escape for him."

"Bit of a balls-squeezing choice, by the sound of it."

She flushed at my careful crudeness.

"He chose me. He had the choice, and he chose me." She spat the words out over her still-folded arms. "You people think you're entitled, that you can crash into other people's lives and take what you want. You think the normal rules that most of us have to live by don't apply to you. That you can do what you want and get away with it.

"Well you can't. Not with me at least, and not with Toby. I won't let you destroy what we've spent all these years building up."

"I'm not the only one, you know." It was an obvious guess, and it hit its mark. Her eyes flickered with self-doubt. "If he's been missing in action at home, it wasn't always with me."

She unfolded her arms and cricked her wrists. "Maybe not, but you're the worst." Then she recovered herself and scanned me up and down in the same way I imagined she looked at her children when they were naughty. "And the oldest."

She refolded her arms. That curious triumphalism appeared in her face again. And then the full extent of Toby's weakness dawned on me.

"Did Toby send you over here?" I asked.

"Yes." The glint in her eye turned into a shaft of undiluted venom. "He says it's better if you don't see each other again—out of office hours, that is."

"What a complete shit."

"You don't have to be so offensive."

"I don't mean you, I mean him."

"He's not." Now she was on the defensive. "He's not a bad man, he's just a bit weak. He's always had women after him, ever since I first met him, and he gets led on."

I snorted. "Led on my foot. D'you really think he was so innocent?"

If she'd been Donna, she'd have spat. But she wasn't. And she hadn't lost anything apart from her pride, and she'd sacrificed that long ago. Drawn up the balance sheet and calculated that a lifetime of compromises and humiliations was a price worth paying to hang onto her lifestyle and the flawed man who went with it. I wondered whether there was still love between them, or whether it had all boiled down to convenience for him and a trophy husband for her.

"He's not going to change, you know Veronica. There'll always be someone else. Maybe like you say, a younger model, maybe safer for you—but there will be someone."

"I know." For a victor in love, she seemed pretty joyless. "But I don't care, so long as he stays with me." I wasn't sure whether she was stubborn or desperate. In that moment, I got some understanding of what her life had been like with Toby, and how she knew it would continue. I might even have felt her pain at being condemned to such a fate if I wasn't hurting too.

"You're welcome to him," I said.

She lifted her hand. For a split second I wondered what came next. But all she did was look at her watch. "I've said what I came for," and then she turned and stomped out the door.

I went into the kitchen window, where I had a view over the front of my block and the carpark. The entrance door below me opened and Veronica appeared. A car reversed in the carpark, one of those chunky cars that cruise around the suburbs proclaiming happy families. I thought it was going to knock Veronica over, but then she dodged behind it and got in the passenger side.

And then the window came down on the driver's side and he looked out. Toby, his face unnaturally thin at this angle, blanched despite the Italian holiday, taut skin over his cheekbones as he craned his neck upwards, his eyes searching for the right window. Before they found it, Veronica clunked the car door shut behind her, he pulled his head back inside, the window closed and off they went.

How had such a creep managed to work his way into my emotional blind spot? I went into the bedroom, took the bottle of wine and one of the glasses into the living room, threw the glass against the wall and got a satisfying smash, then opened the bottle and took a swig from it. Unlike Veronica, I would never have the satisfaction of tipping out his stuff. There was nothing of him in my flat. Apart from my bruised heart.

· · · ● · ● · ● · ·

Gerald gave it an extra kicking. I was sweeping up the broken glass in my living room when he phoned from his London flat, his home since his marriage breakup.

"You coming to the meeting this evening?" He sounded back to his cheerful self.

"Which one is that?"

"The finding-a-new-party-leader meeting."

I'd have admired his persistence if I'd had the headspace to admire anything. "For us or them?"

"The proper functioning of our democracy requires both." He'd also reconnected with his pompous self. "But we only have a say in ours. At least changing that would transform things."

I tucked my phone under my ear, went into the kitchen and tipped the broken glass into the rubbish bin. "Perhaps the problem isn't politics. Perhaps that's not what's responsible for the current shitshow. Perhaps it's got nothing to do with our sclerotic political parties, or our useless parliament, or how crap we've always got on with the French so that half of Kent is turned into a lorry park and all our fresh veg is rotting in a traffic jam at Calais."

"What's this about?"

"Perhaps it's blokes that's the problem. Perhaps it's something wrong with the way you're built."

"Has Toby dumped you?"

"What's that got to do with it?"

"It's just you sound a bit upset."

"The whole country's upset one way or other."

I could imagine him backing off, checking through his list of people to phone, calculating how much time he could spend talking to each one, how little time he could waste on me. And then he surprised me. "Would it make you feel better if I took you out somewhere? For a walk or whatever it is singletons do on a bank holiday?"

"Crystal Palace Park. We can check out those concrete dinosaurs in the pond enclosure."

So, we went for a walk. More of a saunter given the heat. Gerald managed to find a parking space in a side road nearby, but even the short distance to the park was enough to send rivulets of sweat down my thighs. Gerald stripped off his shirt, one of his new ones from France, and checked out his tanned pecs. The dinosaurs strutted their stuff on the island in the pond near the bottom of the park; heat's no problem if you're made of concrete. Unlike the people, who spread themselves out on the grass beyond the pool with picnics and barbecues and sunshades. They abandoned plans to play with their children or dogs and instead drank warm beer and flat coke and traded life stories and insults and jokes about how they'd tell future generations about this epic August bank holiday; the one when it didn't rain.

"They don't look very upset to me," Gerald said.

"They should be."

"'Should' isn't a political term. It's a moralistic one."

"Honestly, Gerald, you can be..."

"Pompous." He laughed. "It has been said."

He bought me an ice cream. He didn't ask me what I wanted, just ordered a double Mr Wonderful vanilla in a cone with a flake and directed the ice cream seller to give it an extra squirt of chocolate topping. The ultimate luxury in his ice-cream buying experience.

"You're a real dad, aren't you?" I said.

"Listen, I won't jump on your hurt feelings if you don't jump on mine."

But as we got into his car, he couldn't help himself. "I always told you that bloke's a bastard."

"Lucky I wasn't invested then." I slammed the door and glared through the windscreen.

Gerald started up the engine. I felt his eyes on me.

"Sure?" he asked.

I couldn't bear to be pitied by him. "Yes."

Gerald dropped me off at home. He wouldn't come in: calls to make, people to persuade, flames to fan before his meeting. Afterwards he was heading up the M1 to his constituency for the final few days of our parliamentary recess.

"You haven't given up on it then?" I asked.

"I miss my kids. The middle one's threatening to run away from home."

"I thought she was doing a blog."

"She can run away from home and do a blog at the same time. She can do pretty much anything she turns her mind to, that one." Pride.

"Like her dad." I kissed his cheek as I got out of his car.

He glowed.

· · · ● ● ● ● · · ·

I stripped off in my flat and stood under a cold shower until I felt cool enough to go and draw the raffle at a community barbecue organised by a tenants' group on a green space near the Thames, after which I was planning to spend a quiet evening checking out emails. On the way up to the river, I passed the Cooper Estate. It was still light and the three tower blocks stood like grey beacons of lost hope. It was impossible to tell whether there was anyone left in them.

There were some flashing blue lights down a side street. I slowed and peered. Only police cars. Nothing more serious. A little voice of warning sounded. But I was tight for time. I put my foot down on the accelerator.

Chapter 18
Ocracoke: June 1643

"Lizzie."

It could be her father's voice. Elizabeth lay on her back, the sun on her face, and felt a kindling of hope. She opened her eyes and looked into the blue eternity above her. It could be the blue sky of London. Like it was the day she saw John Lilburne flogged. Unseasonal the heat had been that day with her father. He'd told her she was freeborn, and she'd felt it then. Now she wasn't so sure. She closed her eyes and wished she was still there.

"Lizzie."

It wasn't her father. It was the insistent voice of her present. She sat up and looked north along the coast, where sand bleached to whiteness by the sun glittered from the headland of their arrival into the shimmering distance, pounded by foam-topped waves from the ocean that had so nearly killed her. She held one hand up to shield her eyes against the glaring brilliance of it.

"Lizzie."

She turned south, to where the ebbing tide coursed out, between sandbanks on which was amassed a throng of birds. Squat white creatures with huge beaks, whose lopsided gait reminded

Elizabeth of Young Will. Elegant brown birds that picked
their way across the banks as graceful as her sister, Sarah.
Grey gulls as raucous as her brother, Richard. Across the
channel, beyond the sandbanks, in the distance was a dark
strip that spoke of more land, but of what type there was
no telling—no cliffs or rocks, no hills, no smoke, no sign
of habitation, nothing. It was all as empty as the watery
wilderness she had just crossed.

"Over here, Lizzie."

She twisted in the direction of the sound, towards Ocracoke's western shore that fronted the inland sea, where
gentler waves broke over a yellow beach on which the
greys, blacks and browns of the survivors were busied. Some
hauled sea chests up the sand to where a line of stunted trees
provided sparse shelter from the sun. Others ran into the sea
to pull ashore rowboats, the sailors aboard shouting as they
set down their oars, handing out passengers who cried with
alarm at the shock of their landing.

Josiah Carver paraded on the tideline, signalling to the
oarsmen, ordering men to lift higher, further, faster.

Hywel Williams waded through swirling water to reach a
rowboat as a prone figure was lifted out, to cries of "Steady
now," and, "Mind him." And then Hywel was struggling
back through the water, placing careful feet in the rushing current, arms around the sick boy Haz slumped over
his shoulder, whom he carried up the beach and laid out
above the high-water mark beside the chest on which Beatrix
Carver sat in her fine silk. Behind them all, beyond the
rushing of the tide and the wheeling of the gulls, loomed the
stricken Speedwell, sails flapping, the captain on the poop
deck surveying the abandonment of his ship.

"Lizzie."

Malachi Balhatchet had broken away from the group on the seashore and was walking towards her.

"Don't you hear me? Are you unwell?" He stood over her, hands on hips, blocking out the sun. She looked up, squinting, seeing only his dark shape against the searing light.

"Papa calls you. He says you must come and work."

His heirs, the papers had said. She was sold to the man and his heirs. She sighed. In this new world, she was still bound by the old order.

"What ails you?"

Elizabeth shook her head, tried to get up, felt the ground move beneath her feet, fell back, squatted, stretched out her hands on the beach, then pushed herself until she stood upright. Was it her legs or the land that teetered? She bent forward and rested her hands on her knees, waited for the undulations to stop, then stood up and brushed the sand off her clothes. Malachi's every feeling showed on his face. Now it was clouded by concern. Whatever the hardships of her life, she knew they weren't his doing.

"Nothing's wrong," she said.

An encampment took shape in the disorder on the seashore. Josiah Carver paced the beach with the passenger list provided by the first mate.

"One hundred and fifteen passengers boarded at Rother-hithe, of which 34 have died and 12 more are sick as like to death. That leaves 78 healthy—no, 68—no, 69, of whom half are men and women, and the rest are children and servants."

"Do I count as passenger or crew?" asked Malachi.

"Plus 26 crew," said Mr Carver. "No, one was lost today. Make that 25."

Ezekiel Balhatchet stood above the tide-line reading his Bible. His daughter, Ruth, squatted at his feet talking to her doll, while her brother, Samuel, skimmed stones across the water to make them jump and scowled when they disappeared below the surface.

To Mr Carver's direction, Elizabeth pulled Ezekiel's chest up the beach, then across the wiry, buff-coloured groundcover that passed for grass to the space allocated. "Suitable for the Reverend's station in life," said Mr Carver. As she was settling the chest under the bushes, she saw a bright green coil wrapped around one of its lower branches. When she looked closer, she saw it was a snake, small and green, more brilliant than a grass snake, a radiant green that at home would signify bursting life. She reached out for it, but the snake flickered its head at her and slipped away.

Malachi rolled barrels of food and water across the sand and set them upright in the shade. Sailors rowed to and fro across the channel, ferrying passengers and supplies from ship to shore. As the tide went out, the channel shrank, the receding water leaving the Speedwell ever higher on her sandbank and uncovering, below the beach, a layer of clinging mud, through which, once the passengers were all ashore, the sailors finally squelched to haul their boats above the tide-line.

· · · · ·· · · · ·

And now the immediate terror of their landing were past, people allowed themselves to enjoy the possibilities of the present. They were, at least, on solid land. They could stand still or walk further than the confines of the ship's deck. They could escape the enforced company of others and find solitude—or privacy to kiss. They could walk on bare feet across hot sand to the water's edge, feel the sea breeze cool their faces, tease the waves that rushed in, washed over their feet, and then fell back, protesting, down the shore. And then they could turn their backs on the ocean and walk away.

Elizabeth sauntered along the beach with Annie Meadowsweet. Her friend had decked out her battered sunhat with yellow flowers that she'd plucked from the bushes on the seashore. Elizabeth held Samuel's hand and scolded the boy for kicking sand in his sister's face as she bent to inspect a crab's shell.

"I thought we was all deadwood on that ship. I never thought I'd walk out ever again." Annie slipped an arm around Elizabeth's waist. "Who did you walk out with in London, Lizzie?"

"No-one."

"I don't believe that. You must have had a sweetheart."

"People thought I was a boy. I dressed like one. I looked like one. My father treated me like one."

"They won't be able to think that much longer."

Ezekiel walked past, lifting his hat to Annie, who smiled and nodded, and then he strode off, his black shoes sinking into the dry sand above the waterline, long black jacket blowing in the wind that came in from the ocean, black hat wedged low on his head, his cane held over his shoulder like a gun.

"Where do you think he's going in such a hurry?" asked Annie.

"He's looking for a new world," Elizabeth said.

"We're all doing that."

"The rest of us talk about it." Elizabeth watched Ezekiel struggle to keep himself erect in the soft sand. "But what most of us mean is somewhere that we don't have to be so poor or work so hard. My father thought England without a king would be new enough. When Reverend Balhatchet talks about a new world, he means a world remade. A new heaven and a new earth, that's what he says the Bible tells him, for the first heaven and the first earth will pass away, and there will be no more sea."

"I'll settle for the no more sea," said Annie. "I don't care if I never get on a boat ever again."

"And God shall wipe away all tears from their eyes; and there shall be no more death, neither sorrow, nor crying," Elizabeth had learned these words from Ezekiel during those long hours spent studying with him on the Speedwell. They'd brought her hope that whatever she found in the new world would not be snatched from her as everything she loved in the old had been.

"That's beautiful, Lizzie. Do you think there really is such a place?"

"Reverend Ezekiel says so." Elizabeth was surprised at her friend's questioning. "I thought you believed him."

"I'd believe anyone who said they'd get me off that bleeding ship alive."

Ahead of them, Ezekiel turned and walked away from the beach and into the dunes with their grey-green grasses, so that only his black hat could be seen, until even it disappeared into the stunted trees.

"Will Papa come back?" asked Ruth.

· · · ● · ● · · · ·

Ezekiel hadn't reappeared when the sun started its journey down the sky, and Elizabeth prepared for the first night in the new world, struggling to close the gap between her expectations and the reality of the encampment among the bushes. People gathered around their opened sea chests, taking out now a shawl, now a petticoat or a pair of breeches. Mr Carver's was the biggest chest ferried from the Speedwell and he pulled from it a rich blue velvet jacket that he put on, stretching out an arm to admire the sheen of it, picking off a fleck of dust, pulling it close across his paunch, patting into place the shining brown curls of a fresh wig.

Elizabeth marked out a space beside Reverend Ezekiel's belongings with branches and filled it with grasses to form a bed for his children. But she felt the fear that Ruth, standing with her doll, turned into words, "Dolly's scared. She wants to go home." Annie spread out her blanket nearby. Hywel swung his chest onto his shoulders and went to camp down among the dunes. Malachi took himself off to join the ship's crew on the beach.

On the foreshore, the sailors assembled a mound of firewood, which they set alight. A cacophony of protests came from the seabirds jostling for space on the sandbanks shrinking under the flooding tide, cackling against the rising water, the sinking sun, the foolish intruders. Soon the comforting smell of cooking carried on the breeze. Elizabeth took Ruth and Samuel's hands and joined the people who stopped their unpacking and arranging and emerged onto the beach, each carrying a tin plate and a spoon to queue for food from a cauldron that stood over the sailors' fire.

Mrs Carver sat on a grassy tussock, presiding. "Only one piece of salt beef, and a ladle of gravy," she shouted. "I said one ship's biscuit each, not two, and half rations for children. Orphans go to the back." She glared at Elizabeth.

"I'm not one of the orphans; I'm with the Reverend Balhatchet's children."

"Hmm." Elizabeth could feel Mrs Carver's disapproval. The older woman was still in her silk dress, sweat-stained from the exertions of supervising the cooking. A grey-brown lock of hair fell across her shoulder and she tucked it back in place under her cap. "For how long I wonder."

The meat was grey and stringy, and the gravy was the colour of mud. But Elizabeth didn't care. It was hot, it was food; her first meal on American soil. She took it and settled down to eat with the two children and Annie among the band of survivors.

But before she could take her first mouthful, Hywel cried out, "We should give thanks."

"Whatever for?" asked Annie.

"For this food and our safe arrival," said Hywel.

"Where's the Reverend?" Josiah Carver stood close to the cooking pot, clutching a plate piled high with salt beef and, by Elizabeth's count, at least three ship's biscuits.

"He hasn't come back yet," she said.

"Then there's no-one to pray for us."

"Any of us can pray." Hywel's eyes burned. "I'll pray for us if you like."

"We can't understand your prayers," said Annie to laughter along the beach.

"I can't pray in English," said Hywel.

"That settles it, then, we'll have to wait for the Reverend to return." Josiah Carver put a big piece of salt beef into his mouth and chewed contentedly.

Across the water, the rising tide had lifted the Speedwell until she approached upright, silhouetted against the evening sky, light from the falling sun illuminating her masts and rigging. A figure appeared on her deck, carrying a lantern—the shambling captain, followed by the wiry first mate and, bringing up the rear, Peggy lurching on his wooden leg.

"I wish he'd come and cook for us," Annie said.

"They'll be making preparations to weigh anchor, I've no doubt," Josiah Carver took another mouthful of food. "I have every confidence."

On the ship's deck the first mate lowered a plumb-line and the captain and Peggy leaned over the railing to watch. Then the first mate pulled it up, and the three men grouped around.

"D'you think the ship will float again?" asked Elizabeth.

"I'm sure it will," Josiah Carver said. "The captain will come and tell us in the morning. We'll get our marching orders," He held his plate in his left hand, and waved his grease-covered right in authoritative fashion.

"Will Father be back then?" asked Ruth.

"If he's not, we'll have to leave without him. Stop snivelling, child, there are bigger considerations at stake. In a word, we can't risk everything for one person." Josiah Carver turned to the survivors with a swagger. "We'll be on our way in no time, you'll see. On board again tomorrow as like as not. I have friends and business to do in Jamestown. They're expecting me before the summer's out." He dabbed one of his ship's biscuits in the gravy on his plate and sucked on it.

"Mr Carver will be a man of consequence in Jamestown." Mrs Carver had settled herself on her tussock as rotundly comfortable, it seemed to Elizabeth, as ever she was at home. "The colony needs men such as him. The governor will give us a reception to mark our safe arrival."

"It's alright for some." Hywel hunched over his plate, picking at the salt meat. "What wouldn't I give to lie down in my cottage in the cool mountains and look up at a thatched roof."

"I'll make you smile, sad Hole, look at me." A flash of red and the little orphan Barty ran in front of them, turned a somersault, missed his footing, and landed flat on his back.

"Fool." Hywel almost joined in the laughter. He broke his ship's biscuit and threw a piece at the boy who jumped up to catch it, then ran off and sat on a tuft of sea grass and started eating.

"Where's your sister?" asked Elizabeth. The boy shrugged.

"Mind this for me," Elizabeth gave her plate to Annie and went off searching among the bushes. She found May crouching over Mrs Carver's open chest. The girl was engrossed in a gold chain with a pearl on it, which she held up to the light and studied intently, then pulled the chain over her head, so the gem lay on her chest, and patted it, then fingered her red curls and cocked her head.

"May, stealing is still stealing, even here." Elizabeth grabbed at her, but May ducked.

"It fell out of the chest all by itself." She whipped the chain from her neck and ran away with it scrunched up in her right hand.

"What will become of them?" Elizabeth said to Annie when she returned to the group, where May was sitting cross-legged beside her brother, munching on a biscuit.

"Never fear, I'll find a good home for them in Jamestown," said Josiah Carver, stuffing more meat into his mouth. "They're pretty little things and they must be strong to have survived the journey. They'll make excellent house servants, I've no doubt." He chewed on the meat, sizing up the two children with calculating eyes.

"I suppose you're thinking you'll get a tidy price for them." Hywel put down his plate and wiped his hands on his trousers. "You shouldn't be doing that. They're God's children, so they are."

"Then why did God fetch them up here?" asked Annie. "Where's your ma?" She called to the children and threw a biscuit at them.

"Dunno," Barty caught the biscuit, and gave half to his sister.

"What's her name?" asked Malachi.

"Ma," said May.

The group on the beach laughed. "Pity's sake," cried out Mrs Carver.

"Her real name?" asked Annie. The children appeared puzzled and whispered to each other.

"What did people call her?" Annie explained.

"Whore," said Barty.

"Heaven's sake," cried Mrs Carver.

Elizabeth giggled, then laughed and once she'd started, couldn't stop until the tears ran down her cheeks and she put her food aside and buried her face in her hands. Annie joined in, throwing her head back and closing her eyes. Malachi roared. Even Hywel gave up the struggle to hold back the laughter that rolled up and down the beach. It was as if a madness came over the group of survivors, cast on this shore, alive at least, but so helpless against their misfortune that all they could do was laugh in the face of it.

From behind them, came a squawking of birds, wings beating among the undergrowth, the sound pierced by a man's scream. Elizabeth reached for Ruth and Samuel. Josiah Carver pushed his wife off her grassy tussock and hid behind it. Annie buried her face in her apron. Then Elizabeth heard the thwack of a cane.

"Papa." Ruth ran to Ezekiel as he emerged onto the beach. He left off brushing leaves from his coat, and focussed on his daughter. He took her hand and stroked her face with a gentleness that Elizabeth remembered from her own father, but hadn't seen in Ezekiel before.

"The Lord has shown me the place." He took off his hat and wiped his arm against his brow. His long black jacket was dotted with burrs and there was a tear across one shoulder. Above the whiteness of his collar, the lowering sun fell directly into his face, which glowed red under the silver streak that shone in his hair. The sailors shifted uneasily. Even Mr Carver fell silent.

"Come and have something to eat and drink, Papa."

Ezekiel turned in Malachi's direction, but his eyes were fixed on something beyond his son. "I have no need. Today, I have eaten the bread of heaven and drunk from the spring of eternal life."

Holding Ruth's hand, he walked into the centre of the group of survivors. "Today the Lord has revealed our destiny to me."

Hywel's dark face burned with conviction. Annie twisted her apron with nervous hands. Josiah Carver frowned in disbelief. Elizabeth felt sick.

"In the shape of a bird, He led me through the woodland, guiding me from tree to tree until we reached a small building."

"People." Mrs Carver turned to her husband.

"You see, I told you." Mr Carver patted her lap.

"From the outside it was a simple shack of rough-hewn wood, weathered grey," Ezekiel continued, "but as I approached, the door opened and inside the floor and walls glowed white, and in the light a figure appeared and pointed. So I followed its direction and sparkling lights led me across open grassland until exhausted I could walk no more and fell to the ground and prayed for a sign."

Elizabeth saw how Ezekiel's eyes passed across the group and settled fleetingly on his older son before moving on, unseeing though not blind. He'd been like this before in the cabin of the Speedwell when his family had feared death by tempest and he, glassy-eyed, had been untouched by their terror.

"I heard a cry—not human, not animal, not of this world at all it sounded—and I crawled towards it. And then the grasses parted, and I found myself before a spring where water seeped from the ground and trickled into a small pool. I dipped my head and drank."

"Water. Then by God's grace we're saved." Hywel clasped his hands in prayer.

"He's found water. That's good, but that's all," Mr Carver muttered to his wife.

"And when I had drunk my fill, a cloud descended from the heavens and from it shone a light, so bright I was blinded, and a voice said, 'Behold, the place.'" Ezekiel's words came so fast he struggled now to get them out. "'This will be the land of the new covenant. You will be my people and I will be your God.'"

Now the most ragged of the survivors—the thinnest, the sickest, those Elizabeth had seen suffer most on the voyage—swept past her and crowded around Ezekiel, laughing, crying, kissing his feet, clutching any part of his clothes they could reach. Hywel stood with one arm across the clergyman's shoulders, the other held aloft like John the Baptist proclaiming a new Messiah.

Mr Carver held back. "We're due in Jamestown, we must travel on," he said. His wife, dutifully nodded and said, "Yes, Mr Carver." But she kept her eyes fixed on Ezekiel, who held his black hat to his chest and raised his glowing face to the reddening sun.

"And as the cloud lifted, a horse galloped away, its hooves the sound of thunder, a mass of writhing snakes flowing from its mane. And it was overtaken by a column of swirling smoke and was lost to my sight."

And now Elizabeth saw that it wasn't any divine light that made Ezekiel's face glow. He was burnt and blistered across his cheekbones, his eyes were bloodshot, and when he spoke again, his tongue seemed to stick to the roof of his mouth and he struggled to form his words.

"Today I have seen our new Jerusalem." Ezekiel swung his arms around, taking in the beach, the fire, the bushes draped with clothing. "Here in this place that the Lord has shown me, we will build our holy city, where we will dwell with God and be his people and he will dwell in us and be our God."

"So we stay here then, so we do," declared Hywel.

"I never wanted to get back on that ship anyway," said Annie.

"Wait." Josiah Carver pushed himself forward and stood in front of Ezekiel, his back to the clergyman, facing the survivors, his plump hands held out in appeal. "Our fate can't be decided in such a fashion. We have only one man's word that this place is even habitable."

"Not one man's word. God's word." Hywel folded his arms.

"We're bound for Jamestown," said Josiah Carver. Elizabeth wondered who among the survivors would listen to him, with his fine blue jacket and tumbling wig. "I've goods aboard the Speedwell destined for the colony; I've business to do there. We can't finish our journey here. When the ship's ready, we must leave."

Only a sliver of red sun remained above the horizon. Elizabeth looked from Ezekiel, on whom the firelight flickered, lighting up the sharpness of his jaw, catching his angular cheekbones, his hawkish nose, his eyes hidden in the darkness of their sockets. To Josiah Carver, around whose double chin the firelight lapped, spilling over the softness of his fleshy cheeks, picking out the richness of his curled wig. Only one of these two men could be the master.

· · · · ●·● · · ·

Nightfall ended their deliberations. Reverend Ezekiel led them in praying for God's protection over their souls. Josiah Carver

had the fire stoked up and posted Hywel with a musket outside
the encampment to protect them against intruders, whether
animal or human. To Elizabeth either would be welcome in the
loneliness of the place.

Darkness deepened, but she couldn't sleep. An insistent
thrumming of insects whirred in her ears above the whispered
conversations, occasional laughter and muffled groans of those
around her. But no more the straining timbers, lapping waters,
thud of sailors on the decks overhead. No more ocean to rock
her to sleep. No more fetid air of lives and deaths played out at
close quarters. The night sky was the only constant. The stars
endured.

She counted them, once, twice, but still could not sleep. Finally, she gave up trying, wrapped her blanket around her, crept
away from the sleeping children, sidled past Hywel asleep over
his musket, and went down to the waterside. Night was kind
to the Speedwell. Only her outline was visible. One mast was
missing, but apart from that she looked the same ship that had
set sail from London. Elizabeth recalled how she'd felt then.
The agony of loss which she thought could never get worse,
but then did. Until she passed through a pain barrier and found
within herself the determination to survive whatever disasters
befell those around her. Such a life lived within the confines of
the ship that appeared at ease now across the water. Could she
bear to get on board again? Or could she find the willpower to
fashion a life in this harsh place?

Soft footsteps padded on the sand, and Malachi sat down
cross-legged beside her. In companionable silence they watched
the ship, their destiny, one way or the other.

"Look how she moves," Malachi said.

A full moon rose behind them and cast its cold light across
the water. Ripples corrugated the centre where the current ran

the strongest; wavelets splashed on the beach close to their feet. The insects' singing was unearthly. Elizabeth felt this was indeed another world.

"She looks like she's floating," said Malachi.

Elizabeth considered the inky shape. "That may only be what you want to see. To me she looks to be stuck as fast as ever."

"No. She'll float off her sandbank with the tide. We'll be on our way in the morning."

"Perhaps you will. But your father won't. You heard what he said. He believes he was destined for this place. Whatever happens, he will stay here."

"I won't." Malachi pulled his knees up to his chest and wrapped his arms around them. "We'd be lucky to survive until the next vessel comes by, if one ever does. Whatever my father says, I'll leave. I'd rather take my chances at sea, even on our damaged ship. We could yet reach Jamestown. You should come too. You'll die if you stay here."

"Would you be sorry for that?" asked Elizabeth. In Malachi's silence, she could feel him blush. "At least you have the choice. I don't. My papers, which are in your father's chest, say I'm indentured to him. So I'm bound to stay here."

"No." Malachi grabbed her hand. It was her turn to blush. "The papers say Richard Gardiner is indentured to my father. You're Elizabeth. You're free to choose."

CHAPTER 19

London: 26 August 2019

N ight brought darkness, but the day's heat lingered as I headed for home. Two police vans shot past me, closely followed by a car that travelled faster than was credible for something so shabby. Above one window was a flashing blue light. The streets around the Cooper were alive with more.

I parked up and ran onto the estate. Hot air rose from the grey concrete of the piazza. Red and yellow clouds from smoke bombs billowed up the front of the tower blocks. Light flooded from the open doors of the community centre. Mobile phones beamed over the heads of the shoving, jostling crowd outside Speedwell House. They were young. They were diverse. Some were dressed up like they were on their way out clubbing. Most were in dark street clothes. What they lacked in numbers, they made up for in anger. Through a loudspeaker, police ordered them to move away. They didn't. The police were no match for the disembodied voice blasting rebellion out of a megaphone.

"Housing is a human right.

"Fight for the Cooper.

"Fight. Fight. Fight."

It was an easy chant, picked up by the crowd, echoed between the tower blocks, amplified and repeated like it was on a loop, led by the ear-splitting voice. It was a woman's voice, piercing the darkness from the far side of the crowd. I couldn't see the person, but I knew the voice, and it didn't need a megaphone.

Laurelle. She started a new chant.

"They say knockdown."

I spotted her then, dressed in tight jeans and a red T-shirt, standing on a green wheelie bin, arms aloft, taut as a whip.

"We say no."

She unleashed her fury across the heads of the crowd who wielded placards that carried a single word. "Occupy." Or a picture of a collapsing cooling tower, or "Hands off our homes."

Two of the tower blocks were enclosed by security fences; that left only Speedwell House as the focus for the protestors' attention. They pushed against the police lined up outside the entrance. Bare arms flailed, a woman screamed, a yellow smoke bomb went off. The police pushed back. If the crowd had been bigger, it might have broken through the police ranks.

There were as many people gathered outside the community centre to watch. Standing at the front, smoking a cigarette, was Donna. It was the first I'd seen of her since the funeral of her murdered grandson Dylan, the second time only since the spitting incident. She was wrapped in a grubby beige dressing gown and her roots were showing, but her hair was sprayed to attention and she had lipstick on.

"She's a right cow, that one." She nodded in the direction of the tower blocks.

"It's Laurelle." I tried to read Donna's expression, but she was holding her cigarette close to her face.

"Who else would it be? Out of harm's way with her fan club around her so she doesn't get nicked and lose her job. Too clever by half." Then Donna turned to me. Whatever else, she hadn't lost her ability to fillet a person. "How about you? I hope you know whose side you're on."

"As in?" I was on shifting sand. I didn't want to make another mistake.

"You said you wanted the estate knocked down." She nipped off the burning end of her cigarette. "Don't you go denying it; I saw your pictures."

"What d'you think of demolishing the estate and doing a complete rebuild?" Donna shifted her feet and opened her mouth, but before she could fix her thoughts by turning them into words, that I guessed would go against me, I qualified things. "The tower blocks at least. They're beyond refurbishing, and besides, two of them are empty. The low-rise is a different story. It's in better condition, so demolition might not be the answer for the whole estate, if you think..."

"It's the best thing that could happen." She put what was left of her cigarette back in its packet.

"Have you told Laurelle that?"

"I haven't got a death wish. Not like you, posting those pictures. What did you think you were doing?"

For Donna this was reaching out. Whether she thought I was being stupid or brave, it wasn't the time for the humdrum truth: that they weren't my pictures.

"Any word on Canvey Island?" I asked.

"Yes." Her face brightened. "Two-bedroomed flat."

"That's wonderful news." At least some good had come out of my affair with Toby.

"Stephanie fixed it."

One day I might explain.

A light appeared in Speedwell House. It was only a single window on the top floor, but it shone like a lighthouse in the darkness and triggered anger and excitement in the crowd of people below. Fingers pointed, phones turned up to capture and share the moment.

"That's Miracle's flat," I said.

"My god. She's still there." Donna couldn't hide her shock.

Laurelle screamed at the police through her megaphone.

"There's a mother and baby up there. Shame on you. Shame on you!"

People joined in. "Shame on you. Shame on you." Placards flew from the back of the crowd towards the police lines.

Out of nowhere, a camera crew appeared, and set up with the reporter positioning herself so that the crowd and Speedwell House were in the background. Laurelle let out a barrage over the megaphone, and a red smoke bomb went off just as the camera lights went on. After the filming of the demo had finished, I sauntered over, and did an interview. Donna followed me and watched gimlet-eyed while I spoke about the housing crisis, understanding local anger, the need for all the tenants to have a decent home, the fears everyone had for the safety of the mother and child on the top floor. But I didn't talk about blowing up the estate.

Donna locked up the community centre after the TV crew had left. That was the signal for most of the other people from the low rise to drift home. I spoke to them as they left, headshaking in equal measure about the demonstration, about the police action, about the plight of the woman trapped by the riot.

"It's good you're here." A woman wrapped in a blue sarong shook my hand and added, "Thankyou."

Donna said she'd stay. "I want to see what they do about Miracle."

Laurelle's voice was replaced by a man's. A young guy in jeans and a black T-shirt with a clenched fist printed on the front was struggling to keep his balance on the wheelie bin.

"Laurelle's probably had to go to work," Donna said. "Wound them all up like yo-yos and now she's left them."

We crossed the piazza to get a better view. The police dragged a young man out of the entrance to Speedwell House and led him to a police van. Then another, and another. The man on the megaphone stumbled over his words. He wasn't as fluent as Laurelle. The crowd at the foot of the tower block looked up to where Miracle's light beamed defiance.

"That's it. All gone except for Miracle," Donna said. "They'll fetch her down now. I wonder if she'll put up a fight."

"She must be desperate, and she's got nothing to lose."

"Oh yes, she has. She's not got a home, she's not got a visa, she's got issues. They'll take her baby away."

A woman's voice came over the megaphone. Not Laurelle's. This one was younger, higher pitched, and its message was more pointed.

"They're going after a helpless mother and child. Shame on you. Shame on you."

It re-galvanised the crowd, and they chanted, "Shame on you, shame on you," until the light at the top of the tower block went out. Red and yellow flares streaked up the front of the building and exploded. Donna coughed. "Bloody smoke bombs."

Across the piazza, lights went on, and doors opened in the low-rise. My phone buzzed. There was a message from Gerald sent at 00.37. *Don't forget the meeting in Church House in the morning.*

"It'll take them time to get her out with the baby," said Donna.

The lift shaft and stairwell formed the core of Speedwell House. It relied on artificial light; there were no windows. So there was no flicker of torches as the police brought my Madonna out of her tower block. We could only wait in the darkness outside, people leaning from the walkways of the low rise to watch, Donna with one hand to her open mouth, the crowd chanting, "Shame on you." My heart thundered. My phone showed 01.02. The woman with the megaphone shrilled, "Here they come." The heavy entrance doors opened; the crowd surged against the police ranks.

But there was no Miracle, and there was no baby.

Instead, the police came out with Stephanie.

Chapter 20
Ocracoke: June 1643

E lizabeth had no choice to make.

Not the next morning when she woke to see a small boat row from the Speedwell, which was still stuck fast on her sandbank. The first mate came ashore, twisting the knot in his grey plaited beard, to say that the captain regretted there would be no sailing that day, the tide not having been sufficient to re-float the ship. Nor the next day, when the first mate rowed across the channel again with more apologies from the captain. And as days drifted past with no change and no captain, Elizabeth felt a snake of fear, a twist of its body, a flick of its tail, a dart of its cusped head, until it turned hating eyes on her and hissed.

Around her, an order took shape. Possessions unloaded onto the beach were reloaded onto rowboats and taken up the western coast to the headland closest to the spring of water Ezekiel had discovered. Barrels of salt meat, flour, salt, saws, hammers, and nails were ferried from the Speedwell and offloaded. Ship's canvas was carried ashore on the same boat that also brought the remnants of the livestock: a clutch of chickens and a young goat that, as soon as its hooves touched solid ground, ran away bleating into the undergrowth.

On the beach of their first landing, they left a grave. Haz, the boy snatched off the streets of London, died. Not so much died; that would be too purposeful for what Haz did. He stopped breathing at some point where he lay on his blanket under a bush and was already stiff when Annie called attention to his passing. Elizabeth remembered her brother, Little Tommy, and how his life had seemed of so little consequence.

Malachi fashioned a cross to mark the spot where Haz was buried.

"What was his name?" asked Elizabeth.

Josiah Carver consulted the Speedwell's passenger list.

"All it says here is 'Haz'."

"That's not enough to mark a life. There must be more."

"Oh," Josiah Carver harumphed. "What does it matter? It says here, 'indentured labourer, aged 16, Redriff.'"

At Elizabeth's instruction, Malachi carved onto the cross, *Harry Redriff, beloved son.* "He was someone's son," she said. "He must have been loved once."

Josiah Carver put on his blue velvet jacket for the burial. Ezekiel presided, hand raised in blessing, face turned to heaven, eyes closed, mind where? wondered Elizabeth. Not with the dead boy.

"I'll sing," said Hywel. Which he did, in a voice of such exquisite purity shot through with such profound sadness, that Annie dissolved, and a tear ran down even Mr Carver's cheeks, although neither could understand the words Hywel sang.

Ezekiel's daughter, Ruth, listened solemn-faced, clutching Elizabeth's hand.

"Will you sing like that for us too, when we die?" she asked Hywel.

"You won't die, bach," said Hywel.

The sailors lowered Haz's shrouded body into the grave. Annie dropped in a spray of beach flowers and the survivors filed past, each person muttering "Amen".

"Don't bury the blanket," said Mrs Carver, stately in her grey silk dress and bonnet. "We may have need of it."

Elizabeth placed a giant conch shell on the grave and hoped it would provide a fitting memorial.

· · · · ●· ●· · · ·

Then craftsmen who had boarded the Speedwell with all the skills needed to build the towns and cities of the new world applied them to a lesser enterprise.

Ezekiel said they would tame the wilderness. Mrs Carver said she feared they would be over-run by it. But it was the sand that overran them, blowing in a great dry storm up the beach. It stung the men's bare chests and the children's legs. It caught in the crevices of the women's clothes and settled in a sullen blanket across the camp until Hywel said it was worse than all the plagues in the desert of Egypt.

"We need a palisade for our protection," declared Mr Carver. At his direction, the men organised themselves into teams to clear land and erect a rough fence. Within it they built shelters, first for the families and then the married couples. The single women would share a lean-to made of reeds with the few remaining orphans. "But not you," Ezekiel told Elizabeth. "My children must be cared for." So Elizabeth carried her bundle of belongings into Ezekiel's shelter under the jealous eyes of Annie and the smirks of the single men, who Josiah Carver directed to sleep in canvas tents outside the palisade. Where Barty and his sister May were also consigned.

Mrs Carver said they needed some fresh food to supple-
ment their supplies and the fish that they caught in quanti-
ties in the inland sea and roasted, dried, boiled and smoked
until Hywel said he never wanted to see another fish ever
again and Annie said he smelt like one.

So Elizabeth set out to find a place where she could create
a garden. She escaped the confines of the camp, Mrs Carver's mean eyes and Ezekiel's increasingly lustful ones, and
walked away from the shore to where the trees grew tallest.
There she found a hovel built of planks, weathered grey and
daubed with fragments of tar, with a deep X carved above
the entrance. Inside, the walls and ceiling were covered with
white shells embedded in dried mud. The hut was divided
by a translucent veil that moved gently in the air. When
Elizabeth drew closer, she saw it was made of discarded
snakeskins. Beyond the veil, the far wall was studded with
mother-of-pearl, which to Elizabeth's eyes glittered as rich
as any altar. She wondered what manner of people had built
this hut and how long they had survived. And whether one
day people would find the remnants of the palisade and
ponder on the lives that had been lived inside it.

Nearby she found a clearing, large and flat enough to turn
into a garden. The soil was dry and sandy, but sufficient for
her purposes, and the surrounding trees sheltered it from
the wind and blocked out all but the midday sun.

Next morning, waking early, she opened her bundle of belongings, put on her working clothes and pulled out the bag
of seeds given to her by her brother Richard. She begged a
shovel from Mr Carver, and then, returning to the clearing
in the woods, she set about digging and planting. She carried
water from the spring to the protests of Mrs Carver until Hywel
opined that if Lizzie managed to grow anything for them to eat,

the fruits of her labours would be worth more than all of Mrs Carver's opinions.

Elizabeth's garden took shape, until one evening, when she had just returned from it and the survivors were gathering for evening prayer, Barty ran among them. His red hair flared out from his head like a burning bush, and desperation was in every bare footstep.

"Where's my sister?"

"Where did you last see her?" Elizabeth asked.

"She can't have gone far," said Hywel.

"Someone has her."

"Silly boy," said Mrs Carver.

"One of yous knows." The boy spat out the words and then retreated into the shelter he shared with May, a lean-to built of branches set against a tree. Elizabeth peered into it and thought the boy snarled at her, but when she looked more closely, she saw he was sobbing.

"Go away. For all I know it was you what took her."

Malachi led a search for the missing girl. Elizabeth followed. Barty came out of his lean-to and stood on the headland watching as the survivors beat around the bushes and poked sticks into the creeks. The Carvers observed from the entrance of the palisade, she with her hands clasped across her silk-clad stomach, he with his hands folded behind his linen-clad back.

"You should come and help us," Malachi called to Barty.

"Why?" the boy shouted back. "One of you knows where she is. They should say where they've hidden her."

Among the long grasses, behind the low trees between the headland and the landing beach, Malachi found some pieces of cotton cloth. When he emerged from the undergrowth, carrying them as carefully as if they were a child, the survivors gathered around. Barty ran down from his vantage point and pushed his way through the people until he reached Malachi.

"It's May's dress." Barty stroked the rags and kissed them.

"You can't be certain, bach," said Hywel.

"They're no more than tatters," said Mrs Carver.

"Someone knows what happened to May," said Barty. "Who knows should tell."

Josiah Carver caught the boy by his neck and shook him. "What are you saying?"

"One of yous knows who killed my sister." Barty screamed, howled, swore, kicked, punched, bit and finally broke free and ran away, red head bobbing through the long grass.

"Good riddance." Josiah Carver wiped his hands on his jacket.

"We must bury her remains." Elizabeth fingered May's rags, which Hywel held reverently in his hands.

"You can't have a burial without a body," said Annie.

"You don't know she's dead," said Mrs Carver.

Malachi turned over the rags, exposing hardened patches of dried blood.

"It must have been an animal," said Mr Carver.

"What kind of savages have we become if we can't respect her passing?" asked Hywel.

So another burial took place. The seabirds cawed in truculent disapproval and the sun beat down from overhead, casting no shadows, exposing no truths. When Elizabeth came to the graveside carrying May's rags, tied up in a yellow ribbon provided by Annie, people shuffled their feet and looked away. Josiah and Beatrix Carver stood apart from each other, just like, remembered Elizabeth, her parents had when Little Tommy's death came between them.

Reverend Ezekiel, presiding, was resolute. "Oh ye of little faith." He gestured to Elizabeth to lay the scraps of clothing into the ground. From behind a tree she caught a glimpse of red hair and hoped that this ceremony, inadequate though it was, might ease Barty's grief.

"What do we put on her cross?" asked Elizabeth.

Josiah Carver adjusted his wig, Annie shrugged.

Hywel said, "May is all we know."

So Malachi carved *May, beloved sister* and the cross was planted on the headland, across the water from the stricken ship.

· · · · · · · · · ·

The Speedwell settled further on her sandbank, her captain appearing rarely now on deck, and the first mate arriving less often on the tide to bring ever fewer prospects of departure and to collect details of the survivors' latest casualties. As Ezekiel won, by default, his ambition to remain, Elizabeth felt a change in his demeanour. At morning prayers he asked her to hold the Bible while Mr Carver read the lesson. Mrs Carver pursed her lips. The single men snickered and nudged Malachi who glowered. Ezekiel commended her gardening as a divine task, and she thought perhaps she had misjudged him, and that he did, after all, recognise her worth. But then in the privacy of his shelter, she felt his hands on her.

"My children need a mother."

Elizabeth wriggled away. He stepped after her.

"I'm a man," he said. He stroked her hair as her father had once done. But when she looked into his eyes, it wasn't a father's love she saw, and she ran outside. One evening, as she bent over, untangling Ruth's hair, she felt something hard brush against her and turning saw him, lips parted, cheeks flushed and a bulge in the front of his breeches.

"And I need a wife." He wasn't asking.

"Not me," she confided in Annie. "It won't be me. It's enough he owns my body; he won't possess it."

"You could do worse," said Annie. She preened her hair, bleached blonder by the American sun.

Elizabeth escaped to her garden. She set a barrier of thorn branches around it to protect her fragile plants against animals that never appeared, not even the missing goat, and constructed a canopy to shield them from the midday sun. Some mornings she took Ruth and Samuel to play while she worked. At Ezekiel's insistence the little girl still wore dark dresses. Having worn out her own, she wore cast-offs from her dead mother, cut down and refashioned by Annie. Elizabeth was content to see Ezekiel's hand settle on her friend's shoulder. It stayed there longer than was needed to show gratitude.

"I'm going to put shells on the walls in my room when we build our proper house," said Ruth, gazing around the hovel among the trees. Mute Samuel found a giant beetle in a corner of the hut, went outside and built a palisade of white shells. He put the beetle in it and squatted to watch it clamber to escape, Every time freedom threatened, he pushed it back inside.

"There's Barty," Ruth pointed among the trees. Samuel forgot his beetle-baiting and jumped up; the beetle, taking its chance, clambered over the shells and made off.

Elizabeth peered into the wood. "I don't see him."

"He's gone," said Ruth. "He's wild. He steals food at night."

"He has to live. At least he's free." And Elizabeth sighed and wondered how much longer she could escape Ezekiel's advances, or if they would shift to Annie.

Her seedlings were a hand high, the beans curling towards their climbing frame, when Malachi came to sit with her on the hottest day yet. Elizabeth's shirt and trousers were tattered and rode up her arms and legs which had tanned under the American skies. Her hair was bundled under a wide-brimmed grass sunhat woven by Annie. A slight figure in browns and yellows and greens, she blended into the landscape.

"What do you suppose happened to the people who built that hut?" Malachi lounged in the shade in the still heat.

"They're dead, of course." Elizabeth hoed between the neat rows of plants.

Malachi took off his hat, his old London black-brimmed hat with the peak beaten flat, and fanned his face with it. "God, it's hot. We'll end up like them unless we get off this island."

"Not me. I don't intend to die." Elizabeth bent over to pick out a stone from among her plants. They were so tender, with an impossible greenness. She wondered if she could nurture them to maturity and how the weather might change before then, and what Malachi would say if she told him about his father's behaviour towards her.

"You fit into the land here like you belong to it."

"I don't," said Elizabeth.

"Then why are you making this garden?"

"It's what I know. It's who I am."

"Papa says you're doing the Lord's work, taming the wilderness as you've been called to do. He says it's a sign that you believe, that you belong to him in spirit as well as in law." Malachi rolled onto his back, put his hands under his head and crossed his legs.

Elizabeth snapped. The garden had been her escape from the settlement, something she could make her own. If she read the soil, the sun, and the water right, it might even produce food.

But it wasn't her destiny. She wasn't going to be trapped by it. She bent and picked up a stone, which she threw at Malachi.

"Ow. What was that for, Lizzie?"

"I'm freeborn. I don't belong to anyone."

"He says you do."

"And you believe him?" Elizabeth stood over him, one hand on her hip, the other holding her hoe like a weapon.

"I did once." Malachi sat up cross-legged and dug a finger into the soil to pick out a fragment of shell. "He told us America would be a land flowing with milk and honey that we could make our own. He read us letters from people of his church who had gone before. Mother said we could get a house not so different from the one we had in England, and that father would be easier in himself. She followed him as was her duty, whether she believed him or not. But when I saw the suffering she endured, and her death and her baby's and my brother's and sister's, then I understood. His vision was about himself and what he wanted."

Malachi extracted the piece of shell, brushed the soil from it, and held it up for inspection. Elizabeth didn't state the obvious, it was only a broken fragment.

"He may yet get his way," Malachi said. "We may all stay here, we may survive, we may even build a village though we'll never manage a city. But it won't be out of choice, or some divine purpose, it will only be because we're stuck. And then he'll take that as a sign he was right all along."

He threw the piece of shell into the trees. "Look, there's Barty. He must have been watching us."

"I think he sleeps in the hut. He doesn't go near anyone, but he's always watching. He knows us better than we know ourselves." Elizabeth felt the pain in Malachi's voice, understood how much it hurt him to break with the past.

"Your father's wrong," she said. "I believe, that much is true, but not in what your father says. I believe in my own survival, that I will find a way out of this place and that one day I will go home."

"Do you miss it so much?"

Elizabeth leaned on her hoe and shut her eyes. She pictured the cottage with the red roses over the door. She smelled the sweet rosemary hedge, heard the milk cow low, saw the fields with their ripening crops, unkempt they would be now in abandonment. Would Sarah be wearing silk dresses? Would Richard be going to school? Baby Arthur would be lifting his head in a different world. Mary alone would be unchanged. And her mother: she imagined Rebecca's soft arms around her. Miss wasn't a sufficient word for what she felt, but it was all she could admit. "Yes. I miss it."

"What did you expect of America?" Malachi leaned back, looking up at her. She returned to her hoeing. So she didn't have to meet his eyes, so he couldn't see the hurt.

"My mother sold me one day, and I was gone the next. I knew nothing of what I would find here."

"What about your father?"

"My father was a visionary too, but not like yours. He believed in this world, not the next. He taught me that we are all freeborn, with rights that no-one can take away. When the war against the king started, my father left to fight for our freedom. I didn't understand then, but I do now. I'm a freeborn girl and I will never be bound to anyone ever again."

"What's freedom worth in a place like this?"

Elizabeth knew her mind now. "Everything." She held out her hand to Malachi and pulled him up. They left the garden and walked past the abandoned hovel. Out of the woodland, they fell into single file, Elizabeth leading the way through the tinder-dry, spikey grasses to the narrow creek that meandered up from the inland sea. Sluggish water trickled through the salt marshes and the reeds rustled in protest at being disturbed by a wind that blew in across the sound. Elizabeth felt the hot air catch at the back of her throat, tighten in her chest, and she tasted the sea saltiness it carried. Around them, insects chirped. From the encampment came the rasping sound of metal on wood as timbers were sawn and a new shelter took shape. Gulls sounded an alert, the cawing noise they make as they wheel around a vessel. If Elizabeth had not been so distracted, she may have heard their warning. If there'd been time. But there wasn't.

Boom!

The day exploded.

CHAPTER 21

London: 27 August 2019

"When did you last see Miracle?" The radio reporter peered at me over her glasses.

I was sitting opposite her in the radio studio at 7.55 a.m. the morning after the demonstration on the Cooper Estate, listening to the weather forecast being broadcast. Next would come the news, then a background piece on the estate and then she'd come to me for a live interview about the mayhem the night before, when Miracle James and her daughter Blessing had disappeared.

"What do the police say?" I asked back. "Have they told you whether they've got any leads?"

"No. All they say is that she was missing after the disturbance at the Cooper Estate and there are concerns about the safety of her baby. They're appealing for help in finding her." The reporter pushed her glasses up her nose and scanned through a piece of paper. "Their statement's a bit short on details."

I tried to remember the last time anyone had told me that they'd seen Miracle. The last time I had, she'd kissed my hands and wept.

"My intern saw her last week."

"Stephanie?"

"You've met her?"

"No. Laurelle mentioned her."

"You've done an interview with Laurelle?"

"She gave us her version of events last night. You'll hear it."

The package on the Cooper Estate came on after the news headlines. It led with Laurelle's interview. I was the villain of her piece, supporting the regeneration that would result in 800 hardworking people losing their homes. While I listened to it, I worked out my lines, and then the reporter nodded to me and turned up the microphones and said: "Strong opposition there to regeneration plans, including demolition of the Cooper Estate, which it's claimed that you, as the local MP, support."

"Whatever happens with the estate," I said in my most listener-friendly voice, "This appeal concerns the welfare of a young mother and her child. Miracle James was an informal tenant of a flat on the Cooper Estate. She was in a difficult position, living on the edge, and now she's disappeared. She and her daughter are vulnerable and we're all desperate to know where they are."

"If the police raid hadn't taken place, she would still be in her flat." The reporter glared at me, critical eyes over her glasses, which had slipped down her nose.

"By any standards, Miracle's flat was unfit for anyone—let alone a young mother and her child."

"You'd been there?" She sounded surprised. That really narked me, so I decided to lay it on thick.

"Yes. The first time I visited, she was living in a single room in a flat at the top of Speedwell House. The lift was broken, and the plumbing was shot to pieces. There was water trickling down the stairwell. All she had was a chair and a mattress, and three bin bags of belongings. The last time I visited, she and her daughter were living alone in the flat under siege conditions. Everyone else had left except for a criminal gang, which had broken into a flat below and were using it as a base. She was terrified for her child."

The reporter looked at me with what—surprise that I'd visited the flat? Grudging respect? I decided not to talk about the child-minding.

"If Miracle comes forward, we can provide her with something more suitable and help her resolve her other issues. So I hope anyone with any information that can help us find her, will share it. It's a terrible situation for Miracle and her baby."

The reporter flashed me a smile.

"Anybody who has any information that could help find Miracle, no matter how small you may feel it is, please report it to the police online or by calling 101."

When the traffic report came on, the reporter took off her glasses.

"Well!" she said.

"You don't know the half of it," I replied.

"Busy times?" She moved on. That was a big part of Miracle's problem. Everyone always moved on from her.

"Apocalyptic," I said.

"Are you one of the rebels?"

"Everyone's a rebel one way or the other these days. I like to think I'm one of the sane."

She laughed. "As in, it's the world that's mad? You're probably right, and it's going to get madder today." She put her glasses on again and returned to the switches and sliders on her sound desk.

On my way along Millbank from the radio studio to Gerald's meeting, I texted Stephanie to find out where she was—as in, which police cell—and Joey to find out if there was any update on Miracle.

Stephanie's reply was instant. *I'm in the office.*

Coffee in five. I texted back. Gerald and his meeting could wait.

Stephanie was sitting at a table near the coffee bar in the atrium with a flat white for herself and a skinny-latte-extra-hot for me. "Joey says it's how you like your coffee," she said. She was wearing a pink silk blouse and her pearl necklace, but not her Alice band. Her brown hair fell around her face; it made her look younger. Not exactly vulnerable but less officious.

"Thank you Stephanie." I felt wrong-footed from the start.

"It wasn't how it looked."

"That was bad enough. After the police marched you out of Speedwell House, I thought I'd be springing you from the nick." She looked puzzled, so I explained, "Rescuing you from the police station."

She smiled. "Oh no, nothing like that. The police were real nice to me." I did a double take, but she wasn't joking. "I explained everything to them. It took a bit of time, and then Joey came in an Uber to collect me. He doesn't like the police, does he?" She drank some coffee. "You see," she tucked her hair behind her ears. "I'd been talking to Laurelle."

"That wasn't such a clever idea."

"I realise that now." Her eyes avoided mine. "I never meant for to cause you trouble." She drank some more coffee, then put her hands in her lap and looked me straight in the eyes. "I guess there's been a bit of a perception issue."

In other circumstances I'd have laughed, but this was more serious. "Was it you who leaked that stuff about the demolition to Laurelle?"

She wilted. "Not exactly; at least, not intentionally. The video of those cooling towers collapsing at the power station was all over social media, so when I mentioned to Laurelle that there were plans to demolish the tower blocks on the Cooper in the same way, she must have put two and two together."

"And made five."

Stephanie hung her head. "I'm so sorry."

"And when exactly did you see the light?"

"When she said there was going to be an occupation on the estate." Stephanie came the closest I'd seen to angry. "Only Speedwell House was left; the others all had security fences around them. So I asked her what would happen to Miracle, and she said—she said—"

It was the first time I'd known Stephanie be lost for words. "Go on."

"She said that having a mother and child stuck at the top of the tower block would help the cause. I said she might get hurt. Laurelle said they wouldn't dare. I said there could be an accident. But Laurelle was determined. So I went to try to get Miracle out before there was any trouble. She wasn't there, but her stuff was, so I waited for her, and then, well, like you saw, I got stuck."

There were a lot of loose ends. Why had she stayed so long? Why not come down? Why hadn't she told me beforehand, or at least texted me for help—not that Stephanie was one to ask for help. But she'd already carried on with her story.

"It made me realise that Laurelle is, well... I don't like to use the word, but a bitch."

This time I did laugh. "Is that the worst word you know, Stephanie?"

She blushed.

My phone buzzed.

Where are you? Message from Gerald.

"Listen, I have to dash." I gulped down my coffee and got up to go.

She reached out a hand to me. "Is it OK if I have a few days off, Frances?"

"Are you shaken up by what's happened?" Unlikely, I thought, but possible.

She shook her head. "Remember I told you I wanted to do some research on my ancestors before I leave. The ones that stayed." Her face lit up. "There were the Gardiners, and then I believe there were some called Balhatchet, originally from Broome. I want to go there and check out the local records."

"OK. But be back by next week. It's going to be busy." For the first time, I felt I'd been allowed to see the real Stephanie. I had a fleeting urge to hug her, but I was already running late.

· · · · · ● ● ● · · · ·

Gerald was disconsolate, hunched over his laptop in the ruins of his meeting in Church House, across the road from Parliament: empty coffee cups, crumpled biscuit wrappers, a phone charger left in a socket behind the top table. "If we had either a leader or some ideas, we'd be alright," he said.

"Well, I couldn't have helped in either department."

"At least you'd have been moral support."

"Sorry." And I was. He'd been there for me when I was at rock bottom.

On our way out of the building we passed Hugh, grinning.

"You look cheerful," I said.

"Another coup bites the dust."

But Gerald came straight back at him. "People haven't given up, they're just knackered, that's all."

We were walking around Parliament Square when my phone went. I recognised the number: Derek Rawlings, the owner of Loverage Development, the man busy destroying—whoops, regenerating—the Cooper Estate. I stopped outside Westminster Abbey to take the call and waved at Gerald, who gave me a thumbs up and went on. I admired his resilience.

"Hello Frances."

"I'm not going to say how can I help."

A chuckle. "Is there any word of the young mum?"

"No. She was in a pretty desperate state before, so goodness knows how she must be feeling now."

"I thought I'd talk you through our plans."

"If I listen to you, it doesn't mean I agree."

A grunt down the phone. Then, "We're planning on putting a security fence around Speedwell House."

"When?"

"Starting tomorrow."

"That's not planning, that's doing."

"We can't risk another attempt to occupy that building."

"Could you hold off a few days? Miracle could come back. She must have found somewhere to stay, but from what I understand her belongings are still there." 'Belongings' was a generous word for three bin bags of stuff.

"We've put security on the entrance. I suppose. we could wait till Monday."

Ahead of me, crowds were already gathering outside Parliament to protest. Against Brexit, against Europe, against the threat to shut the place down. Whatever. We were punch drunk from protests.

"And the demolition?" I asked. "Are you seriously going to go ahead with that?"

A gravelly chuckle. Amusement or embarrassment—impossible to tell.

"In due course."

"There are other options."

"Not viable."

"You mean profitable."

"I'm not a charity, Frances."

I wove my way through the crowd outside Parliament. A few people peered at me with suspicion, but not being any kind of name or face, I wasn't identified as a collaborator. For either side of any row. It was only when I pushed through the gates into New Palace Yard that someone shouted, "Traitor." In the middle of the cobbled courtyard a colleague was taking pictures by the fountain with a group of his constituents. He waved and pointed me out to his people, who also waved. I waved back.

"That intern of yours is mixed up with this," Derek said. "She's one of the ones causing all the trouble."

"Did Toby Davis tell you that?"

"You should keep her out of it."

"You shouldn't believe everything he tells you."

"And you shouldn't mess with me."

By the time I got my car out of the parking garage and into New Palace Yard, the crowds were too thick for the police to open the gates. So I drove along the road that runs through the heart of the parliamentary estate and snuck out the back way.

· · • • • • • • ·

Next day, when I went to visit my mother, Hanna glided me through the corridors like she would glide through a war zone. Her voice was as soothing as it had been the day when my mother hadn't died. Even her words were the same.

"You'll find her changed," she said again as she opened the door.

Mum was sitting in a chair watching television. The French windows were open, and the slightest of slight breezes wafted in the scent of roses. A bowl of them, extravagant pink blooms, was standing on the table beside the television.

Hanna turned the sound down. "You'll want to talk."

"How do you know?" Mum was back to her old self.

"You're looking good, Mum."

"And you're getting even more holidays."

That was her take on the announcement that the Prime Minister had decided to settle the Brexit row by shutting down Parliament and had sent one of his side-kicks to Balmoral to square things with the Queen. All morning I'd been watching developments on television at home, to a background barrage of social media posts and WhatsApp messages.

"It's not holiday, Mum, and it's not right. Parliament shouldn't be shut down on one man's whim. It's a coup."

"The Queen agreed to it."

"She has to do what she's told."

"Well it won't make any difference anyway, will it? They're all the same, these MPs."

"Hello Mum, it's me." I laughed. I was past being hurt by her. I was past being hurt by anyone. I pulled up a chair and sat beside her and we watched the silent screen as crowds thronged down Whitehall.

· · · • • · • • · · ·

The crowds were out in even greater force on Saturday when Stephanie came back, so I met her at a café on the south bank close to Westminster Bridge.

She was back to inscrutable in tan slacks and cream top, her hair safely tucked under its Alice band, her computer bag over her shoulder. She gave me a hand-flutter of a wave.

"How did things go?" I hoped the closeness there'd been between us the previous week hadn't completely disappeared.

"It was complicated." We stood awkwardly together in the queue at the bar, too close for strangers, too distant for friends. She got a fashionable poke bowl, I got a more conventional salad. The tables were too small for all our stuff. As we juggled it all to fit, food, drinks, her laptop, she knocked her coffee over. It caused a bit of a commotion. Unlike her to be so clumsy.

When I'd finished running through the national trauma of the past week, she opened up her laptop and didn't so much start telling as blurting out her story.

"I went to Broome and checked out the parish records. There were Balhatchets living there in the 1600s, including one Ezekiel who married an Agnes Staines. It looks like they had six children: Malachi, Joshua, Ruth, Samuel, Naomi and Zachary. Joshua, born in 1632, died in 1633. There's no record of what became of the rest of the family. They must have been the Balhatchets that went to America. Ezekiel's listed as a landowner, not a clergyman."

Plot point, I thought. I pushed my salad bowl aside.

"Why are you telling me all this?"

"I'm getting to it," she said. "There was a clergyman called Ezekiel Balhatchet in Broome, but he lived in the 19th century. According to church records he moved to Deepening in Kent. I went there to follow him up."

She stopped and took a sip of coffee. Pink flushes appeared on her cheeks. Heat? Or excitement? She continued.

"The family petered out, except for one, Edward Balhatchet. He died in Croydon at the end of last year. I visited his house. It had a For Sale board up outside. A man opened the door. He didn't want to engage. But he did confirm that Edward was his father." She fussed over the last bits of food in her poke bowl, as if they mattered.

"And?" I couldn't understand why she was so agitated. It looked like she'd done a forensic job of tracking down her ancestors that stayed behind.

"I took a picture of Blessing's birth certificate. Did I ever show you?"

"No."

A few clicks on her laptop, and she swivelled it around and pointed to the parents' names:

Mother: Miracle James. Father: Edward Balhatchet.

It was a moment for her. The connection to her roots, the missing part of her family's story, stretching over four centuries and three continents, ending with Blessing.

But to me only one thing mattered.

"D'you know where she is?"

CHAPTER 22

Ocracoke: August 1643

*B*oom!

Elizabeth felt the blast in the pit of her stomach. Around her the reed-beds erupted. Birds flew up, panicked wings flapping, clamours of alarm.

Boom!

It came again. The sound could mean only one thing: a ship had arrived. People of some kind. They must be saved. Elizabeth started running. Her feet fell hard on sharp, dry grass, splashed through salty creeks, were burned in hot sand, as she ran towards the sound. Once the echoes of the cannon had died down, and the birds had flapped and flown away, all she heard was the crackle of the reeds underfoot, the whip of dry grass brushed aside, the squelch of mud and splatter of water as she ran. That and the frantic beating of her heart. Her whole life was in that run. She forgot even Malachi, crashing behind her, "Wait, Lizzie, wait." Every sinew in her body strained towards a point ahead, off shore, where a ship was anchored. She saw it gleaming, sailors in the rigging, men and women on the deck, bright clothes, pink faces, merry smiles, cheering the survivors, food set out to welcome them aboard. She saw the cross of St George waving atop the main mast, the lighters rowing ashore, herself, Ezekiel and the children, the Carvers and Annie, Hywel even, hands stretching out to pull them to safety, the embraces, the tears, the laughter. The miracle of rescue. She saw it all.

Until she reached the land's end. In the channel the newcomer was sleek, low-lying. Smoke clearing on her deck revealed a row of cannons and, around them, figures: men in clothes of every colour and description, scarves tied around their heads, sunlight glinting on their cutlasses and swords, their shouts and laughter filling the void left by the cannon fire. Above them were two masts. Flying above the taller was a red flag.

"Pirates." Malachi's voice behind her. "And a red flag. No mercy."

Another blow to her gut, harder than the first. "Ohhh." Hot tears of fury came to her eyes. "Why is life so cruel?"

Malachi's hand on her shoulder. "Who else would come here?"

Smoke drifted across the water from the cannons on the pirate ship. Metal clattered from the deck as she dropped anchor mid-current, close to the stricken Speedwell. Seabirds returned and swooped round the two ships. One bristled with malice. The other lay supine, her captain on deck staring at the tangled ruins of her remaining masts, shattered by the pirates' barrage.

"It's the end," said Elizabeth.

"It can't be. We can't let it be. Not for us."

We. Us. Elizabeth had been so lonely for so long, she'd forgotten what it was to feel part of someone else's life. She turned to Malachi to see if she could read more of his emotions. But he was intent on the pirates and all she could see was a desperation that matched her own. She took his hand and said, "I understand. I feel the same."

They watched hand in hand as two longboats were launched from the pirate ship. Men leapt into them and rowed towards the Speedwell with all the evil intent, thought Elizabeth, of a fox closing in on a wounded chicken.

She wished that whichever of the Speedwell's crew was left cowering below deck, they would dig into whatever courage they could summon, and fire their cannons on the longboats. She yearned to see Peggy stump onto the deck and drive away the marauders. Such suffering she'd witnessed on that ship, herself had plummeted such deep despair. Now she could only feel pity as the longboats reached their prey, and the pirates scaled the ship as lithe and cunning as foxes.

"What will they do to the men on board?"

A gunshot, and then another. Gulls flew shrieking into the air. Three pirates appeared at the deckside, heaving a bundle which they swung, to and fro, to and fro, then let it go. The figure of a man flew from the ship, limbs spread-eagled, coat flapping. The body landed splat on the water, held on the surface for a second, and then sank. The gulls returned and wheeled above it.

"That's what," said Malachi. "Such an ending."

"Who will be next?" Elizabeth asked.

They set off again, through the dunes, between the bushes, towards the settlement.

· · · ● · ● · · ·

At the headland, in the shelter of a tree, they found Josiah Carver perched on a tussock of grass. His blue velvet jacket sat loosely on shoulders that had shrunk during the weeks on the island. Ezekiel Balhatchet was cross-legged in the sand, skeletal in his clerical black. One the colour of water, the other the colour of death, thought Elizabeth, but not mine, not yet.

"We feared you were both lost," said Josiah Carver.

"Is that all you can say?" Malachi turned away in disgust. "Papa?"

Ezekiel had his Bible open on his lap, but his eyes were shut. Only his lips moved.

Josiah Carver heaved himself up, flexed his shoulders, and cleared his throat. "I can tell you that as governor of this settlement, I have made provisions to ensure our safety. In a word, we are prepared for battle."

"How can we fight them?" Elizabeth saw this man, who claimed to be their leader, had no more substance than a cockerel in a bear pit. He was like Oliver taking her father off to war when he himself lacked the courage to fight.

"We can, God willing, although Reverend Balhatchet has yet to divine God's precise wishes." Josiah Carver rolled the reverend's name round his mouth and spat it out at the clergyman's feet.

Ezekiel folded his hands round his Bible and rested his forehead on it.

"You cheated us." Elizabeth shouted at both men. "You brought us here, to this place, which is nowhere and now that we face death, you don't know what to do."

"We got you ashore in good order, didn't we? We built an encampment with a palisade for your protection," said Josiah Carver. "You should be grateful."

Ezekiel opened his eyes. "It wasn't our will that we came here. We were led by God."

"And them, Father?" Malachi pointed across the water. "Who led them?"

Ezekiel's eyes followed the direction of Malachi's finger, but Elizabeth saw them glaze over before they reached the pirate ship. "The Lord will soften their hard hearts and show us a way through our adversities," he said.

"We've posted guards." Josiah Carver straightened his jacket, folded his hands behind his back, thrust out his chest, tilted up his chin and stood erect, as if he was a statue in Westminster. "As your governor, I've ordered the pirates be shot if they come ashore."

"Who will shoot them?" asked Malachi.

"Hywel Williams," said Mr Carver.

Across the channel, the longboat, piled high with loot, rowed away from the ravaged Speedwell. Something slithered across Elizabeth's feet. She looked down. A flick of green. She stamped at it, but the snake had already slipped away.

All her life there'd been someone who told her what to do. Her father, her mother, her master, someone who was in control of events or claimed to be. Now they were all gone; dead, fled or failed. There were no certainties. She felt more adrift than she ever had at sea. She left Malachi talking with his father and walked from the headland towards the palisade.

At its entrance stood Hywel, matted hair and beard, tattered clothes hanging on soldier-straight shoulders. By his side was a gun, a musket, which he lifted and pointed at her.

"Friend or foe?" His sing-song voice.

"What do you mean?" she asked.

Hywel let the muzzle of the gun fall. "I have to ask everyone. Are you with us, or them?"

"I thought you were a man of peace."

Hywel rested the butt of his gun against his groin, caressed the smooth shaft, ran his finger over the flint, held it to his face and sniffed at its oil and gunpowder. He flexed a finger on the trigger, held the gun up to his shoulder again and pointed it at the pirate ship.

"Pow." He feigned recoil from his gunshot. "Peace is for us, not them. They're pirates." He grinned.

Elizabeth had never seen him so purposeful.

Beyond him, inside the palisade, she found Mrs Carver sitting on a sea chest. Locks of hair escaped from her bun, stains of sweat darkened her crumpled dress, her panicked eyes darted around the encampment. Annie, wearing only a shift, hair loose around brown shoulders, waved a fan of grasses over the older woman's head.

"This is the death of us." Mrs Carver put her hands on her knees, rocked back and forth, and breathed in deep gulps of air that she exhaled noisily. "Oooh."

"Please don't take on so, Mrs Carver. You're scaring us." Annie's fan-waving was frantic.

Elizabeth could smell the fear. It radiated from the woman rocking on her sea chest, from the heat of her silk-encased body, from the red terror on her face. It rose in tendrils from her drying sweat, twisting through the still, hot air dispersed by Annie's panicked fanning. It infected the dust that hung in the afternoon sun, thrown up by the bare feet of children running amok chanting, "Pow-pow-pow, we're pirates," by chickens that fled clucking before them, by men grappling with logs to reinforce the palisade to make it proof against cannonballs. Elizabeth felt herself choking on the fear.

Into which commotion ran Barty, dangling in one hand a gold chain with a pearl on it.

"I found this in your shelter." He swung the pearl in front of Mrs Carver. "My sister had it before she died. She kept it with her all the time. She'd never let it go."

"It's mine, she stole it from me." Mrs Carver, snatched at the necklace. "What were you doing going through my things?"

"Looking for it." Barty skipped out of reach, still holding aloft the chain, jiggling the pearl.

"You little devil. Just like her." Mrs Carver struggled to her feet, grasping for the jewel.

"You're evil. All of yous. I know what happened to my sister. You killed her. All for this." Barty wrapped the chain around his fist, and ducked the woman's outstretched arm.

"Stop him." Mrs Carver lunged at the boy. Annie grabbed his shirt, but it tore in her hands and he ran free just as Hywel walked into the settlement, his gun held to his shoulder.

"Shoot him," screamed Mrs Carver.

"No." Elizabeth grabbed at the gun.

It fell from Hywel's hands and landed in the dust with a weak "phut."

There was silence. So profound that Elizabeth heard the swishing of the fan that Annie beat with even more frenzied desperation.

"Do stop that." Mrs Carver reached out a hand and placed it on Annie's wrist. "You're driving me to distraction."

Hywel picked up his gun. He held it to his shoulder again and trained it on Barty, whose red hair bobbed above the long grass close to the woodland. "He's running too fast." Hywel let down his gun and looked around sheepishly. "Besides, the gunpowder's wet. It will never go off."

"So how will you shoot the pirates?" asked Elizabeth.

CHAPTER 23

London: midday 9 September 2019

Donna must have been watching. Because as soon as I walked from the carpark onto the piazza at the Cooper Estate that final Monday morning, she came out of her flat. From the way she strode towards me, head down, shoulders rounded like a boxer's, it looked like her mood fitted the fractious day. She was wearing a smart jade track suit and a pair of black trainers. Her hair was a darker shade of blonde and she wore it pulled away from her face and fixed at the back. She cut a younger figure, but when she got close, I could see the lines on her face had deepened and her mouth had a downward sag.

It was a sultry morning. Sullen light radiated from behind morose clouds. Sweat trickled down my back. I took off my jacket and tied it around my waist.

"Hello, Donna."

She pulled out a pack of cigarettes and a lighter and lit up, took a deep drag and blew a stream of smoke over my head. "Don't tell me I shouldn't. Cancer would be easier than what's gone on here."

"How've you been?"

She clenched her lips and raised her eyebrows, which I guessed meant she didn't have the words to express what she felt. The last time we'd spoken was the night we'd stood outside the community centre, listening to Laurelle wind up a group of activists to occupy Speedwell House. That hadn't been an occasion to talk emotions either, just to feel them.

"It must have been hard for you." I put the words out there.

The quiver in her lips told me she didn't trust herself not to cry. She flicked away the ash on her cigarette.

"No-show from the police then?" she said.

"We're early. I was going to come to your flat."

"If you could remember the way. It's been a while."

We were shadow boxing, jabbing at what we thought were each other's soft spots.

"It's been busy."

"You should have brought Stephanie."

"We agreed it would be best if she didn't come today. She told me where she thought Miracle might be; that was enough. It's been quite traumatic for her, all this."

"She's a good girl, but..." Donna twiddled her cigarette between finger and thumb. "Is she in cahoots with Laurelle?"

"No. She's seen through Laurelle."

"I always thought she was sensible."

When the police arrived, it was with council officials. Three carloads decanted and walked onto the piazza, led by the chief inspector and including a woman officer. A car emblazoned with *Loverage Development, regenerating London*, parked up and a beefy man in khaki clothes ran out to join us.

Donna looked the police up and down. "Mob-handed, eh? Has there been a crime?" She pinched out her cigarette and put it back in the packet.

"We did a very thorough search of the building last time," said the chief inspector. "I don't see how we can have missed her."

"You wouldn't have seen the door." I said. "The lights inside the stairwell are broken so it would have been pitch dark."

The inspector turned to Donna. "Did you know about this place?"

"Of course." Donna gave him such a withering look he must have regretted asking. "It's like a studio flat on top of the building. People used to live there. But then it was left empty and got vandalised. The lifts don't go up that far, so it was always awkward. The stairwell to it has been blocked off for years."

The council officers dished out builders' helmets and hi viz jackets and we set off. The entrance door to Speedwell House was broken, so we got in easily enough. The lifts were barricaded, but in any event, the power was off so they wouldn't be working. A grille screen across the stairwell had been levered away enough for someone small to slip through. The Loverage man used his brute force to remove it. The police put on torches; I put on my phone. The stairs were covered with rubbish, bits of concrete, tin cans and fast-food cartons, some of which looked new. Water trickled down the wall. The Loverage man stopped and shone a torch onto the sole of his shoe. Whatever he'd stepped in smelt bad, even by the stairwell's standards.

We'd only gone up two floors when Donna said she'd got a bit of grit in her shoes. So we stopped, and she took off one of her trainers and emptied it out.

"You don't have to do this," I whispered to her.

"Oh yes I do," she whispered back.

"Did you really know about that place?"

"Yes, of course. I sort of forgot. Last time I went there it was a complete shithole."

At the fifth floor, with Donna flagging again, I said I needed a breather. She heaved herself up beside me. "Not so young then, eh?" she said when she got her breath back.

"So who lived there?"

"In that flat?"

"Yes."

"The last person was Stella."

Her dead daughter. Mother of her murdered grandson. I was glad of the darkness.

At the eighth floor, the chief inspector stopped. He shone his torch down to where I was a flight of stairs behind.

"We're only halfway. Everyone still up for this?"

Donna was struggling behind me, wheezing. She looked at me and nodded. "Of course," I said for both of us.

"And keep those helmets on."

"You'll have to stop smoking," I whispered to Donna.

"No. I'll have to stop climbing tower blocks," she whispered back.

"Are you sure you're OK with going up there? I mean, old wounds and all that."

"They're not old. They still bleed."

When the police started off again, I felt for her hand in the darkness. It was leathery, dry and strong. She grasped mine back. At the eleventh floor I felt her straining to keep up, and at the twelfth floor she gave my hand a double squeeze. I shouted up the stairs that I'd got some dust in my eyes and needed to stop for a minute. From above me in the stairwell there came the sound of someone panting, and a disembodied voice said, "Bloody hell."

After that, Donna and I linked arms.

"I'm sorry," I whispered to her.

"What for?"

"Everything. Dylan. This."

"You couldn't have changed anything."

That made me feel worse.

When we got to Miracle's floor, the police went out onto the landing and shone their torches around. All the flats were barricaded off, Miracle's included.

"What happened to her things?" I asked the council officer, who flicked through her notes. "There was nothing there apart from a broken chair and a mattress that had to be destroyed." The police officers wiped the grime off their faces. They looked unbearably young.

We went back into the stairwell. "There it is," said Donna. Tucked away behind the lift was a grey metal door, barely noticeable. The police turned the handle and pushed. Nothing. They thumped, kicked and rattled; the noise racketed around us.

In the silence that followed we heard a baby cry. We all froze in that cramped stairwell. None of us could say the sound was unexpected. We had climbed all the way up the building to find this child. But the reality of what might lie on the other side of the grey door was another matter.

"Miracle." I put my head to the door. There was no sound from inside. "Are you there? It's Frances. Your MP. We've come to help you." Silence. "And Blessing."

No response.

"Here let me try." Donna pushed past the police. She stood facing the door, as if she could will it away. "Miracle, we're so sorry about what's happened. We'll try to make things better for you."

"There's nothing you can do." Her voice. Weepy, but strong enough. I felt a spasm of relief.

"We managed to find some keys in the office." The woman from the council rummaged in her handbag and pulled out a whole jangling bunch of them.

"It's blocked inside," said the police officer.

Donna put her head to the door, "Will you let us in, love?"

"I can't. The lock broke."

None of us liked to ask when.

The Loverage man came up trumps. "We'll need a bolt-cutter," he said. "I've got one in the car. Hang on and I'll run and fetch it."

He was a few floors down, his footsteps were only a rumble in the stairwell, when I put an ear to the door again. Nothing from inside. So I started talking to Miracle. About what we could do for her when she came down with us, how we'd get a flat for herself and Blessing, somewhere away from the Cooper, with proper furniture, where she could get a job when Blessing was older.

"Stephanie said to say hello to both of you," I said.

I thought I heard a muffled sob.

Donna took over. "We can get it sorted. I'm just sorry it's been so tough on you, love."

"I'm sorry, too." Miracle must have been standing right by the door at that point because her voice was as sharp as broken glass.

A collective intake of breath from us outside.

"Whatever for?" asked Donna.

"Dylan."

For a minute, Donna was overcome. Then she recovered herself. "That's not your fault, love."

Thuds echoing around the stairwell and then torchlight, and the Loverage man appeared, sprinting up the stairs in his khaki shorts, with his equipment. To me he looked like an angel. He'd brought a pair of protectors for his ears. The rest of us had to block ours. "Stand back," he said. "And you inside." When the noise had died down, and the dust cleared, the woman police

officer pushed the door open. "OK Miracle, we're coming up."
She led the way with Donna and I behind.

When the Cooper Estate was new, the unit on top of Speedwell House must have been a wonderful place. A penthouse,
technically. Now derelict was a generous description. A short
flight of stairs led up to the unit, a flat which was wrapped
around two sides of the engine room above the lift shift. The
stairs were caked white with pigeon shit. There was a window
halfway up, but the glass was gone and even the frame was
missing.

"You alright love?" Donna called out as we picked our way up
through the mess.

"Hang on in there, Miracle," I shouted.

The door to the unit was loose, and a tatty curtain hung
inside the entrance. Rubbish bags were piled up, from which
ready-meal containers spilled out, along with the smell of used
nappies. The police officer pushed aside the curtain, and Donna
and I followed her past the remains of a kitchenette into the
main room: grey concrete walls covered in garish graffiti, the
floor swept clean. Against one wall were three black bin liners,
against another was a pile of blankets with a pillow on top.
Along the far wall were huge windows, empty of any glass,
through which could be seen The Shard. Silhouetted against
the grey sky stood Miracle, in her yellow dress, with her red
headwrap, clutching Blessing.

"Fuck me," muttered Donna.

We stood in a semicircle, the woman police officer, Donna
and me. The others had the sense to stay outside.

"We're here to help you, Miracle," I said.

"You know you can trust us," said Donna.

Miracle's body language said she didn't.

"There's nothing that can't be sorted," I said.

The police officer moved around, as if she was trying to close in on Miracle, who swivelled to face her. The officer froze.

"Think of your little girl," said Donna.

"She'd be better off without me." Miracle buried her face in her daughter's hair.

"No she wouldn't, she needs her Mum," said Donna. "Believe me, I'm a Mum myself, I know."

Miracle swung round and glared at each of us in turn. "Where's Stephanie?"

"D'you want us to get her?" I asked.

"She understands." Miracle shut her eyes, cradled Blessing, sang gently and swayed with her, feet moving in time with her song. I was mesmerised. I didn't dare look at the others.

"All we want is to help you, my lovely," said the police officer. She took a step towards Miracle, who stopped dancing and jerked upright.

"There's nothing anyone can do." Her despair was tangible.

"Come down with us. You and Blessing can rest at mine till things get sorted. You must be knackered." Donna's voice was hypnotic.

Miracle stepped forward. So did Donna, arms outstretched to make this a happy ever after moment. But then Miracle got agitated; her face twisted with pain. "I'm a bad person."

"Let me hold her for a bit for you." It was like there was no one else in that room, in the entire tower block, except the woman in the jade tracksuit and the girl in the yellow dress holding her baby.

"Will you look after her?" asked Miracle.

"Of course I will, love."

"Promise?"

"I promise."

I held my breath as Miracle edged forward, step by cautious step. The woman police officer tensed like a cat ready to spring. I prayed the beefy Loverage bloke in his khaki shorts would manage to stay stum outside. That high up, the city's hubbub was no more than a gentle hum that dissolved into the sound of the wind blowing through the empty window as Miracle edged ever closer. When she finally laid Blessing in Donna's arms, I did an inner fist pump. This story would end well after all.

"Be kind to her," said Miracle. Then she said some words I couldn't understand, and before my jangled brain could begin to register what was happening, the police officer leapt towards her.

Quickly. But not quickly enough.

CHAPTER 24
Ocracoke: September 1643

H ot day gave way to suffocating night.

Inside the confines of the palisade, Elizabeth sat on the baked ground, comforting Ruth and Samuel. The little girl cuddled her doll, "Papa will fight the pirates and kill them dead." Samuel squashed a beetle and flicked it into the dirt.

No fires, no candles to betray the presence of the huddled band of survivors. Only moonlight on figures thinned by weeks of hunger, faces blanched with fear. No breeze to ease the fevered stillness, only Annie's fan agitating the air over a prostrate Beatrix Carver. No sound beyond the whispered arguments of Ezekiel and Josiah Carver, sitting with the men of the encampment, debating how best to deal with this new threat to their existence.

Until Beatrix Carver sat up, pushed Annie to one side and hissed at her husband, "Your noise could wake the dead."

And then there was only the singing of the insects. Their disembodied sound reverberated until Elizabeth thought it came from inside her own throbbing head.

When Ruth and Samuel fell asleep, she laid them down, and crept out of the encampment, past Annie slumped over a snoring Mrs Carver, past the flagging men, past Hywel slumbering

over his gun at the entrance to the palisade. She sensed someone following her, but when she turned, all she saw was her
moon shadow. She waved at it, and the moon shadow waved
back. She danced, and it danced with her. She listened, but
all she heard was the insistent call of the cicadas.

Another shadow stretched across the beach. Malachi
stood at the waterline, arms folded, silhouetted by the moon
which hung full and yellow over the sound. He turned and
smiled as she came up beside him, opposite the Speedwell
high on her sandbank, her broken masts like black teeth. All
was dark on board and Elizabeth wondered whether any of
the crew were still alive. Alongside was her deadly twin, the
pirate ship.

"Next time the tide goes out, I'll go with it," Malachi said.

"How can you say that? The Speedwell will never sail
again. All this time we've deceived ourselves that she could be
floated off. But now we must face the truth. She never will."

"I'll go on the pirate ship," said Malachi. "They've taken
everything of value off the Speedwell. They'll go with the tide
and will leave us marooned here to die."

"I thought they'd kill us."

"We aren't worth it."

"You'll be an outlaw if you go with them."

"At least I'll be alive."

The pirate ship rocked on her anchor. Light glowed from
the cabins at her stern, then a lantern flickered across the deck.
Laughter, shouts. More lights darting the length of the ship.
Elizabeth thought of the encampment, with its wooden palisade that would provide no protection against this wild bunch
if they came ashore. Neither would Hywel with his gun that
didn't work, or Ezekiel with his religion and lechery. Or Josiah Carver with his rules-based order and murderous wife. She

knew that Malachi was right about one thing: that in a world turned upside down, the pirate ship was their best hope.

"I'll come with you," she said. "We only have to get as far as Jamestown."

"But you're a girl."

"My papers say I'm a boy, Richard Gardiner. I will travel as such. You told me that I'm free to choose. I choose to leave."

• • • • •• • • • •

Back in the encampment, she carried the sleeping Ruth and Samuel into their shelter and laid them on their blanket. They nestled together, comforting each other in sleep as they never did when awake. Then she untied her bundle from home, took out the dress her mother had made and the trousers and smock, the silk shawl and lavender bag, what was left of the seeds and John Lilburne's leaflet. She folded up the dress and put it at Ruth's feet. Perhaps she would wear it when she was older, if she got to be older. For Samuel, she had nothing but a kiss. He stirred and smiled. She hoped that someone else would kiss him again before too long. Perhaps Annie. She wondered about the children she'd left behind, her brothers and sisters. Whether Young Will still sang as sweetly and how Mary was managing without him.

Then she crawled to Ezekiel's sea chest and rifled through his papers until she found the document of her indentureship. Signed R. Her mother. For all that had happened since then, she still felt the bitterness of her betrayal. She folded it up in the silk shawl, repacked her bundle, tied it up and crept out.

All was quiet in the encampment. The men were slumped in their circle, Ezekiel and Josiah propped against each other at their centre. The women slumbered cuddling their children.

As Elizabeth snuck past, Annie sat up. She looked around, confused, caught Elizabeth's eye, smiled, opened her mouth. Elizabeth froze, expecting her to speak, an innocent word that would dash her chance of freedom. But Annie made do with a yawn, a smirk, a blown kiss and sank down again.

· · · · ●●·●·· · ·

Malachi was waiting on the beach. They sat together and watched the moon disappear, dark water merging into dark sky, against which two even blacker shades marked out the ships. Elizabeth remembered another night when she'd tried to stay awake, and hoped she wouldn't fall asleep like she'd done then. The tide was flowing in across the sandbanks and up the beach, as silent as a thief. In the east a bright star glistened.

"The dog star," said Elizabeth. "The sun will rise soon."

"Then it's time to go," said Malachi.

They ran to one of the rowboats tied to a bush above the high-water mark. Malachi untied it and they stood on either side and pulled. The boat inched forward, scraping across the sand. A bird crashed through the undergrowth and flapped into the air. Elizabeth waited for a shout, or a shot from Hywel to stop them, then weighed the distance still to cover and despaired. They pulled again, until at last they reached the water's edge and launched the boat. Malachi held it while Elizabeth put her bundle on board and climbed in after it. He was about to follow her when an imp of a figure jumped aboard and shot past Elizabeth.

"Take me with you." Barty squatted on the seat at the end of the boat. "I can't stay here. Them's bad people what killed my sister."

"What will you do on a pirate ship?" asked Malachi.

"I can make myself handy. If you don't take me with you, I'll holler and people will come running."

Which left Elizabeth and Malachi no choice. They rowed the boat, Barty crouching at the back, giving directions. "To the right, straight ahead, harder, wotcher, there's the Speedwell." They drifted past the silent wreck. "Poor cow," the boy said. "She won't move again."

As they reached the pirate ship, the darkness thinned to the east. They dipped their oars into the water, then pulled them inside their little boat and drew alongside. Barty jumped up on his seat. "Look." He pointed to the prow, where Elizabeth saw the carved figure of a woman, one breast uncovered, the human face replaced by a bird's head.

"Godwit." Elizabeth read the ship's name painted below.

They pulled themselves amidships and Malachi held the rowboat steady while Elizabeth stood and reached up to pull herself aboard.

"Stand on the seat," he whispered.

She stretched again, curled her fingers over the edge of the railings, but then fell back. She stood on her toes and tried again.

"Climb onto my shoulders," said Malachi.

She put one unsteady foot on his shoulder and felt it give. The boat rocked. She pushed herself up and reached out. And then she felt a hand grab her in her armpit, then under her stomach and she hung, suspended. Her arms flailed, her hands clutched only air, and then she was landed like a giant fish onto the pirate deck. She looked up to see a face smiling down at her. Dark, this face was in the half-light. She knew that in the midday sun it would be the same.

"Peggy."

"Tssss. On this ship my name is Shekaru."

There was a soft thump and Elizabeth's bundle landed on the deck.

Shekaru turned from her and leaned over the side of the ship again and pulled up Barty.

"You," said Shekaru.

"I'll be good, I promise."

Malachi pulled himself aboard.

"You three are lucky," Shekaru said. "Now, follow me."

He rolled up his prayer mat, tucked it under his arm, and set off between two rows of canons, his wooden leg tapping on the deck. A man lay spread-eagled in front of the main hatch. In the half-light he looked dead, but when Shekaru took his legs and pulled him out of the way, he grunted.

Shekaru chuckled and swung himself down the hatch. Elizabeth followed into darkness. She couldn't see, but she could hear: the familiar creak of a ship's timbers, the ripple of water, and over it the snores, grunts, and mutterings of men. And she could smell: drink, tobacco, sweat, piss—all the stinking waste of London overlaid with sea salt and tar. In the dim light that filtered in through the gun-ports, she could make out the shapes of hammocks swinging from low beams.

"That you, Shakey?" A voice came from the darkness. "Who's them with you?"

"Nobodies," said Shekaru. "Quick," he whispered to Elizabeth and hobbled to the stern of the ship as quietly as his wooden leg would allow, weaving his way between the hammocks. From one, a bare arm was flung out in front of Elizabeth. Etched on it was a tattoo of a woman with a fish's tail, and the hand at its end had only four fingers; the fifth was a blackened stump. Elizabeth peered over the edge of the hammock to see what kind of man owned such an arm. The pirate slept on his side with a crimson jacket across his shoulder, not unlike, thought Elizabeth, one Josiah Carver would wear aboard the Speedwell. He was clean-shaven, or perhaps he was too young to grow a beard. A scar ran from his jawline to his left eye, which was wide open, although the man himself was asleep, Elizabeth concluded from the steady rise and fall of the crimson jacket. The breath from his open mouth was so rotten that she gagged. She ducked down and crept under the hammocks. When she got to the far side, she found Shekaru and Malachi waiting.

"Where's Barty?" she whispered. Malachi shrugged.

So she crept back and found him perched under a hammock, stroking a kitten.

"Can it be mine?" Barty asked. "I could love it."

Elizabeth grabbed him and the kitten and when she reached Malachi, he beckoned her through a door, into a small galley, suffused with the aroma of spices. There was a fire box at the far end, barrels down one side and, on the other, a wooden surface with a large metal cleaver on it. Malachi sat on one of the barrels, while Shekaru stowed his mat under beams.

"The men on this boat may cut your throats," he told them. "If you have anything, they will steal it. If you break their rules, they will put you overboard without a thought, whether at land or sea. They believe in nothing; they care for nothing. But they need hands for their ship, and they will accept anyone for that."

"Is that why you joined them?" asked Elizabeth.

"I'm an outcast, like them. I have nowhere else to go."

"No more do we." Elizabeth faced the enormity of what she'd done.

"Yes, you do. You will find somewhere that you can be yourself." Shekarau said. "But for now, you must be Richard. You can be my galley boy and I'll protect you as best I can until we get to Jamestown. Unless they find another job for you or discover you're a girl. If that happens, no one can protect you.

At Jamestown I'll get you put ashore, and you can be Elizabeth again.

"It will be different for you, Malachi. You're a sailor, you'll be alright on board the Godwit. But the longer you stay with the pirates, the harder it will be for you to get away. I'll try to get you ashore with Lizzie."

"How about me?" asked Barty. He'd retrieved his kitten from Elizabeth and sat playing with it on the floor.

"You will never leave," said Shekaru. "Now all of you have to persuade the pirates that you're one of them."

CHAPTER 25

London: afternoon 9 September 2019

It only took a second. Miracle went out of the window and all that was left was a space. Outside was blank grey sky and in the distance the Shard. And inside there was Donna holding little Blessing and me and the woman police officer standing among the pigeon shit and graffiti. Silent apart from the wind that blew in through the window. Then a siren wailed; and then another and another. Every service that ever was, mobilised—too late.

· · · · · ● · ● · · ·

We stumbled back down the tower block. The chief inspector went ahead so he could light the way he said, and then spent a lot of time fiddling with his torch. When he looked up his face was in professional mode, but a muscle twitched above his left eye. Donna insisted on carrying Blessing. I staggered alongside, to help, I said, not that I was capable. The Loverage man walked in front of her so she could lean on him if she wanted, so he claimed, not that he looked up to that either. Halfway down she did. When we reached the bottom, his face was grey. The woman police officer was in tears. A white tent was being erected outside Speedwell House where Miracle had... where she'd... I still can't find a way to say what happened that doesn't involve screaming.

Later, Donna and I sat side-by-side on the settee in her flat with little Blessing between us and watched the woman on the lunchtime news speak to camera with the white tent and the block of flats behind her and describe "as it happened" how the young woman had handed over her baby before jumping to her death. But then she hadn't been there, hadn't known Miracle. And even she looked shaken.

Donna defaulted to anger. She refused to hand over Blessing to the social workers, held her close and seethed, said she'd promised the mother, had the space, had been police-checked. "I brought up my Dylan, and he turned out alright till some shit knifed him."

"But we've got a court order."

"So take me to court." Donna clung to the baby.

I told them to back off and respect Donna's loss. She'd been as close to Miracle as anyone, and the tragic mother's last words were to ask Donna to take care of her baby.

They looked to the police officer for help. She flipped through her notebook and chewed her lips, until I said to the social workers, "Are you accusing me of lying?" At which point they blurted out, "No," although their eyes shouted, "Yes," and then they took themselves off around Donna's flat, making notes and checking the electric sockets until I suggested perhaps that could wait till another day and they mumbled condolences and pushed off.

When I left, Loverage workers were already putting up steel fencing around Speedwell House. A few heart-shaped balloons floated from it, and some bouquets of flowers lay close by, huge cellophane-covered creations.

That's when my phone buzzed, just as I'd pulled Donna's front door shut, and I stood and read Hugh's message which returned me to reality.

Friendly reminder. You're on the sixth delegated legislation committee to consider the draft Statutory Auditors, Third Country and International Accounting Standards (Amendment) EU Exit Regulations 2019. Committee Room 12. Today 4.30. Don't be late. Hugh.

To be fair to him, not that there was room in my heart just then for fairness, he wasn't to know where I was when he sent that message.

A small crowd had gathered outside the community centre. One of the women hurried over to me.

"I'm sorry," I said. "I can't..."

She gave me a hug. "Jesus Christ, kiddo."

"The baby's staying with Donna."

"Is she...?" The woman pointed at Donna's flat.

"Yes, she's there, but give her a bit of time. It was tough."

The woman scuttled back to the group, and they crowded around her to hear the latest. I walked to my car and texted to Hugh, *F* off*, and was about to get in when Laurelle appeared, dragging along her daughter. Her face was twisted with what I mistook for anger. It made me flip.

"You knew she was up there, didn't you, Laurelle?"

"You could have saved her. It was your fault she died." She stopped, but didn't stand still, fidgeting instead from foot to foot.

"A whole week and no one saw her. I don't think so. Someone had pushed that security grille aside at the stairwell in Speedwell House. Someone had slipped up and down."

"She was such a sweet girl. All she needed was a visa and a place to live." Laurelle tried to purse her lips, but she couldn't stop them trembling.

"Someone must have provided all those ready meals."

"Perhaps it was Stephanie."

I wanted to slap her. "Stephanie was on holiday."

"You're all the same, aren't you? Finger never points here." She touched her chest with one finger, then her whole hand. Then she let go of Sherine and clutched her face.

"You'll never know..." I started.

"Oh, what's the point of you, if you can't even sort out something as simple as a visa and a flat?" It was like a dam burst when the tears poured down her cheeks.

· · · · ● · ● · · ·

I wasn't even on autopilot as I drove along the Old Kent Road. At a minimum at least the real pilots have to be present and paying some kind of attention, I guess. I wasn't there at all. Instead I was caught in a virtual reality on replay.

"We want to make things better."

"There's nothing anyone can do."

And then, "Will you look after her?"

"Of course I will, love. Promise."

"Be kind to her."

And then those words I couldn't understand.

And then Miracle disappearing through the window.

Over and over like a viral video. And me scrutinising each clip for the one when things could have turned out different. The pigeon-shitted flat. Miracle and the baby. The police officer circling. Donna reaching out. And then the frame of me, the police, Donna and the baby. And the empty window where Miracle had been.

Outside Parliament, the protesters and banners belonged to another world in a parallel universe. Or I did. We couldn't both be real. The police opened the gates, and I drove in over the cobbles around the Jubilee Fountain, where a group of visitors were doing selfies, and down into the darkness of the underground carpark.

For once, I was glad of Hugh and his mindless delegated legislation committee. It meant I had an excuse not to loiter and gossip, to expose emotions that were still so raw they could only be spewed out unprocessed. I could scoot through the nerve-racked corridors. Past men in sweaty suits show-talking. Past women with bright jackets and lipsticked smiles. Past Gerald, busily directing a flow of words at one of our political commissars, a rakish man whose bored expression said, "I hold your future in the palm of my hands, so don't push your luck."

I tried to smile at Gerald, but it must have misfired because his face registered concern. He stopped talking mid flow, held one hand up to the commissar, and the other in a phone gesture, ear-to-mouth. I shrugged, he frowned. But then I was gone, running up the stairs to the committee corridor and into room 12, where a poker-faced Hugh, sitting at the end of the row of desks, ticked my name off his list just as the meeting started.

I didn't even mind if Hugh felt he'd achieved something by having us all sat in line behind our history-splattered desks like a bunch of schoolkids. Me, some fading stars from when we were last in government, and rising stars who wanted to be part of the next. We sat and checked emails, did our social media, signed some actual letters. Or they did. I sat and pretended to read the committee papers in minute detail. But what I saw wasn't black and white. It was heart-stopping colour. A young woman in a yellow dress and a scarlet bandana clutching a baby. Three grey tower blocks against a blue sky. Dazzling graffiti. A blonde *Jesus loves you* poster with *Occupy* plastered across in bright red. And then the jade track suit among the white pigeon shit with an empty space where a woman should be. And outside the window, only the wind. Unless you went over and looked down.

From the committee meeting I went to my office on the third floor of Portcullis House to wait for the final votes in the frantic final session before Parliament was shut down. It was empty apart from a pile of letters for me to sign, and a note. *So sorry. Know how much you cared about her and how hard you tried to help. Joey x*

And below that, *Beyond heartbroken. Stephanie xx*

I promised myself I'd sign the letters, but as soon as I sat down in the easy chair, I passed out. And came to sometime after midnight when the division bells rang, calling me over to vote. I stumbled out of my office to the lift and ran across to the Chamber of the House of Commons. There, frenzied desperation had disintegrated into molten hysteria. Bare-knuckle fighting would have been gentler and more honest than what went on in the voting lobbies.

After it was over, and we'd returned more or less to our places on the green benches and the microphones were put on again so the world could hear what was happening, Gerald leaned over from the row behind me and said, "Where've you been hiding today? You missed all the action. The Speaker's resigned. We beat the government over closing Parliament down. Sort of. They're still packing us off for a month, but the bastards have got to disclose all their WhatsApp messages about it." His words were a blur of sound that didn't connect with anything inside my head. "Plus they've agreed to comply with the law when it comes to Brexit. Personally, I think we've got a better chance of seeing the WhatsApp messages. But there you go. How was your day?"

"So so," I said.

My phone went.

They found the knife. A message from Stephanie.

? My reply.

The one that killed Dylan Stafford.

"Are you alright Frances? You look a bit off." Gerald's voice in my ear.

Where? I texted Stephanie.

In one of Miracle's black bin liners.

Those colours. Yellow dress, blue sky, grey towers. They morphed into the grey suits, bright jackets and green benches around me. And the words, "Be kind to her," and "I promise," became the finger-pointing fury of men and women holding up signs that read, "Silenced." It whirled around me while over it all I heard Gerald's voice, "They're shutting us down," and Laurelle's, "What's the point of you, what's the point of you." Louder and louder. "What's the point of you?" And then I don't remember anything.

Chapter 26

Ocracoke: September 1643

Elizabeth was on the deck of the Godwit when the pirates left Ocracoke.

Above her gulls cawed in protest at the disturbance of the ship weighing anchor. From the east, the first tendrils of sunlight reached for the island's white sands. In the undergrowth beyond the dunes there was no movement. No sign that among the trees there was a clearing with a wooden palisade that sheltered the survivors from the Speedwell. They would be waking to find that two of their number were missing: Elizabeth and Malachi. They wouldn't miss Barty.

Beside Elizabeth, the pirate with the mermaid tattoo brushed out the barrel of a cannon. Another primed its fuse. He wore an emerald jacket that looked like one of Josiah Carver's, and a third, wielding a cannonball, had a yellow scarf tied round his head that was the colour of one of Mrs Carver's dresses.

The pirate captain gave her a box of gunpowder. "Take this to each of the cannons. If you blow yourself up, we'll know we can trust you."

Such a stillness, the wind barely filled the sail as the captain turned his ship to ease out between sandbanks that lurked below the waters of the high tide. Ahead of the Godwit was a

small boat, the rower dipping his oars into the water while
a boy leaned over the bows with a plumb-line in the water.
Beside him was a pirate with a pistol held to the boy's head.
The boy pulled up his plumb-line and checked the depth and
nodded, and the oarsmen rowed forward. The pirate with the
gun didn't move.

The Godwit's captain shouted to his crew to set the sails.
A shaft of red light shot across the horizon. Behind them, the
Speedwell sat upright in the high tide over her sandbank. No
sound, no movement from her.

And as the Godwit turned, the captain ordered, "Fire"
and beside Elizabeth the gunner set a light to the fuse on his
cannon. The deck shook, Elizabeth flinched. A cannonball
arched through the air and landed in the middle of the Speedwell's main deck. It was followed by another, which fell short,
and splashed into the water, and then two more fired in quick
succession. They found their mark. There was an explosion
aboard the Speedwell—flames shot up from below, and when
the smoke cleared, Elizabeth saw that the ship had become
a floating inferno. The pirates cheered and when desperate
figures appeared, staggering out of the fire, they laughed.

"They're for the devil."

A man leapt off the Speedwell and tried to swim away
but was caught in the current and slipped under it. Another
threw an empty barrel overboard, jumped in and scrambled
onto it. He drifted towards the Godwit. The pirate with the
mermaid tattoo took a pistol out of his belt, primed it, took
aim, and fired.

"Missed. Hell's teeth."

The barrel hit a cross-current and rolled over; the man lost
his grip and disappeared below the surface, and the pirates
doubled over with laughter.

"What's wrong with you that you're not laughing?" The pirate turned on Elizabeth. "Are you on their side?" He swung his arm with its mermaid tattoo and hit Elizabeth on the back. She skittered across the deck, landed against the side, looked down, saw the water foaming below, and laughed.

The wind strengthened. At the entrance to the Ocracoke inlet, the rowboat was pulled aboard with the gunman, the pilot and his boy, plumb-line clutched to his chest.

Whatever the difficulties ahead, Elizabeth felt relief standing on the deck, watching Ocracoke slip by. Then figures emerged from the sand dunes, and Ezekiel appeared with Ruth and Samuel. The three stood at the high-tide mark, where the waves gave up and collapsed into the beach. Ezekiel was unchanged since their first encounter: black clothes, black hat, silver-topped cane. He fell to his knees on the sand and raised folded hands to his face. Ruth held up her doll and waved its hand at the Godwit. They were so close that Elizabeth could hear Ruth's words, "Say goodbye baby, we won't see Lizzie anymore." Or perhaps she imagined it. Samuel saluted: Elizabeth knew the turmoil behind that blank face.

In that instant, she knew she'd made the wrong choice: she should have stayed. She felt a deserter's guilt. If the distance had been less, perhaps she would have jumped. But then Ezekiel dropped his hands. A beatific smile wreathed his face. He got to his feet, lifted his hat to the heavens, revealing hair now snowy-white, pointed his silver-topped cane skywards—and laughed. Eyes up, head back, great howls of laughter that rolled across the water and echoed around Elizabeth's head.

"That man's mad," said the pirate in the emerald jacket.

The Godwit sailed on.

Elizabeth's guilt pricked less, the figures on the beach grew smaller, and became her past.

An Atlantic blast hit her face; gusts of wind that blew up from the south. She steadied herself as the ship pitched when the water from the sound met the ocean currents. Canvas slapped as the sails filled, rhythmic cries and the screech of rope on wood as men raised the great mainsail. Laughter as they ran around the deck and over rigging, relief that their ship was out of dangerous waters and free again in the open sea. The captain handed over to his helmsman, shouted orders to his crew and went below deck.

A lookout sounded overhead. Malachi sat astride the yardarm, pointing south, to where a bank of clouds was forming. A group of pirates gathered at the stern of the ship, watching the whiteness billow up. So fast the clouds built, their soft white darkening to grey, and then tumbling outward and spreading forwards.

Elizabeth ran along the deck, rolling with the swell. White sea-foam in the Godwit's wake pointed towards Ocracoke. The receding land lay green and golden under the western sky, but out to sea the bank of clouds was turning from grey to black, seething with a fury. Then from its midst came bolts of incandescent light, flung through air as if to set the sea on fire.

"It's like there's devils in there, fighting." The pirate with the yellow headscarf hunched over the railings of the ship. The rest of the crew was silent. Elizabeth heard only the smacking of water on the ship and the cry of gulls following behind.

The cloud bank formed into a great circle above which trails of vapour curled out like the locks of an angry god. Below, the sea boiled black. The circle started to turn, slowly at first, a celestial wheel that moved through the sky while above it the clouds grew higher until they blocked out the light, and the once-blue sky glowed red. To the far west the sun still shone, but Ocracoke, caught between these two worlds, was in darkness.

"I'm glad we ain't there now." Barty had crept onto the deck and clambered, wide-eyed, up the railing in front of Elizabeth.

"It's god's judgement on us." A harsh voice sounded behind Elizabeth.

And then another, "Or damnation for them on shore. Look."

As she watched the sea rose up, a sheet that lifted and fell back, then rose again and twisted, forming a column that stretched up to the sky like a great sea-snake risen from the abyss to chase them away from Ocracoke. The column grew thicker, darker, wider at the top where it disappeared into the whirling wheel of cloud, and narrower at the bottom where its point met the surface of the water. And then it started to move across the face of the ocean like a living thing.

"Like a demon." The pirate with the yellow headscarf crossed himself.

Elizabeth heard the tap-tapping of Shekaru's wooden leg, felt his hand on her shoulder.

Malachi climbed down from the rigging. "It's a curse on my father."

"Revenge for my sister, more like," said Barty.

"Don't stand there." The captain appeared on the deck shouting at his crew. "If it catches us, we're finished."

His men ran around, trimming the sails, and the Godwit cut her fastest course. Beside her, the gulls flew low across the waves, then soared, circled overhead and flew away.

"They know," Shekaru said. "They always know."

First the column of water moved uncertainly, as if searching for its prey, snaking to and fro across the ocean with the giant circle of cloud hovering overhead. Then it strengthened, steadied, and set its course. The whirling grey wheel with the blackness overhead and the pillar below moved landwards.

Elizabeth could see the ocean churn, its waters rise and fight the swirling vortex so that the blackness of the water was at one with the blackness of the sky. In front was the column of water, tearing towards Ocracoke. The sky closed in; clouds covered the sun; lightning bolted through the darkness, and thunder rumbled across the surface of the water away from the ship now speeding north. Elizabeth couldn't see the column's landfall, but she could imagine.

CHAPTER 27
London: 9 September 2020

I like happy endings.

I'd like to think that Ezekiel and his children survived the hurricane. It would have scattered the burning embers of the Speedwell, flattened the island's misshapen trees, and wiped out Elizabeth's garden. The waterspout would have turned to a twister on land, tearing up the palisade and the mean shelters inside. But I'd like to think that after the storm had blown away across the inland water, from somewhere on the island bedraggled survivors crept out onto the beach and Ezekiel gave a service of thanksgiving—before they salvaged what they could of their belongings and started over.

And then I'd like to think that one bright day, Ezekiel and his children set out across that inland water, Pamlico Sound, in a little boat built with whatever they could scavenge, with a makeshift sail fashioned by Annie. I can see him in the stern, tiller in one hand and in the other the Bible that would lead him to his destiny. I can see Ruth cuddling her doll on her lap, saying, "No need to be frightened, baby, no need," and Samuel with his blank face threading a live worm onto a fishing line and letting it over the side. I'd like to think that somewhere up the river, they pulled into shore and Ezekiel found people to whom he could bring his particular version of the truth. Perhaps where Ruth and Samuel could learn to be children again. Maybe they even had Annie along as a stepmother.

Perhaps Josiah Carver was picked up by some passing ship and got to Jamestown where he and Beatrix managed to ride out the misfortunes that beset that colony. There was a Carver living there some years later, although he wasn't called Josiah. And maybe Hywel found his way to the mountains inland where he could build a cottage and sleep under a thatched roof again.

But history was against them. More than 50,000 people left England between the sailing of the Mayflower and the first years of civil war: children kidnapped off the streets of London, jobless men and women indentured into little more than slavery, would-be revolutionaries, adventurers and saints all taking their chances in the relentless drive to create a new world order. Few of their lives were recorded. Little left other than flotsam on the troubled waters of their times.

Elizabeth, at least, survived. Stephanie was proof of that. She left London the week after my meltdown. When I picked her up to take her to the airport, she was wearing a black tracksuit and had her hair in a ponytail. "For comfort, for the journey," she said, lifting her suitcase into the back of my car. But I thought there must be something more for her to pack away her grey suit and tan slacks. Then I noticed the label on her track-suit.

"Designer trackies?" I asked.

"Joey chose them."

On the way to the airport, she finished off what she knew of Elizabeth's story. "She was set ashore from the Godwit somewhere along the eastern seaboard. Around Chesapeake Bay, so far as I can tell. It was plagued by pirates back then, and there were Gardiners recorded as living there some time later. It's not so far from where I grew up."

"Was there any record of what happened to Malachi?"

"Not that we've found. I always assumed he was my zillionth great-grandfather. Elizabeth's indenture paper survived. We found it in a museum near the coast. There's a framed copy on the wall in my grandfather's house."

"So the circle's complete?"

"For me."

We were heading out along Westway and I was concentrating on my driving. Even so, the silence in the car was unnerving.

"And?" I asked.

"And now I go finish up at school, do my masters, practise law, loose ends of my life sorted."

She lapsed into a silence so portentous it hurt. It was she who broke it.

"But if you don't mind me saying, not yours."

"My what?"

"Loose ends."

For once, silence was easier than finding an answer.

As she disappeared through security with her regulation-sized cabin baggage and her neck cushion, I waved and shouted, "Stay in touch." She called back, "Sure." And being Stephanie, I knew she would.

· · · ● · ● · · · ·

After the security fence went up round Speedwell House, there was an exhibition in the community centre of plans for the estate. The piazza would make way for a development of expensive apartments with an urban garden in the middle. The low-rise would morph into upmarket duplexes. The tower blocks would be knocked down. The fight to save them died with Miracle.

Loverage Development put on the exhibition. I declined the invitation to open it, and when I went down found Toby Davis presiding over a hall full of hostility.

"He's not got much in the way of balls." Donna stood beside me at the back of the hall with Blessing in her arms.

"He's not got any at all," I said.

From the middle of the hall, Laurelle stood up and got stuck into Toby for saying that residents would be allowed to choose the names for the new buildings.

"You mean the tenants could organise a competition?" she asked. When he made the mistake of saying, "Yes," she went in for the kill. "And explain to me, how does running a competition to choose a name compensate us for losing our homes? What planet are you on exactly?"

I joined in the laughter.

Donna fought off all comers to keep Blessing. She even gave up smoking. I wrote to the council about how I'd known her since childhood, and had been a witness to Miracle's final words. The vicar wrote an effusive character reference, ditto the solicitor at the local law centre, and the wife of a former cabinet member, now ennobled, who lived nearby. Long before any legalities were completed, Donna's parenting of Blessing was an immutable fact. She bought out the babywear section of the local supermarket, and one bright autumn day I helped her pack it all into a rental van that her sister Leigh drove up from Canvey Island. Donna and I might have been reconciled but Leigh refused to be in the same space as me and pushed off to the pub for the duration.

"We'll never know if it was Miracle who killed my Dylan," Donna said. "No fingerprints, no witnesses that would come forward. But whatever happened, it wasn't Blessing's fault. If I can give her a chance in life, at least some good will have come of it all."

. . . .

As for me, I joined the flotsam. When the General Election was sprung on us that winter, I bailed out and left my local party to find another candidate. They chose Laurelle. Her smiling face was on the leaflets that filled my letterbox. When I went to put them in the recycling bin, I bumped into my nerdy neighbour.

"What d'you reckon to this new woman?" he asked. "She looks like she'll be a real fighter for us. Not that you weren't, of course. You always did your best. It's just that..." His words tailed off. He bit his lip. Laurelle's face beamed out of the leaflets.

"Don't worry about me," I said. "I'm absolutely fine." It was true, too.

. . . .

The election re-energised Gerald. He cut his fragile ties with the north and rushed around London sorting out his portfolio life. One night in mid-January he turned up at my flat with a bottle of champagne to celebrate his latest directorship. When I woke up the next morning, he was snoring beside me in bed.

"Not snoring, breathing heavily," he said.

"Whatever."

We stayed in bed all day. After that we divided our time between my flat and his north of the Thames, until in the new year we defaulted to his, which was larger but crammed with expansive furniture and floor to ceiling bookshelves. We agreed my minimalist lounge suite would replace his bulging settees.

When I went to arrange its delivery, my flat already had that chill of abandonment.

There was a determined humming from my fridge, like if there was a sign of life after a nuclear war it would turn out to be my fridge. All it contained was a bottle of curdled milk and a manky lemon. In the bedroom, framed photographs of my graduation, my first election victory, and my mother as a '60's dolly bird stood on the dressing table along with a packet of dried-out wet wipes. I packed up the photos with some books from the sitting room and cooking stuff to take to Gerald's.

There was nothing else I wanted from my old life.

Soon after, Gerald's rebellious middle child, Ruby, moved into the spare room with a backpack and a ring in her nose and an attitude. "You try coping with her," said the email from Gerald's soon-to-be ex-wife.

When the pandemic came, Mum moved in too. Hanna was hollow-eyed with exhaustion when I arrived for the last time at the care home.

"Here's your daughter come to collect you, Mrs Garvey," she said through her mask. There was no hair-stroking or arm-rubbing. "Aren't you the lucky one?"

"Sometimes."

Mum got the spare room. Ruby showed good grace about being shunted into a fold-out bed in an alcove by the front door. The two of them soon spotted kindred spirits and spent long hours together in Mum's room. They called themselves the bad girls. Sometimes when I'd look in, they'd be laughing together or watching a video, Mum stretched out on her bed, Ruby curled up at her feet. Other times, Ruby would be doing her remote learning with her laptop on her knees, and Mum would be dozing, under the influence, it turned out, of whisky that Ruby filched from Gerald's stash in the sideboard. Both of them refused to wear masks when Ruby pushed Mum around the neighbourhood in her wheelchair.

Gerald took a picture of Ruby hoovering Mum's room and emailed it to his ex with the caption, "Look what Dad-care achieved."

"That is such an overclaim," I told him.

One Thursday evening. when Gerald and Ruby and I came in from clapping for carers on the street corner, we found Mum had slipped on from dozing. Ruby was heartbroken.

"I wanted her to be at my graduation," she sobbed.

"She probably wouldn't have come. She hated that kind of thing," I said. "She had her best life drinking your Dad's whisky with you."

Eventually, I got a job running a charity for trafficked women. Gerald and I decided to make things permanent. No—I didn't marry him. I said I like happy endings, not marshmallow ones. It was only selling our flats and buying a house together, with space for Ruby, if she'd have us.

To find out, I took her to see Joey at his comedy club across London Bridge, past Borough Market, and out along the Old Kent Road.

"You used to be an MP down here, didn't you?" she asked. "Back in the day."

"Yes. Before that they used to grow asparagus on farms here."

"How random is that."

We crawled with the traffic past the retail parks and run-down blocks of flats. At New Cross I turned left and battled through the petrol fumes and noise of commuter traffic along darkening streets, where people were scurrying home from stations and bus stops to start their weekends. I turned right up a side street of dingy warehouses. There was an arc of multi-coloured lights over one and Ruby perked up in her seat and peered out.

"Is that it?"

I tried to think myself back to studenthood as I parked
the car and we walked into the comedy club where we had
bands stuck round our wrists and I bought a diet coke for
me, beer for her, and then we went down some steps and
along a narrow passage. And found ourselves in the middle
of a ruckus. Ruby was transfixed. By the dim red lighting cast
over the brave, the extroverts and the unwary in the front row.
By the mob shouting the odds from the back as we slid into
our seats. And by the barrage of abuse coming from the low
platform where the shaven-headed compere was working the
audience into near riot,

"Where you from then Kev? Peckham? Wot, Peckham?
You out on good behaviour? Wot you laughing at?" He spun
round to a neat blond man along the front row. "You look a
bit posh for here. What's your name? Hugo? You a banker or
something? You are? Here Kev, here's yer dinner."

Ruby joined in the chanting, "Wanker, wanker," rolled
round in her seat, slurped at her beer, spilt it on the floor, then
carried on laughing as the compere went through the ritual
humiliation of anyone who stood out from the crowd. Or
tried to hide from it. It was brutal, but hysterical, and while
I laughed along, I wondered how Joey would manage to top
it.

"And now let's hear it. No," the compere waved his con-
tempt at the crowd, "not that arse-tickling patter. Bring the
fucking roof down for Joe Malone."

It was Joey, just. He'd shaved the back and side of his head
and bleached the hair on top into corkscrew curls that stood
erect from his face. I don't know if it was the way he swaggered
on stage, or the challenge in his eyes as he took the mic off its
stand, but he had the audience before he'd even said a word.

He had Ruby. She turned to me with glowing eyes and shout-whispered in the mayhem, "You mean you actually breathed the same air as him?"

He had me, too, right through his tirade about the state of our nation, he had me laughing. Right up till I heard the words:

"I worked for an MP once. No abuse, please. I'm sensitive, and besides, it was a woman. I did the creative stuff, you know, the media, as in 'yesterday I saved the planet' quote unquote, filled in the expense forms, as in 'yesterday I recycled my toilet paper.' But I could live with that. I could live with anything. Just not the Joey-be-a-darling-and-get-me-a -skinny-latte-extra-hot-please."

And then with a shimmy of his glittering self, there I was. Under the spotlight in that comedy club. The lift of the chin, the tilt of the head, the sleight of the hand.

"It's you, Franny!" Ruby was hysterical.

"Frances."

He had me skewered, kebabbed. He teetered across the stage on my self-important high heels, pretend-preened his hair, and one hand on teasing hip, turned smooching over his shoulder to his mesmerised audience, and winked.

"Babe," he smarmed into the microphone.

"Babe, babe," the crowd shouted back.

Beside me, Ruby screamed along with the best of them, then grabbed her crotch. "I've fucking wet myself." She kicked over her glass—carbonate luckily so it didn't break, but the man in front turned round when the beer hit his trousers and looked ready to thump her. Only then Joey started up again.

"I thought politics could change the world. But then I discovered politics is just stand-up for sad people."

Afterwards, Ruby plopped her wet bottom onto the newspaper I spread out on my car seat and laughed all the way home.

"He was just the best. Politics is for sad people. Dad will die. What must it have been like to work with him? How did you manage to fix that?"

"So you will come and live with us."

"What?"

"Your Dad and I are setting up home together. We wondered if you'd like to live with us?"

"I already do." She sniffed the air as if she was about to cry, and for a microsecond I wondered if it would be for joy. "God, I stink like an old pisshead."

And so she went on, which meant I didn't have to say anything. She was so busy rehashing as many of Joey's jokes as she could remember that she didn't notice my silence. Why should she, and what, after all, could I say?

That ignore the cocoon of Westminster comfort, the artifice of our battles, the sometimes-cheating duplicity, strip it all away and politics is still about the struggle to build a new world in which life chances aren't determined by the fault lines of injustice that run through the old. That's how it all started for me, whatever it became. How could I explain this to Ruby, sitting chortling next to me in the car, and anyway, would she listen?

It wasn't that I gave up. I'd like to think I was like Elizabeth. Like her, I preferred to take my chances with the unknown. Like her, I wanted a future that was more than sitting about waiting for whatever the tide brought in. I imagined how she must have felt, stepping ashore off the pirate ship and getting a second chance in a new world where the old rules didn't apply. A world that was at once brasher and more precarious, with no allegiances, no preconceptions about what came next. I can picture her gazing in wonderment at the generous land, fertile soil, thick forests, rich wildlife, and thinking, "I can do this." And then she must have looked around at the assortment of people and thought, "What the heck," or her era's equivalent, before she got stuck in.

There must have been times when she longed for what she'd left behind, the family, the farm, the old life, however difficult. Until finally, the tide of history closed over her head too. And all that endured were folk memories and a line of freeborn girls, including Stephanie, who came back.

A letter from Sally Keeble

Thankyou for choosing *Freeborn Girls*. I hope you've enjoyed reading about Frances and Elizabeth and their remarkable life stories. They're fiction, but based on research that took me to some wonderful places where I met some extraordinary people.

I'll do the same for my next book to bring you a very special novel. If you'd like to find out more about my that, you'll be welcome to add your name to my mailing list—I'll send you a free copy of my novella *Flora's Choice* and an occasional newsletter.

You can sign up on my website at www.sallykeeblebooks.com or by using the QR code below.

She, You, I, my debut novel, received widespread acclaim. It's available on Amazon and via your local bookshop.

It tells the story of Skye Stanhope who returns to her grandmother's childhood home, searching for the roots. As she strips away layers of secrecy, she confronts inner torments: the forces that bound her family together, but also tore them apart. It's an emotional journey from a poverty-stricken tenement block in pre-war Scotland, to a wartime airbase in Suffolk, through boomtime London to a coffee cart beside the sea.

Book blogger Becca Scammell praised it as: "A brilliant first novel from a talented and skilled writer."

CJ Mason, The Fallen Librarian called it: "A gem of a novel...captivating, clever, and considered and a reading experience that I highly recommend you try for yourself."

Flora's Choice, my free novella, tells the story of Flora Munro and her search for a new life after her violent husband dies.

"It's your choice what happens now," says her daughter Maisie. So what does Flora do with her newfound freedom? How does she move on after the years of abuse? And what choice does she make when a former admirer comes calling? This novella takes a deep dive into the emotions of a woman as she reclaims her life.

You can find me on **social media:**
on facebook at Sally Keeble Author
or on Instagram at SallyKeebleBooks
or Twitter at SallyKBooks

Most of all, I'd like to hear from you direct: about what you think of my books, and about your favourite reading. You can reach me at www.sallykeeblebooks.com/contact

I hope you'll keep in touch and share in my writing.

Best wishes

Sally Keeble

Acknowledgements

There's a real Stephanie Gardiner—but she's very different from the person in the book. She came from the USA to intern with me in the summer of 2009 and wrote a brilliant report on the impact of the recession on people in Northampton North where I was MP.

We went for a farewell lunch to the Mayflower pub in Rotherhithe, which features in Chapter 11. There she told me about her ancestors who farmed in south London and sailed to America on the Mayflower. The story stuck with me.

So first acknowledgements go to Stephanie—thank you for providing the inspiration for this book and for lending your name.

Stephanie's family farm was in the area of south London where I started my political career as a local councillor. My experiences there were formative for me as a person and a writer. So thankyou to the people of Consort Ward in Southwark. Special thanks also to residents of the nearby Aylesbury Estate for later sharing your experiences of regeneration.

More acknowledgements and thanks are due.

First, to the British Library with its stunning collection of Leveller leaflets. It includes a leaflet published shortly before John Lilburne's public flogging, which I guessed was the one he threw to the crowds. My close encounter with the original leaflet was memorable. Even the indentations of the printing press were still visible on the fragile paper.

How I wish any leaflet I've ever delivered had as much impact.

On a family holiday to America, we visited Ocracoke, rated as one of the world's best beaches. There, I learned about the island's pirate history and experienced its remarkable ecology. Both feature in this book. So thankyou Andrew for insisting we go there, and also to Luise Parsons, whose friends Thomas and Grace Wilson filled in the gaps in my knowledge.

I made several visits to the replica of the Golden Hinde in London. From these, I got a sense of the conditions endured by people crammed onto similar ships for the audacious voyage to America. The Mayflower was only slightly bigger.

Thanks to Barry Gardiner, who provided an insight into what it was like being an MP during the frenetic summer of 2019.

Writing is a learning process. Thank you to Jonathan Barnes for your guidance, and to you and Mary Hargreaves for editing my novel: also to the Faber Academy and to the writing group there for your feedback; to the Olivier Group of writers who read an earlier iteration, and to friends and family members who read and reviewed many versions. Special thanks to Gwyn Bennett who has mentored me through this process.

Finally, at our lunch in the Mayflower, Stephanie and I were joined by my excellent parliamentary researchers, Luke and Danny. Unlike the fictional Joey, they didn't despair, but went on to political and, hopefully, parliamentary careers. Wishing them both every success. Dreams never die. Hope never fades. Tomorrow can always be better.

Sally Keeble

February 2024

Historical Note

History is recorded by the rich, the powerful and the educated. Elizabeth Gardiner was none of these.

But look around London and you'll find traces of her story.

Many of them are included in the *Freeborn Girls Heritage Trail* which you'll find at sallykeeblebooks.com. It's a fantastic walk that follows the steps of Elizabeth and Sarah Gardiner and takes in many of the landmarks that have survived 400 years.

You can also see New Palace Yard, where John Lilburne was slapped into the pillory and threw leaflets to the crowd. It's behind the railings round the entrance to Parliament's carpark. The man himself, the populist hero of his times, is mostly forgotten, although his legacy lives on. Some argue that his belief in freeborn rights contributed to the theory of unalienable rights that underpin the American constitution.

There's a wonderful collection of John Lilburne's leaflets in the British Library, along with others by his movement, the Levellers. Yes, according to contemporary accounts, he did throw leaflets to the crowd in New Palace Yard, and did use the words attributed to him in this book. Lilburne's belief in freeborn rights is thought by some to lie behind the theory of unalienable rights that underpins the American constitution.

Every May there's a colourful procession through Burford, a picturesque village in Oxfordshire, in honour of the Levellers.

Hundreds of them were imprisoned there, and three of their leaders were hanged.

Turnham Green, site of a key battle in the Civil War, is now a tube station on the District line. A fragment of green space survives as part of a conservation area. The passion Londoners feel for their city, that turned them out in such force there to fight their king, still burns strong.

South London is much transformed, although poverty and injustice endures. Once beyond Southwark, there were market gardens along what is now the Old Kent Road. One of the prize crops grown there was asparagus—sparrow-grass, as it was called—for sale in the City. The Cooper Estate is fictional. The local folk hero it's named after is not. Henry Cooper was one of a string of famous boxers who sparred at the famous Thomas a Becket pub that stands close to where Elizabeth once farmed.

Rotherhithe's starring role in the peopling of the United States of America is marked by a modest blue plaque on the wall of St Mary the Virgin's Church. Close by is the Mayflower public house. The tavern on that site in Elizabeth's time was destroyed by fire. The present building is a replacement built in 1780, full of historical pictures and artefacts. The George Inn that she visited with her father, Will, was also destroyed by fire. Rebuilt in 1677, it's the oldest galleried pub in London.

Today, Borough Market is a foodie paradise. Four hundred years ago, it was where Elizabeth sold her sparrow-grass. The route that she and her sister, Sarah, took from the market remains a vibrant walk through history; past Southwark Cathedral along Bankside to the Globe Theatre, closed by the Puritans, and rebuilt by American film director Sam Wanamaker. It forms the *Freeborn Girls Heritage Trail*.

Across the Atlantic, Ocracoke's pirates are now confined to the island's museum. Ocracoke Island was a favourite spot for them, where the infamous pirate Albert Teach met his end. Teach is better known as Blackbeard, said by some to be one of the inspirations for Captain Jack Sparrow in the Pirates of the Caribbean.

There's more about the stories behind the story on Sally's website at www.sallykeeblebooks.com. Best of all, follow Elizabeth and Sarah's *Freeborn Girls* walk—and experience their story for yourself.

About Sally Keeble

Sally dug deep into her lived experience to write *Freeborn Girls*.

After working as a journalist, she went into politics. She became Leader of Southwark Council in south London, and then MP for Northampton North and a government minister. *Freeborn Girls* draws from her experience of tackling the entrenched poverty in Southwark, as well as the foibles of Westminster bureaucracy and political life.

Her debut novel, *She, You, I,* published last year, was acclaimed as, "a brilliant novel" and, "a book of our time." It drew from her family's East Anglian and Scottish roots. It was followed by a novella, *Flora's Choice,* and a work of non-fiction about conflict-related sexual violence, *In Plain Sight,* co-authored with two other women.

Growing up in a diplomatic family, she spent much of her early years in the USA, Switzerland and Australia, returning home to the UK after working as a journalist in South Africa. She made the switch from journalism to politics, first to work at Labour HQ as a press officer, and then standing for election to Southwark Council in the turbulent 1980s. After serving as the council's Leader, she was selected as a parliamentary candidate in Northampton, and became one of the big intake of Labour women MPs who changed the face of British politics in 1997.

She served as a minister for local government and then international development.

Itchy feet don't stand still. After losing her seat, she set up an international development agency for the Anglican Communion, and travelled widely, especially in Africa and South Asia. Sally splits her time between Northampton, where she was MP, and Bawdsey, a village in coastal Suffolk. She and her husband Andrew have two adult children. She remains active in politics, still working for a better future.

Printed in Great Britain
by Amazon

38800232R00159